The Thrice Na...

CW00509393

Part VIII

Roxolani

The Thrice Named Man

Part VIII

Roxolani

by

Hector Miller

www.HectorMillerBooks.com

The Thrice Named Man

Part VIII

Roxolani

All characters and events in this publication, other than those clearly in the public domain, are fictitious and any resemblance to real persons, living or dead, is purely coincidental.

Author: Hector Miller

Proofreading: Kira Miller, J van Rensburg

First edition, 2020, Hector Miller

Part VIII in the book series The Thrice Named Man

ISBN: 9798556402232

Contents

Contents (continued)

Chapter 1 – Gallienus (July 254 AD)

For long, Gallienus glared at us down his nose. Slowly his eyes narrowed.

"My father, Valerian Augustus, informed me that you have spent your own gold to raise a force of cavalry", he said, and his lips slowly morphed into a sneer. "He told me to seek your counsel in all things martial."

"Augustus is wise indeed", Marcus replied.

After a handspan of heartbeats the emperor leaned in and whispered, "It would be best not to get ideas above your station." He retreated a step, smiled without humour, and took another swallow from his chalice. "You will do well to remember that the glory of victory belongs to me - to me alone."

Marcus returned Gallienus's stare in a way that could easily have been interpreted as a show of defiance.

"Caesar", I said in an attempt to mitigate the tension. "The Illyrians are at your disposal."

"What would I want with a bunch of barbarians?" he said, laughed out loud, and waved us from his presence.

Marcus slowly exhaled as we walked from the chamber. "May the gods help me, Lucius", he whispered, "but I find him difficult to endure."

"He is insufferable", I said, "but what he says cannot be faulted. The Empire has been plagued by a never-ending line of usurpers. To set it right, Valerian and Gallienus have to win glory to rise in the esteem of the legions."

Marcus nodded with pursed lips without offering a reply.

When we arrived in his office, my friend dismissed his clerk and poured two cups of wine. He drank deeply and refilled his to the brim.

"I am sure Gallienus will only be here for a couple of days", I said. "He seems to prefer spending his time in Colonia Agrippina in Germania Inferior where cultural activities of a more diverse nature are available."

"If by that you mean the theatres and brothels our emperor prefers", Marcus said with a scowl, "I agree with you."

The door opened without a knock and Hostilius burst into the room with Vibius on his heels.

"There has been a breach", the Primus Pilus said, and poured himself a cup of wine. "A warband of Franks crossed the limes near Saalburg, twenty-five miles to the northwest. The savages are raiding the farms and settlements between there and Nida to the south. Seems to be a large band, more than two thousand of the bastards."

Marcus's shoulders visibly slumped, drawing a frown from Hostilius.

The Primus Pilus grinned. "We've been waiting for the opportunity", he said. "Why the long face?"

"We will have to invite Emperor Gallienus to join us", I said. "He desires glory."

Hostilius's shoulders slumped, his demeanour suddenly mirroring Marcus's.

"Maybe he won't notice our departure", Vibius said, his voice tainted with desperation.

"Best we can hope for is that there is a new play opening at the theatre in Colonia Agrippina", I said, and retraced my steps to inform Gallienus of our plans.

* * *

Three legionary cohorts were drawn up in battle formation on the plain north of the Moenus River, a few miles south of the low ridge of the Taunus Mountains. Four hundred paces distant stood the shield wall of the Franks.

The Illyrian cavalry, as we called the black-clad, armoured riders, was arrayed in a standard formation at the rear of the infantry. Gallienus, surrounded by his praetorian guards, trotted to where I sat on Kasirga, beside the draconarius in the centre of the column.

I removed my black-plumed helmet and inclined my head. "Lord Emperor", I said.

Gallienus stole a glance down the lines of horsemen encased in black scale.

With lances grounded, they stared straight ahead, their eyes remaining hidden behind the oil-blackened chain riveted to their helmets. The only hint of their affiliation to Rome was their red cloaks fluttering in the breeze. But the one thing that was meant to make them look more human had the opposite effect – it appeared as if they were unworldly beings drifting in a sea of blood.

"They look to be…, er, well trained", Gallienus said, and it was clear that he was intimidated by the Illyrians.

4

Hostilius approached at a trot, saluted Gallienus, then turned to me.

The emperor nodded for the Primus Pilus to continue.

"We will engage at your signal, Tribune Domitius", he said, and returned to his position at the rear of the infantry.

"What happens now, Domitius?" Gallienus asked.

"Now, lord, we will win the glory you seek", I replied, nodded to the signifier, and as one the Illyrians wheeled to the left and accelerated to a canter.

The column skirted the orderly ranks of the VI Gallicana and formed up in front of the cohorts, four hundred paces from the shield wall of the Germani.

I gave the order to the draconarius. On his signal the column went to a trot, then a canter. The draco standard swallowed the wind, its black tail billowing while a low moan emanated from its snarling maw. Three hundred paces from the enemy, our line extended, and the five hundred riders split into ten groups of fifty, evenly spread out along the width of the shield wall of the Franks. Seamlessly, each group arrayed in arrow formation.

I kicked Kasirga to a gallop, dropped the reins, and took five *plumbatae* in my left hand. A hundred paces from the shield wall we hurled the darts high into the air. More than two thousand of the missiles rained down on the enemy. Skilfully the Illyrians swerved to the right, keeping out of range of the deadly axes of the Franks. Behind us the shouts and moans of injured Germani could be heard.

We wheeled and came around again. I slipped my strung horn bow from its case, took four arrows in my draw hand, and guided Kasirga with my knees. A hundred paces from the shield wall, the men who did not carry bows, loosed another volley of *plumbatae*, and readied their light throwing spears. As the Germani in the front rank raised their shields to protect themselves from the deadly rain of darts, hundreds of javelins struck low. But we had strayed into the range of the Franks' axes. Many lowered their shields, drew back their franciscas, and skipped forward to cast their deadly weapons. A wave of armour-piercing arrows struck the Germani who had exposed themselves. Again and again our shafts slammed into the Franks while the rain of deadly darts continued. Slowly their shield wall disintegrated.

For the third time the horsemen wheeled, wide this time, and came around again. I nodded to the signifier, who tilted the draco's head forward, altering the pitch of the howl emanating from the standard. The Illyrians opened their ranks, broadened their line, and charged. The black riders rode boot to boot in a near straight line five hundred paces wide and two ranks deep.

This time there was no sign of the defiant, grinning, bearded giants of moments before. The eyes that peered from behind the tattered wall of shields were wide and filled with fear. We went to a canter, and the draco's wail changed pitch, strangely resonating with the moans of the wounded Germani.

I took three arrows in my hand and gave the signal.

The lancers lowered their long, heavy spears as we went to a gallop. Waves of shafts slammed into the Franks facing the spearmen - again and again and again the arrows struck while darts rained from above. The Germani warrior who faced me fell with an arrow through the eye. Two heartbeats later the heavy lancers decimated what remained of the crumbling shield wall.

It was the last straw, and as one the Franks turned tail and ran. The rout soon turned into a slaughter.

I sat on Kasirga's back, grimly staring at my handiwork. Hostilius arrived then, interrupting my musings.

"By the gods, Lucius", he whispered and slowly shook his head.

He turned in the saddle, glancing at the Roman infantry still arrayed in a neat formation behind us.

"You did this with five hundred horsemen", he said, and gestured to the hundreds of Germani corpses. "They outnumbered you four to one."

I experienced a strange feeling of intense pride mixed with guilt.

"Here he comes", Hostilius said.

I noticed the approach of Gallienus and his guards.

The emperor reined in and whispered words to the praetorian centurion. Caesar ignored the guard's objections and approached on his own. He dismissed Hostilius with the wave of a hand.

"We need to talk", Gallienus said, and gestured for me to follow him out of earshot of his guards.

Chapter 2 – Glory

Marcus and Vibius arrived soon after Gallienus and his escort had trotted off.

"Word will spread", Marcus said. "You have put the fear of the gods into the Franks. They will think twice before crossing the limes again."

"What did Caesar want?" Hostilius asked.

I shrugged noncommittally. "He didn't say", I replied. "He told me that we would be called to meet with him after he had applied his mind."

Hostilius snorted in derision. "What in Hades is that supposed to mean?"

"It means that he is concerned that some of the glory will accrue to us", Marcus said with a scowl. "And he will seek to remedy that."

"We all knew that would happen", Vibius said. "Let's just hope that he doesn't do anything stupid."

I nodded my agreement. "I never desired glory", I confirmed. "Arash gave me a vision - one that demanded my obedience."

Hostilius nudged his horse closer and placed a hand on my shoulder. "And you can be proud of what you have achieved, Lucius", he said. "No matter the scheme which Gallienus comes up with."

Just then Gordas arrived at an easy trot.

"The Illyrians suffered no casualties", he said proudly. "Five horses had to be put out of their misery, and eight men are wounded. One of them lost a finger. Looks like half of the Franks have been killed." He took a long swig from his wineskin. "Arash smiles on us."

"Have the men gather the loot, Gordas", I said. "Tonight, we will feast."

I had great difficulty putting the imminent meeting with Gallienus from my mind, and I found that I became irritable, which did not go unnoticed.

A few days later, Hostilius, Cai, Gordas and I sat around the hearth inside the villa, sipping on wine.

As always, Gordas, who was blessed with a simpler view of the world, came up with a suggestion. "You are concerned about the actions of Gallienus", the Hun said. It was an observation and not a question, so he continued without waiting for my reply. "I will slit his throat in the middle of the night", he said, which made me choke on my wine.

"I tend to agree with the Hun", Hostilius said.

"And then what?" I asked with a scowl. "At least his father, Valerian, is still in charge. If Gallienus is killed, it will weaken Valerian, and some other usurper will try to grab the purple. Someone like Philip the Arab or his evil brother."

"The future is for the gods to decide", Gordas countered. "You think too far ahead."

"We have all helped to put Valerian on the Roman throne", Hostilius said. "There comes a time when enough is enough. If you ever decide to go live with Bradakos, I, for one, will be at your side."

It was an alluring thought.

"Let me first hear the words of Gallienus, then we will see", I said.

Later, when Hostilius and Gordas had both retired to their furs, I sat alone with Cai.

"Lucius of the Da Qin", he said, "Man must be careful who he listens to."

I waved away his concerns. "They mean well", I said.

11

"Not talking about Primus Pilus and Hun", he said, which served to grab my attention.

Cai placed his open hand upon his chest. "Two live inside heart. One seek power, glory and gold. The other refuse glory, it prefer humility and pity. All men have two voice inside. Before make decision, know which voice give advice."

"Do you always know?" I asked the Easterner.

"No", he said. "But I try. Way of Dao not easy."

"Sometimes", he added, "best is keep eye on goal. Gordas right, whatever Caesar say, it gods who decide future. Not Gallienus."

I found much comfort in the words of my friend from Serica. When morning arrived, I felt at peace until we arrived at my quarters in Mogantiacum, where Marcus was waiting for me.

"We have been summoned", he said, and immediately the knot in my stomach returned.

* * *

Three days later, Marcus, Hostilius, Vibius, Gordas, Diocles and I, escorted by fifty Illyrians, set out for Colonia Agrippina, the capital of Germania Inferior.

Some still referred to the city by its original name, Ubiorum, which had been changed to honour Emperor Claudius's wife. She was born in the city while her father, the famed Germanicus, was punishing the Germani under Arminius for Varus's defeat in the Teutoberg Forest.

With two spare mounts each, Gordas and I could have completed the ninety-mile trip within a single day, but this was Germania, not Hunnia. Marcus insisted that we take the long route north, along the Roman road following the Limes Germanicus. We visited every fort, spending at least two thirds of a watch in discussions with commanders and inspecting the fortifications, turning what could have been a day trip into a laborious, five-day affair.

On the afternoon of the third day we approached Niederbieber, the most northerly fort of the limes in Germania Superior north of the Rhine.

"Impressive", Hostilius said, gesturing with his chin towards the iron-reinforced wooden gates recessed between two enormous three-levelled towers. The fort was constructed upon a raised earthen berm, fronted by a ditch seven paces

13

wide, and as deep as the height of a man. Every fifty paces, a large, robust tower protruded from the stone wall. The sun glinted off the polished helmets and whetted spears of the sentries patrolling the rampart.

"Niederbieber is a large one", Marcus said. "Two hundred paces by two hundred and seventy. The auxiliary units stationed here are up to full strength again, thanks to the intervention of Emperor Valerian."

The gate creaked open. Five mounted officers emerged from the fort and approached at a walk, halting ten paces from us.

The lead officer saluted when he recognized Marcus. "Prefect Caius Vitale, *Numerus Brittonum*", he said. "We were not aware of your visit, legate."

As with the other forts, the visit was planned to be a surprise.

"Let us inspect the ditch before we enter the fort, prefect", Marcus said curtly, causing the prefect's complexion to turn ashen.

"As you wish, Legate Claudius", Caius Vitale said and led us around the fort.

It turned out that Vitale had nothing to be nervous about, as the ditch was well maintained and the stakes lining the bottom had recently been sharpened, but we kept our counsel.

On the northern side, between the fort and limes, lay a sprawling village inhabited by retired legionaries, craftsmen, and hangers-on.

Marcus nodded his approval when he noticed that at least a hundred paces separated the nearest buildings of the village from the wall of the fort. It was not uncommon for a *vicus* to encroach upon the walls. This situation was not ideal, as it could provide invaders with a hiding place. The firing of the buildings in the village, paired with a wind that favoured the enemy, could potentially put the fort at risk.

When we had completed the inspection of the ditch, we entered through the southern gate, the *porta praetoria*, from which the officers had earlier exited. While an underling showed the Illyrians to their accommodations, we circled the inside perimeter of the fort along the ring road, and inspected the barracks, granary and workshops.

A centurion escorted Gordas, Vibius and Diocles to the guest quarters within the praetorium, allowing Marcus, Hostilius and me to conclude our business with Vitale. Neither of us made any comments until the decidedly nervous prefect closed the door behind Hostilius, who was the last one to enter.

"Strength report?" Marcus asked when all were seated.

"Four hundred and eighty auxiliaries from Britannia", Vitale said, "and the same number of Germani. Eighty of the men from Britannia are *exploratores*, highly-trained mounted scouts. Five of the Germani and three of the Britons are unfit for duty due to injuries sustained while training."

"You are doing a fine job under difficult circumstances, prefect", Marcus said. "There is very little to fault, although I would suggest that you turn the cleared area into a killing field. Dig holes and line them with stakes and caltrops. Place large stones randomly to break up an enemy charge. And when you have time, extend the width to one hundred and fifty paces."

Vitale nodded, clearly relieved. Senior commanders were known for being capricious.

"Prefect, there is one area of the fort we would still like to inspect – the officers' baths", Marcus added, and broke out in a grin. "And make sure you join us with a large pitcher of your best wine."

The evening in the company of the prefect turned out to be an enjoyable affair. He was a hard, unsophisticated officer who had been under the standard all his adult life. Only a man who had stood on the walls of a fort facing thousands of barbarians is truly able to comprehend the value of well-maintained defences.

We departed early on the morrow, crossing the shallow Wied without getting wet. The road led us north and west along the fortifications for eight miles until we reached the last watchtower on the northern bank of the Rhine, where a large military barge was waiting on our arrival. It took two trips to ferry all the riders across the river. When the middle hour of the day arrived, we were on our way to the massive legionary fort at Bonna, the home of the I Minervia.

Days before, Marcus had dispatched a messenger to the commander of the fort, informing him that we would be passing through his domain. In reply we had received an invitation to dinner.

The duty centurion manning the entrance recognized us from afar. The thick gates swung open when our approach was noticed, and he personally escorted us to the praetorium.

As was the case with Marcus, the legate of the I Minervia had recently been promoted at the behest of Valerian.

While the others were shown to our accommodation, Marcus and I went to meet the legate.

The accepted practice was for a junior tribune to man the reception area which gave access to the legate's office, but he was nowhere to be seen. Rather, the door to the office stood wide open. A tall, heavily muscled man ducked from the door of the general's office. He wore the scarred mail armour of a common soldier, but his thick-woven crimson cloak, ivory-hilted spatha and expensive soft leather boots identified him as a senior officer. His eyes were blue and piercing, his blonde hair curly and thick. It was clear that he had the blood of the Germani.

"Welcome to Bonna", he boomed in a powerful voice. "I am Legate Postumus of the I Minervia", he added and clasped arms with Marcus and me.

He must have noticed our scrutiny, rubbed his thick beard and said, "If you are wondering - my father was a Batavian."

"And my mother a Scythian", I said.

"At least there is one Roman between the two of us", he replied, and laughed loudly at his own jest.

He waved us into his office. "Ale or wine?" he asked.

"Red", I said.

He filled three wooden cups from a clay amphora and joined us on couches arranged in a corner of his spartan office.

He took a large mouthful of wine. "I will travel with you tomorrow", he said. "I have been summoned as well."

"Do you know why?" Marcus asked.

Postumus's smile vanished in an instant, hinting that there was another side to the jovial legate. "We will have to wait and see what Caesar will command in his infinite wisdom", he said, a frown creasing his brow.

Then the anger seemed to dissipate and the glint returned to his eyes. He dismissed his own words with a wave of a hand. "I have heard a rumour that Emperor Valerian is on his way north. He is travelling up the Rhine by boat. Let us pray to the gods that it is true."

We all shared the same sentiment, but to criticise Gallienus openly would have been tantamount to treason. "I will pray to Fortuna for Emperor Valerian's safe arrival", Marcus said instead, and we exchanged knowing glances.

"So, Valerian is on his way to Colonia Agrippina", Hostilius said when we returned to our quarters. "Doesn't surprise me in the least. I've spent the afternoon with an old friend of mine, the primus pilus of the I Minervia. We shared a few cups. Don't be fooled by Postumus's jovial appearance. He can be an iron-hard bastard if he wants to - the men adore and fear him in equal measures. He's a bloody good soldier but no friend of Caesar Gallienus."

"What did you tell your friend about us?" I asked.

"Pretty much the same thing", Hostilius replied.

Chapter 3 – Two men

We continued our journey north on the morrow along the Roman road following the western bank of the Rhine.

Postumus travelled with us, but insisted on bringing his own escort of mounted Batavi – rough, spear-wielding brutes. They rode fine Gallic horses, drawing envious stares from Gordas.

"Who is he?" Postumus asked, gesturing with his chin to Gordas who rode ten paces ahead of us.

"My bodyguard", I replied.

"A Goth?" he asked.

"No", Marcus said. "The Goths tremble with fear when the name of his kind is mentioned. I pray to the gods the tribes of the Hun never covet these lands."

Postumus eyed Gordas warily, but he was unconvinced. "Never seen a bow like the one he carries."

I took my Hun bow from its case, slipped a string into the groove, and handed it to the legate, who turned the weapon in his hand, raising his eyebrows. "It is lopsided", he observed. "Is it any good?"

"It works reasonably well", I said.

Postumus nodded, then pointed to the river where a Roman ship powered north under oar. "The liburnians are fast, but we need smaller boats to pursue the tribes into shallower waters. They raid with flat-bottomed boats and flee back up the small tributaries leading into Barbaricum. They taunt us as soon as they reach the shallows."

I had no answer for Postumus, as I was well aware that the finances of the Empire were in a parlous state.

Colonia Agrippina was but fifteen miles north of Bonna, and soon the imposing walls of the provincial capital came into view.

"Seems awfully quiet", Marcus said when we were three hundred paces from the southern gate.

Postumus frowned and gestured to a flat expanse of land between the eastern walls of the city and the river, connected to the far bank by a wooden bridge. On the barbarian side of the river, a square fort, surrounded by thick walls and a moat, guarded the access to the bridge.

"The flat area is usually a bustling market", he said. "Trade between Rome and the Germani is flourishing despite the conflict. There should be hundreds of people, vending their wares."

Vibius pointed to a purple sail obscured by one of the large warehouses close to the wharf. "They wouldn't want Valerian to have to push his way through the market, eh?" he said with a grin.

"Our prayers have been answered", Postumus said, and I felt a weight lift from my shoulders.

We would not have to suffer Gallienus without the oversight of his father.

* * *

The scarred centurion extended his hand – a clear gesture for me to surrender my weapons. Ten paces behind him Valerian sat on a purple couch, flanked by two hulking praetorians.

"Leave him be", commanded the emperor. "Do you really think you would be able to stop the tribune if he had violence on his mind? Do you know not his reputation?"

The praetorians exchanged glances, doubting the words of the emperor.

"Leave us", Valerian said.

The centurion eyed me for a span of heartbeats, then nodded to his men. He bowed to the emperor before closing the door behind him.

I approached and went down on one knee.

Valerian stood and raised me to my feet, his hand remaining on my shoulder. "It is good to see you again, Lucius", he said in a tired voice. "You remind me of the fact that Rome is not only a bunch of conniving old men. It is why I labour every day, to support the men of iron, the warriors who keep the darkness from overwhelming us."

"My father gave his life for the Empire, lord", I said. "I have taken that burden upon my shoulders."

He slumped down on the couch. "Pour for us", he said.

I filled two golden chalices with rich, dark purple wine and handed one to Valerian.

"I desire to speak with you alone, Lucius", he said. "Tonight, my son will make announcements. I wish for you to know the reasoning behind it."

I trusted the old man, and nodded my acceptance of his words.

He drank deeply. "I believe that I have steadied the ship", he said. "The next step is to reclaim the East, to win back the

Roman lands conquered by the Sasanians. But it will all be in vain if Germania and the Danubian Provinces are lost to the barbarians."

"Your words are wise", I said.

"It is but the ramblings of an old man", he said and waved away my objections before I could air them.

"I have decided to relocate to the East in the coming months, to personally oversee the reconquest of Syria. It is too big a responsibility to delegate. While I am away, my son will ensure the integrity of the Rhine and Danubian frontiers."

Valerian was no fool and he must have noticed the doubt in my eyes.

"I know he is no warrior", he said, his eyes cast down. "Therefore, I have decided to appoint imperial legates, true soldiers, to share his burden. Postumus, the fierce Batavian, will protect Gaul and Germania Inferior. Marcus Claudius, your friend, will be the shield of Germania Superior and Raetia. General Ingenuus, a man as hard as iron, will defend the Danube. They are all loyal to me and I trust them implicitly."

"It is true", I said. "They are all men of reputation."

"But", he sighed. "I cannot go east alone because I, too, am no warrior. At least I am not fool enough to think that I am."

He took another swallow and continued. "And there is only one man I wish to have at my side – the favourite of Mars, the god of war. And that man, Lucius, is you."

I suspected that there was more to Valerian's request and decided to probe. "But there is something else?"

"He fears you, Lucius", Valerian replied. "Gallienus has seen what you are capable of. And fear makes men do foolish things. I am concerned that he may try to do you harm because of this. If he succeeds, Rome will lose much, but if he fails, nothing will be able to save us from what you will unleash. You not only command the loyalty of Romans - I know that the hordes of the Scythians will also answer your call."

For a moment I was stunned. "And what about the Illyrians?" I asked.

"Gallienus told me what he had witnessed", Valerian said. "No man could stand against them. It was as if the army of the underworld had been unleashed."

He drank again, carefully considering his words before he spoke. "Although your horsemen are a force to be reckoned with, there are not enough of them. Their numbers need to be increased to five, maybe ten thousand. Only then will they make a difference in a major battle."

The old senator was right. I did not possess enough gold to recruit and equip more Illyrians, although I had hoped that I would be the one to oversee their expansion on behalf of the Empire.

Valerian misinterpreted my hesitation. "Lucius", he said. "I will make it worth your while. Trust me and you will be well rewarded."

"I will accompany you", I said, "but I wish to be involved with the Illyrians until I leave."

"I expect that we will be ready to depart for the East towards the end of next year's campaigning season", he said. "I first need to replenish the army. Thousands of soldiers' lives were thrown away at Barbalissos. It will be of no use if we go to the East understrength."

"That will allow enough time to break the will of the Franks and hand over the Illyrians", he added.

There was still one issue that bothered me. "Who will command the Illyrians in my absence?" I asked.

Valerian stared into his cup of wine, clearly reluctant to meet my gaze. "To ensure harmony, sacrifices have to be made", he sighed.

"Will the Illyrians be such a sacrifice?" I asked, and became aware of a sudden chill in my voice.

Valerian did not reply. I felt the anger rise inside, but focused on the words of Cai, realising that the old senator was doing his best to keep the Empire from unravelling.

"May I suggest a compromise?" I asked, my tone reconciliatory.

Valerian nodded.

"Allow Marcus to remain involved with the Illyrians", I said.

"I will see what can be done", Valerian Augustus replied while I drained my cup in one swallow – the priceless wine suddenly tasteless.

* * *

Hostilius pursed his lips and looked me straight in the eye.

"It's not too late to unleash the Hun", he said.

"I was also tempted to listen to the wrong voice from inside", I replied, which served to deepen the Primus Pilus's frown, but Gordas nodded his understanding.

"Huns have a legend like that", he said. "My father told me that two spirits reside within each man. A weak one, prone to pity – the other, strong, proud and brave."

He turned away, and continued to rub the limbs of his horn bow with some vile-smelling concoction.

"And?" Hostilius asked. "Who do you listen to?"

Gordas grinned like a wolf. "The weak one has been silent for years", he said. "I think it is dead."

I ignored the Hun's remarks. "Don't forget who assisted us when the Arab wished to kill us. Valerian risked all to help us."

"He also gained the Roman throne in the process", Marcus added dryly.

"I believe that the happenings are the machinations of the gods", I said. "I have done what Arash had asked of me. The future is for them to decide, not for me to mould according to my will."

None gainsaid me.

"There is more", I said. "As soon as they are old enough, Valerian is planning to send Gallienus's two sons, Valerian the Younger and Saloninus, to the frontiers to gain experience."

"Who is being placed in charge of the Illyrians?" Vibius asked.

"A man called Aureolus", I said.

"The name does not seem familiar", Marcus said, frowning.

"He's the head of the imperial stables", Diocles said from behind his desk in the corner. "Word is that he is a confidant of Emperor Gallienus, as they are kindred spirits."

In response, Marcus issued a groan.

Chapter 4 – Sacrifice

Later the same evening, a few select men attended a private dinner hosted by the emperors.

When Marcus and I arrived at the venue, we found Emperor Valerian in conversation with Legate Ingenuus. He was not much older than me, tall and lean with dark brown hair and a neatly trimmed beard. Hostilius had told us that he was a well-liked commander – strict, yet honest and fair.

We clasped arms. "It is good to meet you, Tribune Domitius", he said and regarded me with dark brown eyes. "Your reputation precedes you."

"As does yours", I said.

Just then Gallienus walked into the room, leaving his escort of praetorians at the door. The co-emperor was deep in discussion with a clean-shaven, blonde-haired man. His handsome features were slightly tainted by overly large, fleshy lips, and eyes that seemed to protrude from his head, giving him a strange, toad-like appearance when viewed from a certain angle. Gallienus must have said something in jest because a heartbeat later his companion issued a suppressed snicker.

"Aureolus would benefit from a beard", I heard Postumus whisper to Ingenuus, which earned him a hard look from Valerian. "Maybe you could suggest it, lord", Ingenuus said, a smile playing around the corners of his mouth. The emperor dismissed the stab with a flick of his hand and walked towards Gallienus. Father and son embraced – a message to all that the leaders of the Empire were united.

Servants entered with large silver platters heaped with food. They moved with practised efficiency, laying the tables in the prescribed manner. The watchful eyes of the praetorians standing guard around the perimeter followed their every move.

"Although father and son embrace each other", Postumus said, "Valerian still brings his own servants and tasters to test the food. It pays to be careful, eh? Just in case."

I realised then that these men endured Gallienus for the sake of his father. Valerian knew the shortcomings of his son, but his fatherly love blinded him to a certain extent, not unlike the great Marcus Aurelius who was one of the wisest, but still could not see the failings of his own blood.

The last of the servants scrambled from the room and the guards closed the doors behind them.

"Friends", Valerian said, and raised his hand for silence. "Yes, you are all my friends", he emphasized. "Together we have struggled against the forces of darkness, from outside and within. Eventually the gods answered our prayers and provided us with an opportunity to make the name of Rome great once again."

Murmurs of agreement rose from the powerful men gathered in the room.

Valerian continued and announced his decision to relocate to the East. He then allowed Gallienus to name the men who would be the imperial legates of the West - Postumus, Marcus and Ingenuus. Gallienus heaped much praise on Aureolus, announcing that he would be the master of the imperial cavalry. My name was not mentioned, and while he spoke, a war raged inside my heart, as the voice of reason was trying to suppress the rage of the one who longed for glory.

When all had been said, Aureolus sought me out.

"Tribune Domitius", he said in a haughty voice, not dissimilar to that of the co-emperor. "I am Legate Aureolus. I am honoured that our beloved Emperor Gallienus wishes that I take control of the newly formed imperial cavalry. I want to give you the assurance that it is not because of incompetence on your side, it is just that I have worked with horses since I was a child."

It took five heartbeats to subdue the anger which rose like black bile. "Thank you, legate", I said, and prayed to Arash to help me stay my hand.

"I knew you would understand", he replied, and smiled a smile that accentuated his fleshy lips.

"I will remain in Colonia Agrippina for the duration of the campaigning season, as it will allow me to discuss my plans with Caesar Gallienus. Be ready to relinquish command to me before the end of the next year."

He turned around to leave, but then hesitated. "Oh yes, before I forget", he said. "I would like your escort of fifty men to remain behind in Colonia Agrippina for seven days. It will allow me the opportunity to gauge their skills. If you feel that you are in need of protection on the journey home, Caesar will gladly make available as many praetorians as you and Legate Claudius require."

He leaned in, lowering his voice. "I have the ear of Emperor Gallienus", he said. "Please me, and it will go well with you."

My sword hand was shaking, but Arash somehow calmed me. "Thank you, legate", I said and inclined my head so he would not see the murder in my eyes.

Later that evening Valerian Augustus took me aside and said, "Are you beginning to understand what I mean when I say that sacrifices have to be made?"

"Yes, lord", I said, and I meant every word.

* * *

"Over my dead body", Hostilius growled. "Those bloody praetorians can't be trusted. There's a good chance they'll turn on us and slit our throats in the middle hour of the night. The answer is no. We'll return via the same route, and spend the nights inside the safety of a fort."

Just then there was a knock at the door. Hostilius jerked it open.

"Sir", the praetorian centurion said and saluted. "I have fifty of my best men ready to escort you south."

"That won't be necessary", Hostilius said, then realised that he was probably required to provide a reason, as the centurion was simply following Gallienus's commands. "We have urgent business at Fort Niederbieber", he said, offering an explanation. "An ala of their cavalry will escort us south."

The centurion nodded. "Should I arrange for a barge to ferry you across the river, sir?"

"Do that", Hostilius said, and dismissed him.

The praetorian saluted and stomped back down the colonnaded portico.

"Thank you for making sure that we will be taking the long way home, Centurion", Marcus said with a grin.

"It will be much better than being in the company of those dour, nose-in-the-air praetorians who will listen to our every word", Hostilius said, and waved away Marcus's complaint. "You'll thank me eventually."

For a change, Hostilius would soon be proved wrong.

* * *

Less than a third of a watch later, Marcus, Vibius, Hostilius, Gordas, Diocles and I departed the capital of Germania

36

Inferior, riding south along the main Roman road which bordered the Rhine.

"What is your impression of Aureolus?" Marcus asked.

Before I could answer, Hostilius interjected. "That one's got shifty eyes", he said. "He's a schemer who's made a life by sucking up to Gallienus, who has been fool enough to fall for it."

He took a swig from his wineskin, reconsidering his words. "Mind you", he said, "they're probably cut from the same cloth, so I take back that Gallienus is a fool."

"I tend to agree with the Primus Pilus", I said, "although my judgement is clouded because I have been forced to relinquish command of the Illyrians."

"Clouded?" Hostilius asked. "It's Cai who has filled your head with all that nonsense. I will have a chat with him when we get back. In the meantime, I will pray to Mars to set you right."

We arrived at the crossing point of the Rhine mid-afternoon, where a Roman barge was pulled up against the bank. Soon we glided across the mirror-like surface of the calm water while barn swallows darted around our heads to feed on the little flying critters that spawn in the shallows.

When we dismounted on the far bank, Gordas pointed to a white stork that eyed us warily and then took flight. "The bird that brings good luck is avoiding us", he said with a grim expression.

"You scared it", I replied, but still said a quick prayer to Fortuna, just in case.

We continued our trek towards the fort at Niederbieber, following the paved road on the Roman side of the limes. It was built to follow the crest of a natural ridge to allow the towers unrestricted lines of sight. The lands north of the Rhine and south of the limes were mostly devoid of farms and covered in thick, ancient forests of oak, silver birch and beech.

Two miles down the road Gordas suddenly slowed, then vaulted from his horse. He lifted the animal's right front leg, inspecting its hoof.

We reined in and I turned in the saddle. Gordas met my gaze from beside his horse, and by the look in his eyes I immediately realised something was amiss.

"Do you need help?" I said in Latin.

He nodded. I dismounted and casually walked over, holding the horse's leg while he struggled to remove an imaginary splinter.

"There are Germani concealed in the forest up ahead", he whispered. "The wind carries their smell."

"Fall off the horse", I said, "and I will string our bows amid the confusion."

I slapped his back and laughed out loud in an attempt to mislead the Germani, who must have been watching.

"Come, let us ride", I said. "I am hungry and thirsty."

My strange behaviour drew a frown from both Hostilius and Marcus. "When Gordas falls from his horse, loosen your swords in their scabbards and come to his aid", I whispered under my breath. "And for the sake of the gods", I added, "stop frowning."

Twenty paces farther along the road, Gordas's horse reared up, throwing him from the saddle. I watched him do it – a performance that could have earned him a role in one of the plays favoured by Gallienus.

"Are you hurt?" I shouted and we all congregated around the Hun. I took the opportunity to string both our bows and to take a handful of arrows from my quiver.

"We will help Gordas back onto his horse", I said, and placed his strung bow and five arrows beside him.

"The Germani are about to ambush us", I said. "We will trot for twenty paces and then go to a full gallop as we pass the giant beech. Hostilius and I will lead, with Diocles riding between us. Gordas, Marcus and Vibius, take the rear."

None argued.

We struggled to get Gordas back in the saddle, insomuch that I suspected that he had genuinely injured himself. But he met my eyes for a heartbeat before he slumped, and I knew that it was no more than a masterful performance.

When I was level with the ancient tree, I kicked Kasirga to a gallop. He was a powerful animal and within a few paces we were flying along the cobbled road.

I dropped the reins and plucked my strung horn bow from its case, taking five arrows in my draw hand. To my left, a dark shape streaked through the mogshade. I pulled the string to my ear, tracked the shape which was moving towards the road, and released the broad-headed hunting arrow. Before the dead Frank's momentum carried him into our path, a second shaft left the string. The armour-piercing head slammed into a Germani's helmet, split the iron plate, and lodged deep inside his skull. A third, a big man with long braided hair and a blonde beard, made it to the side of the road, his throwing axe drawn back. Gordas's arrow skewered his neck, his weapon clattering onto the cobbles. He clutched his throat with both hands and swayed into Kasirga's path, the shoulder of the huge horse crushing the Frank before hurling him into the mud.

Hostilius launched four *plumbatae* into the undergrowth in quick succession and was rewarded with a scream. He drew his spatha and slashed backhanded at a warrior trying to lay a hand upon him.

I dodged an axe whirling from the shadows and heard a horse grunt in agony. Gordas somehow forced his gelding in behind Diocles, grabbing the boy's arm before his mount collapsed, and swung him onto the back of his horse.

Three Germani with locked shields stepped into the road in an attempt to block our way. Gordas's arrow pierced the one in the middle's thigh and he stumbled backwards. No horse runs into a shield wall, but in the fraction of a heartbeat after their comrade had fallen, the other two did not realise that they no longer presented a solid barrier.

Their shields helped naught as our horses slammed into them, and they disappeared underneath the hooves.

I assessed the damage. A spear, cast in desperation, had scored a deep line along Kasirga's rump and a francisca, thrown in haste, had ripped scales from my armour. I looked over my shoulder and saw more Germani spill from the woods – a noble on horseback among them.

I slipped two shafts from my quiver without slowing down, turned in the saddle, and released in quick succession. Three heartbeats later the mounted Germani toppled from his horse. The shouts of the barbarians turned into roars of anger and hundreds of screaming Franks surged towards us in pursuit.

We continued our flight south, thundering along the road. Gordas gestured to blood pouring down his horse's flank.

No words were required.

"We should seek shelter inside Niederbieber", I said, and deferred to Marcus for confirmation.

He nodded and I noticed blood dripping from underneath his helmet.

"Gordas's horse needs a medicus more than I do", he said, his eyes glassy.

I had seen the look before, reached out, and caught my friend by the arm just before he fell from the saddle.

Chapter 5 – The Bearded One

Marcus banged his fist on the table in anger, cringed, and gingerly touched his bandaged head. "Remind me not to do that again", he said.

"Aureolus was the one who stripped us of our escort", I said, and filled Marcus's cup.

"Maybe Gallienus put him up to it", Marcus said, taking a sip.

"Why?" I asked.

"He fears you, Domitius", Hostilius said, leaning in with his palms on the table. "Getting rid of you and Marcus in one fell swoop isn't something I would put past him. Actually", he added, "I might be giving him too much credit."

"Postumus could have arranged it", Diocles said. "He's half Germani. He most probably knows the Frankish nobles and speaks their tongue. With Legate Marcus out of the way, he would be able to take control of Germania Superior as well as Inferior."

Hostilius had realised long before that Diocles was no fool. "To what end?" the Primus Pilus asked cautiously.

"Maybe he is nurturing greater ambitions", the young Greek said. "Or do you believe that Postumus is the kind of man who would be willing to take instructions from Gallienus, Centurion?"

"By the gods, boy", Hostilius said. "You've got a scheming mind."

Diocles grinned in acceptance of the veiled compliment. "Blame my Greek blood, Centurion", he said.

We heard the clatter of hobnails on cobbles, followed by a knock on wood.

Prefect Caius Vitale pushed open the door. "Legate", he said. "I need your counsel."

"Are they here?" Gordas asked.

The prefect would most probably simply have ignored the words of the Hun, but Marcus's stare drew the answer. "They are", he said.

The day had turned dark, the sun obscured by grey clouds which leaked an interminable drizzle.

Wrapped in our sealskin cloaks, we followed Vitale, who led us to the battlements beside the western gate. The first thing I noticed was not the horde of savages milling at the treeline, but the thousands of freshly dug pits in the cleared area in front of the fort.

"Well done, Prefect Vitale", I said, gesturing to the pits. "It seems that you are not a man plagued by procrastination."

My words pleased the commander of the fort, who issued a smug smile. "Every one of those have a sharpened stake at the bottom", he said. "We've collected a wagon load of the stones you wanted placed in the clearing, but it's still parked next to the stables."

Marcus squinted at the hundreds of Franks gathered at the treeline.

"It is the same on all sides", Vitale volunteered. "Except to the north, where they are looting the village. Your early arrival afforded us enough time to get all the civilians inside the fort, legate. Most of the garrisons of the watchtowers made it back as well."

"How many barbarians?" Marcus asked.

"Three, maybe four thousand", the prefect said. "But there may be more hiding in the woods."

"Open the gate, prefect", I said. "I wish to speak with them."

For a span of heartbeats Vitale stared at me with his mouth agape, not being able to divine whether I was jesting or not.

"That is an order", I said. "And ready my bodyguard's horse as well", I added, which clearly pleased Gordas.

"And mine", Hostilius growled, not wishing to be outdone by the Hun.

Marcus was in no state to join us. Vibius agreed to stay behind in case our negotiations ended badly. Diocles remained silent – I could see in his eyes that the Greek viewed my suggestion as madness.

The prefect led us down the stone steps while a legionary jogged to the stables to retrieve our horses. He returned forthwith, followed by two grooms, each leading two horses.

"I will not hide behind the walls while my superiors risk their lives", Vitale said, a hint of defiance in his voice.

I nodded my approval.

We mounted, Vitale issuing the order for the gates to be opened. It took four legionaries to lift the heavy oak beams from their iron brackets.

"Order them to close the gate behind us", I said.

We walked our horses towards the Franks, reining in roughly halfway between the fort and the treeline. Our weapons were on open display as it was not the way of the Germani to parley unarmed.

"Will they come?" the prefect asked.

"I believe so", I said.

A heartbeat later four thousand screaming savages stormed from the woods.

We were saved by the insubordination of the centurion in charge of the gate. He had not replaced the locking bars as instructed, and a contubernium of his men were ready to open the gate. As the last of our group galloped through the archway, the legionaries were already heaving the iron-reinforced gate into place. Franciscas slammed into the wood as the enormous beams clunked into their brackets. The shouts of centurions echoed through the compound and I heard the familiar snaps of bolts flying from ballistae.

Hostilius gestured with his chin to the centurion at the gate. "Now there's a man who's going to be rewarded for not following orders", he said and exchanged nods with the tough-as-nails Briton.

"It is not the way of the Germani", I said with a frown, dismounted, and handed the reins to a waiting groom.

Hostilius nodded. "Something's not right, Domitius."

Less than a heartbeat later, a tremendous impact rocked the western gate, causing a puff of dust and shards of plaster to erupt from where the brackets of the beams were mounted to the wall.

"The bastards have a ram", Hostilius shouted.

Gordas and I followed the Primus Pilus up the broad stairwell leading to the third level of the northern tower, one of two flanking the gate. At the top was a roofed platform, six paces square, where we found a contubernium crew operating a bolt thrower. They released another thick wooden bolt with a broad iron head at the attackers assaulting the gate - a group of Germani wielding the bole of a felled oak by means of thick leather straps.

The barbarians were no fools because the ram bearers were protected by warriors wielding thick wooden shields constructed from rough-hewn planks – so heavy that each had to be handled by two men. We saw a bolt slam into such a shield. It split the wood and threw the warriors backwards, but did nothing to impede the progress of the ram-bearers.

"Ten strikes with the ram", Hostilius shouted to be heard above the roars of the attackers. "That's all it takes."

The barbarians were swarming through the ditch. I noticed groups of warriors carrying scaling ladders. Many were injured in the pits while others fell to pila and artillery bolts, but still hundreds bore down on the walls.

"Come", I said. "We need to stop the ram."

We ran into Vitale, who directed a reserve of legionaries, carrying three pila each, up to the towers in an attempt to hold the gate.

"It's the first time I've seen Germani use a ram", he shouted, his voice barely audible above the din of battle as another impact rattled the gate.

"Get the eight strongest men in the fort to the gate and draw one contubernium tent from the stores", I ordered, "and meet us here."

Vitale knew better than to question my orders.

Gordas, Hostilius and I rushed to the stables where we found a wagon, loaded with two enormous stones. I shouted instructions to a stable hand who appeared sixty heartbeats later, leading Kasirga and Gordas's horse. We tied our lassos to the neck yoke of the wagon and the other ends to the saddles, then nudged our horses forward. Hostilius pushed from behind.

We arrived at the gate soon after, just as another strike of the ram shook the foundations of the wall. Beside the prefect stood eight Britons. All had the look of powerful men – thick necks, bulging arms and squat legs.

"Four strikes", Vitale said, his voice laced with concern. "We're killing them from the towers, but as soon as one goes down, another one takes his place. There are too many."

I rolled open the tent with my foot, drew my jian, and cut two large squares of tough canvas with the razor-sharp edge, then placed it on the ground at the rear of the wagon – one on top of the other. Before I stepped away, I rotated the top square to allow for eight handholds should the corners of the canvas be grasped.

I pointed to four of the men. "Roll a stone onto the canvas."

When the stone lay in place, I called four more men. "Grab a corner and follow me", I said.

It was the moment of truth. The eight men each took hold of a corner and heaved, the veins bulging in their thick necks, the muscles in their forearms rippling. The stone lifted off the ground.

"Bring the other stone if you are able", I said to a gaping Vitale, and led the eight groaning men up the stairs.

When the seventh strike of the ram reverberated through our bodies, we arrived on the second level right above the gate. Legionaries were launching spears, pila and stones at the attackers, whose large wooden shields deflected most of the missiles. I saw a Frank go down with a pilum in the leg. Immediately he was replaced by another - the injured man staggering back to safety. All around, the horde assaulted the wall, trying to gain a foothold. As soon as a Frank managed to get onto the rampart, a well-armoured auxiliary dispatched him.

Below us, the ram-bearing Germani retreated ten paces to gain momentum for the charge. I caught a glimpse of the hulking, bearded men carrying the ram, all kitted out in Roman mail and helmets, brown furs draped over their powerful shoulders.

With bulging muscles, the auxiliaries lifted the stone, balancing it on the inside edge of the breastwork between two merlons. I knew that it would take great effort to topple the stone over the wall and waited until the ram bearers had begun their charge.

51

"Now", I said, and the men heaved with all their might. I had underestimated the effort required - the stone lifted, but did not budge.

Hostilius met my gaze. "I'm not bloody well spending my last years as a latrine slave of the Germani", he said, and joined the effort of the men.

As usual Hostilius had a way with words. Gordas and I immediately added our strength to the push. Just then the ninth strike rocked the gatehouse. Whether it was the strike, or the effort caused by it, I will never know. But at that moment we won the battle with the stone. I felt it move away from us, slowly toppling over the wall.

Fortuna smiled on us – and frowned on the attackers. The massive rock struck the business end of the oak ram as the Germani retreated for the next charge, crushing the shield bearers as if they were mere vermin, and shaking the ground like the hammer of the bearded, red-haired god. The log split, ripping apart the bodies of the men carrying it, launching deadly splinters in all directions, impaling many attackers.

"By the gods", Hostilius said, gesturing at the carnage in front of the gate.

There was another deep, guttural rumble, and I thought for a moment that another gate was under attack, but a streak of lightning arced from within the dark clouds and struck the roof of the praetorium in the centre of the fort. The roar of thunder that followed shook the ground and chilled my blood.

A heartbeat later, a collective sigh emanated from the horde before the wall. As one their hands moved to their amulets.

"What in Hades is going on?" Hostilius said, gaping at the thousands of savages fleeing through the mud to disappear into the distant treeline.

"It was the lightning", I said. "Donar has shown whom he favours. No Germani is fool enough to stand against the will of the red-bearded god."

Chapter 6 – Narjan (September 254 AD)

Vitale removed the helmet from one of the mangled corpses sprawled on the cobbles in front of the western gate. "Made in a Roman *fabrica*", he said, and nudged the body with his foot. "And so was the mail."

"They've been looting Roman weapons and armour for years", he added.

The helmets were all in the modern style, untarnished and shiny. I kept my counsel.

"Keep the men inside the fort", I commanded Vitale.

He returned to the fort to give effect to my orders, leaving Hostilius, Gordas and me among the dead and injured. I noticed movement at the side of the road and we sloshed through the mire to investigate. A scarred, bearded warrior, with lank blonde hair caked with mud, was pinned underneath a piece of the split ram.

"Careful", Hostilius growled. "They are treacherous bastards. Best is to put four inches of iron into their hearts before you get too close." He picked up a Germani spear lying in the mud and tested it for balance.

"I will be careful", I said.

"Hades is filled with men who spoke about being careful", Hostilius replied with a scowl.

The warrior, whose legs were stuck, turned his head towards us. "Have you come to gloat, Roman swine?" he spat in the tongue of the Germani.

Hostilius drew back his spear to thrust it through the Germani's neck.

"No", I said, and gripped my friend's arm in order to stay his hand.

At that moment, when he believed I was distracted, the Germani lunged for my chest with a spear he had concealed beside him in the mud. Expecting the strike, I stepped to the side and grabbed hold of the haft of the weapon behind the crude iron point, and plucked it from his grasp.

"I might be a swine, but at least I am not a fool", I said in the language of the North. "Now you will have to cross the bridge of stars without a weapon in your hand. Do you think that the Red-Bearded One will allow you to enter the mead hall empty-handed?"

The Germani clenched his teeth in a show of defiance, confirming my suspicion.

I rammed the spear into the ground and took hold of the log. "Help me lift it", I said.

"I hope you know what you're doing", Hostilius whispered.

"He still has a sword or dagger", I whispered as we rolled the log off the Germani's legs. "For the sake of the gods, Primus Pilus, I need him. Please don't kill him."

Hostilius was far from happy, but issued a curt nod.

"And keep Gordas from splitting his skull with a battle-axe", I added.

I plucked the spear from the mud while the Germani slowly came to his feet. Reluctantly, Hostilius and Gordas retreated.

The warrior rubbed his stiff limbs and rolled his shoulders, inhaling deeply. I realised then how big the man was – nearly a head taller than me. Silver and gold torques decorated his bulging arms.

"When you arrive at the door of the corpse hall, tell Donar that it was Narjan, champion of the Amsivarii who sent you", the giant growled and drew his blade. "Around the feasting table you will find many who have succumbed to my iron."

He lunged at my chest. I skipped back and to the side, narrowly avoiding his longsword. In the same movement, I crouched low, and swung the haft of the spear in a sweeping motion, like the Easterners do with a staff. The butt struck Narjan's ankle, and he stumbled backwards.

Again, he attacked, sweeping his sword diagonally from low to high. I stepped in close to get inside his guard. The haft of my spear met his blade near the hilt, where it held little power. Before he could react I headbutted him in the face – the brow of my helmet crushing his nose. He staggered backwards, and the butt of my spear struck him against the side of the head.

The impact would have killed a lesser man, but only served to stun the Germani. The sword fell from his hand and he collapsed to his knees in the mud.

I drew my jian. "Tell Teiwaz that Eochar of the Roxolani sent you", I said, and drew back my blade. "Maybe he will allow you entry, although you have no weapon."

For the first time I saw fear in his eyes. "The Scythian who walks with the god", he mumbled, eyes wide.

I sheathed my blade.

"Or you could do my bidding and drink mead beside your hearth overmorrow", I said, and helped him to his feet.

Not long after, we watched as the hulking Germani, sitting atop a Roman horse, melted into the greenwood.

"Waste of a good gelding", Hostilius said.

"He has given his oath", I countered. "You know it is sacred to them."

Hostilius nodded reluctantly. "We will see."

Then the ground began to tremble underneath our feet, and hundreds of black-clad Illyrians arrived, cantering down the Roman road. "Lord", the lead rider said when he reined in five paces from us, "we rode as soon as we received word."

By the condition of his horse, it was clear that they had pushed the animals to their limits. "You have done well", I said and turned to Vitale. "Please see to my men."

* * *

We spent the evening inside the fort while the rain continued unabated.

As before, Vitale had insisted that we take up accommodation in his personal quarters. The commander was well aware that expecting an imperial legate to suffer the indignity of overnighting in guest rooms could result in dire consequences at best.

The storm had ushered in the first chill of autumn. Marcus, Vibius, Hostilius and I reclined on couches draped with furs, while Diocles heated red wine on a brazier, stirring in honey. He filled our cups to the brim before joining us on the comfortable seats.

"How is the head, Marcus?" I asked.

"Better than the Germani's who tried to spear you today", he said with a chuckle. "What did you bid him do?"

"Very little", I replied. "I sent him with a message to Haldagates, to meet us on the night of the next full moon."

There was a knock at the door and Diocles stood to usher in the cook, followed by two serving slaves who carried large covered trays of fare.

The cook, who had no doubt personally overseen the preparation of the food, wiped sweat from his brow with a cotton cloth. He watched the slaves with an eagle eye while they arrayed the platters on a low table. "Please look past the simplicity of tonight's meal, legate", he said. "To find the desired ingredients for a repast befitting your exalted status is not an easy task."

Hostilius leaned forward from the couch, sniffing the air. "What have you prepared?"

The cook smiled with satisfaction, having anticipated the question. "As appetizer, fried pumpkin fritters stuffed with sheep's brains and herbs, all smothered in a raisin wine and black pepper sauce", the man said. "On the side you will find spicy chicken livers with vegetable relish."

"And the mains?" Hostilius asked.

"Honeyed, fig-braised pork shoulder, covered in a crispy dough", the cook said. "And for those who prefer the delicate taste of fowl, there is roast duck with herbs and turnips."

He removed the silver cloches with a flourish, revealing the steaming dishes, then bowed low and closed the door behind him.

Hostilius reached for a piece of dough-covered pork, only to find Diocles's hand on his arm. "It might be poisoned, Primus Pilus", he said, and took the morsel from Hostilius's hand before he could argue, swallowing it down with a gulp of wine.

"How do you feel?" Hostilius asked after Diocles had sampled all the fare.

"Still hungry", he said, and reached for more.

* * *

Two weeks later, on the night of the full moon, Hostilius, Gordas and I slipped through a gate in the limes near Holzhausen.

Haldagates, Hlodwig and Fardinanth waited for us at the treeline. We dismounted, and the Franks followed suit.

"Narjan of the Amsivarii visited my hall bearing a message", Haldagates said. "He told me that he had been defeated by some man-god who walks with Teiwaz. But it could not have been you, Eochar, because he mentioned that the being was twice the size of a man."

I grinned, aware of the Germani's talents for exaggeration. "It was raining", I said, which made him laugh out loud.

My Germani friend turned serious. "I am no traitor to my people", he said, "but neither am I fond of deceit. A Roman messenger from Colonia Agrippina arrived at the camp of the

61

Amsivarii shortly before they crossed the limes. Even if I knew more, I would not tell."

"Thank you", I replied. "That was all I wished to know."

I embraced Haldagates and clasped arms with his men. "Farewell", I said. "Mayhap one day we will fight on the same side."

The big Frank noble nodded and slipped away into the forest.

Chapter 7 – Blame

"It's either Gallienus, Postumus or Aureolus", I said. "Or a combination of them."

"I do not believe it matters who it is", Diocles said. "What is important is that we know that we have to be mindful of a blade in the back."

"Let us assume that it was Postumus or Aureolus", he continued. "How would you remedy the situation, tribune? Would Gallienus believe Aureolus is capable of deceit? Would Valerian act against Postumus, whom he regards with the same affection as one would a son?"

Diocles displayed insight well beyond his years. He must have noticed my surprise.

"I read while you train with blades", he said.

Diocles had shown remarkable natural skill with weapons, but an even greater reluctance to spend time on anything of a martial nature.

"We will have to remedy your lack of weapon skills", Hostilius said while bouncing little Maximiam on his knee.

"Reciting Greek scribblings is not going to save you when some savage or other wants to bury his iron in your gut."

"Hostilius is right", I said. "No more excuses."

"Excuse me", he said, and stood from his seat on the furs. "I still have much reading to do, as there will be little time for it tomorrow."

"That boy has potential", Hostilius growled when Diocles had left the hearth. "He needs to experience what it feels like to face thousands of screaming barbarians with only a gladius separating you from the far bank of the Styx. Then he'll be keen to learn blade craft."

* * *

Gallienus did not grace us with his presence that winter.

To his credit, before the snows blocked the Alpine passes, chests of gold arrived from Rome, escorted by five hundred farm boys, all chosen for their equestrian skills.

We put the episode at Niederbieber from our minds, but vowed to stay vigilant when dealing with the men occupying the seats of power.

Diocles reluctantly joined us each day when we trained with the sword and the spear. As a consequence, his martial skills improved hand over fist, although he complained regularly that it was at the cost of leaving the Greek scrolls unread.

Hostilius, Gordas and I immersed ourselves in training the new recruits and equipping them in the way of the Illyrians. When the month of the war god finally arrived with the meltwater of spring, the cavalry had grown from five hundred to a thousand. Sometimes, when they practised their manoeuvres on the training ground, I imagined the devastating power that a force numbering ten thousand would wield. In those moments, sadness and desperation overcame me because my time with the Illyrians was measured.

Late one afternoon, two days after the Ides of March, Hostilius, Gordas, Cai, Ursa and I sat on the furs around the hearth in my hall. Diocles sat apart, reading his scrolls, while Segelinde and Aritê were engaged in what can only be called a subdued argument. Adelgunde busied herself with restraining Maximian, who was trying to get hold of Diocles's scroll.

It was cold, so we drank heated, honeyed wine while rain pattered on the rooftiles.

"I have decided to leave Roman lands", Aritê announced out of the blue, stunning us all into silence.

In a traditional Roman household, my daughter's words would most probably have earned her confinement to her chamber for at least a moon, but in her veins flowed the blood of the Scythians, who regarded women equal to men.

I noticed that all, including Aritê, was staring at me, waiting for a response.

"I believe that it is the will of the gods", she added when I was too slow to answer, her eyes narrowing.

As a child, I had watched countless flies getting entangled beyond escape while attempting to extricate themselves from a spider's web. Without exception, the spider would always sit a handspan away, watching patiently while its prey toiled to bring about its own downfall.

On that night my daughter's gaze reminded me of a spider. And there was little doubt in my mind who represented the fly.

I decided not to struggle.

"When do you wish to leave?" I asked, and took a swallow from my cup to disguise my tenuous hold over my emotions.

It was too much for Aritê, who had prepared for a confrontation. She buried her head in her hands and started sobbing before fleeing into the night with Little Nik following close behind.

"That was harsh", Gordas growled, defending his favourite member of the opposite sex.

I scowled in reply, draped my bear cloak over my shoulders, and went in search of my daughter.

Aritê stood on the rampart above the gate, staring into the blackness. "I did not think that you would let me go so easily", she said. "I believed that you cared for me."

It was my turn to shed a tear, trusting that it would not be discernible from the rain spattering my face. I said naught for a handspan of heartbeats until I had composed myself.

"It is not that", I said, using the tongue of the Roxolani. "Remember that I, too, have the blood of the Scythian." I gestured to the forest surrounding us. "Sometimes it feels as if the dark woods are suffocating me", I revealed. "I despise the incessant rain and the muddy bogs of this cursed land of the Germani. I wish to ride Kasirga across the endless plains of the Sea of Grass with the wind in my hair. When evening comes, I long to sit on the furs beside the cooking fire in front of my tent underneath the bridge of stars, surrounded by my mother's people. I wish to ride to battle with my kin and stand shoulder to shoulder with Bradakos, my sword brother."

"Why do you stay here?" she asked, her words suddenly devoid of blame or hostility.

"Because Arash has led me here", I said. "Because I have taken up Nik's burden."

She took a step towards me and buried her head in the thick cloak, sobbing. "I will leave as soon as you have the opportunity to accompany me on my journey", she said.

"You know that I cannot remain there", I sighed.

She nodded.

"How do you know that it is the will of the gods?" I asked in an attempt to lighten the mood.

"Because Arash spoke to me in a dream", she said.

Before I could reply Little Nik issued a low growl. Moments later we heard the sound of hooves sloshing through mud.

* * *

Marcus and Vibius accepted the proffered cups with grateful nods.

"The Marcomanni are swarming across the Danube near Vindobona in Pannonia. Ingenuus, who is still rebuilding his understrength legions, have asked Gallienus for assistance."

"And he wants the Illyrians?" I asked.

"More than that, Gallienus wishes for you to accompany him", Marcus said. "He mentioned in his letter that Aureolus is not yet ready to take command. Apparently he is currently indisposed, to use the words of Caesar."

"I'll tell you why he's indisposed", Hostilius said. "Because he had to change his braccae after Gallienus told him he'll be meeting the Marcomanni."

"It appears that the Marcomanni are willing to negotiate", Marcus said. "After the last round of talks with Chrocus and the Alemanni had ended in disaster, Gallienus is wary. He said that he wants you at his side due to your cultural sensitivity."

"The Marcomanni are not known for their negotiating skills", I replied. "Their preferred method of communication involves wielding blades."

"That will give me the opportunity to travel east with you", Aritê said.

"East?" Segelinde asked.

And then my daughter doomed me with her actions.

She embraced me and kissed me on the cheek. "Papa said that I could go live with Grandfather Bradakos", she announced.

"Oh", Segelinde said. "Did he really?" and there was no mistaking the chill in her voice.

"I've purchased a new boar spear from a travelling Germani merchant", Hostilius said, and gestured for Marcus and Vibius to follow him. "It's been blessed by one of their priests to fly true. Come, let me show you the magic markings."

I suddenly found myself alone with Aritê and Segelinde, and for the second time that evening I felt like a fly caught in a spider's web.

Chapter 8 – Struggle (April 255 AD)

A week later we departed for Vindobona in Pannonia.

Gallienus and his praetorians led the way with my Illyrians acting as a rearguard. Gordas, Diocles and Aritê were in conversation a few strides behind Hostilius and me.

"So how did you manage to convince Segelinde?" Hostilius asked.

"I didn't struggle", I said and dismissed his frown with a wave of my hand. "It's a long story."

Hostilius looked over his shoulder to ascertain whether anyone was listening and lowered his voice. "Have you seen the way Diocles looks at Aritê?"

"He can look all he wants", I said. "But she's not ready for a serious relationship. Not yet, anyway."

Hostilius narrowed his eyes. "That's what all fathers say", he said.

"She follows the old ways", I said. "Remember, she is Bradakos's only grandchild. She is a princess of the Royal Scythians, and wishes to uphold the ancient traditions."

"What kind of traditions?" he asked.

"She has to kill a man in battle before she is allowed to marry", I explained.

Hostilius raised his eyebrows. "Bloody hell", he said, "that's asking a lot."

"Not really", I replied. "Have you seen her practise with a bow recently?"

"No", he said.

"If you did, you would not have believed that it is asking a lot", I said, causing Hostilius to peek over his shoulder again, staring at the sweet girl giggling at Diocles's jests.

Gallienus and his entourage set a slow pace, scarcely advancing thirty miles a day. It soon became apparent that they had planned it, as the way stations where we spent most evenings were thirty miles apart.

During the afternoon break on the third day on the road I decided to speak with Gallienus regarding our slow progress. I found the emperor seated underneath a purple silk canopy. A team of cooks, servants and praetorians rode ahead every day to prepare this small indulgence for the co-ruler of the known world.

"Ah, Tribune Domitius", he said when he noticed me, and indicated for the praetorians to allow me through.

He flicked his fingers and a servant appeared with a foldable wooden stool and an additional plate. Before I could state the reason for my visit, the cook approached with a silver platter filled with steaming fare. Another carried a plate stacked with flatbread. A pouring slave carefully balanced a tray with a silver pitcher and two golden goblets.

"My favourite", Gallienus exclaimed, and clapped his hands together in delight. "Parthian style chicken with chilled shirazi."

With a nod of the emperor's head, two plates were dished. A taster stepped forward, bowed his head, and produced a silver spoon and a small goblet. Gallienus inhaled the aroma of the food and leaned back, allowing the taster to scoop out a morsel and decant a swallow of wine into his own goblet, which he consumed before moving away, yet remaining within sight of the emperor.

Gallienus leaned in conspiratorially. "If you allow them out of your sight, they can empty the contents of their stomachs", he explained.

He regarded the taster for another thirty heartbeats. Apparently satisfied, he then took a swallow of wine. "You know Domitius, this journey is turning out to be a gift from the gods. It feels like a holiday, being away from all the sycophants and courtiers."

The emperor gestured to the lands surrounding him. "I feel alive again", he said and inhaled deeply, "sharing the hardships of campaign with my men. I just wish that the journey could be longer."

He removed a drumstick from the rich sauce and savoured it while gesturing for me to eat. When he was done, he licked the sauce from his fingers and took another swallow of wine. "And there are no nobles to frown and whisper behind my back when I act like a base barbarian", he added.

"Before I forget, Domitius", he said. "What is the reason for your visit?"

* * *

"Did he heed your advice?" Hostilius asked when I returned.

"I did not ask him", I said.

"Why were you away for a watch then?" he asked. "And why do you smell like a bloody Parthian?"

In any event, I abandoned the idea of hastening our progress and decided to view the trip as a holiday, attempting to enjoy the days spent in the company of my daughter who I would most probably not see again soon.

Changing my mindset took the best part of two days. I had just begun to relax when the trouble started.

"Emperor Gallienus has requested that I dine with him tonight", Aritê said, which nearly caused me to fall off my horse.

After I had composed myself, I asked, "At what time are we to join him?"

"The invitation is for me alone", she said. "He took pity on me, a noble *femina* forced to associate with rough soldiers. He said that he too would enjoy to spend the evening in refined, educated company."

I tried to talk her out of it because I did not doubt for a moment that Gallienus's intentions were less than honourable, but she had already accepted the invitation and her mind was made up. Since I had insisted that she be raised to be independent, in the way of the Scythians, it was much too late to change my mind.

75

As was the norm, the praetorians took control of the entire way station even before we arrived, evicting the garrison soldiers and travellers to fend for themselves. The Illyrians made camp around the perimeter while the emperor and his entourage were accommodated within the relative safety of the walls.

I spent the evening beside the fire with my friends, worrying about my daughter's safety.

My companions shared my concern.

Hostilius spoke little, rather spending his time running a stone along the edge of his dagger. Gordas stared into the fire, no doubt berating himself for not opening Gallienus's throat months before. Diocles faked reading a scroll, wearing a generally dejected expression.

Not long after the buccina announced the start of the second watch of the night, Aritê returned, escorted by two praetorians. She nodded, confirming that she was safe, and sat down beside me on the furs.

"And?" I asked.

"I don't want to talk about it", she replied, stood, and retired to her tent.

I spent the night in anguish, dreaming up all kinds of horrific scenarios, all ending up with my sword buried in Gallienus's chest.

When morning arrived, I was determined to assert my rights as the *paterfamilias* and stormed to my daughter's tent. Hostilius and Gordas must have been waiting for me to appear and fell in beside me. We found her outside, dressed in her Scythian garb – a green long-sleeved woollen tunic matched with blue, loose-fitting trousers tucked into undyed soft leather boots. For protection she wore a short-sleeved scale vest that extended to her knees. Her sword and dagger were attached to a broad red leather belt. The limb of a strung bow protruded from a case hanging from her saddle.

"If you must know", she said, "he touched my arm without asking for permission."

I had heard enough and my hand went to my sword.

Hostilius grabbed my arm in his vice-like grip. "Let's hear the full story", he said.

She nodded, nonplussed. "He had dismissed his guards and I was alone in his company", she said.

Hostilius tightened his grip on my arm.

Aritê then turned her gaze on me, her grey-blue eyes devoid of emotion. In that moment it felt as if Kniva was staring at me. I realised that in her veins flowed the blood of the fearsome Goths and the vicious, untameable Scythians. "I threw him to the floor", she said, "and pressed my blade against his jugular. I told him that if he even so much as looks at me again, I will take his scalp", she hissed through clenched teeth.

Equally intimidated, we all retreated a step.

"And I warned him that if I find out that he had told anyone, the Ilyrians that are loyal to you alone, Father, will have his head."

She turned to inspect the tack of her horse. "And I told him I would keep it a secret", she added.

"But you've just told us?" Hostilius asked, suddenly cautious.

She turned to face us, smiling sweetly. "He is a fool", she said. "He did not ask for my oath, and neither did I volunteer it."

Then she vaulted onto her horse and rode off.

"By the gods", Hostilius said. "I feared for her, but I was wrong. I should have feared for Gallienus."

I was too shocked to answer, but I did notice Gordas wearing a smug expression, clearly proud of Aritê.

* * *

No harm was done, and for the greater good I put the incident from my mind, although it did say a lot about Gallienus's character.

I avoided him for the remainder of the journey and I suspect he did the same.

Chapter 9 – Marcomanni

Little Nik lay down on the furs, resting his enormous head on Aritê's lap.

I placed another thick oak log in the flames. "He's getting old", I said.

My daughter nodded. "It is his last journey, Father", she said, and averted her gaze for obvious reasons. "I can see it in his eyes – he knows we are travelling to the Sea of Grass."

Gordas nodded his agreement. "The spirit of the wolf longs for the plains. It wishes to return."

"It's an overgrown dog, for Hades's sake", Hostilius said, drawing a guttural growl from the wolf.

"Tomorrow we will arrive at Vindobona", he continued. "Where do we go from there?"

"If Rome wishes to negotiate with the Marcomanni, we need to understand why they have breached the border", I said. "We will cross the Danube and visit with my friend Belimar, the prince of the Quadi. The Quadi and the Marcomanni are kin. Belimar will know why they have invaded Roman lands."

I placed a hand on my daughter's shoulder. "You and the wolf will accompany Gordas, Hostilius, Diocles and me. The Quadi will regard it as an honour to be visited by the princess of the Roxolani."

"The great Marcus Aurelius died at Vindobona, you know", I said. "He was planning his final campaign against the Marcomanni and the Quadi when he passed away."

Aritê nodded, clearly disinterested, preferring to concentrate on scratching the wolf's ears.

"Your grandfather, Nik, was at the emperor's side when he crossed the river", I said.

The mention of her grandfather, who doted on her, served to rouse her curiosity. "Nik told me that Marcus Aurelius, when close to death, asked him for an oath to look after Commodus. In his last days the emperor must have realised that he had doomed the Empire by placing a madman on the throne."

"So, did he give his oath?" Gordas asked.

"He did", I said with a grin. "But he gave an oath to do his utmost to make sure that the Empire survived."

"Which is an oath that he honoured", Hostilius said, and raised his cup to Nik.

We all followed suit.

* * *

Gallienus listened to my words, then nodded. "I approve", he said. "Will your daughter be travelling with you?" he asked, and I thought I noticed a flicker of fear in his eyes.

"She will", I replied, deciding not to mention that she would remain in Barbaricum.

"I have much to do in Carnuntum, the capital of Pannonia", he said. "There is no need to make haste. The amber trade flows through the city, therefore it is important from an economic perspective. I wish for the people of Pannonia to come to know and love their emperor."

His words made me cringe on the inside. "Caesar is most gracious", I said. "I will return in one month's time."

* * *

Hostilius guffawed. "No doubt he has much to do in Carnuntum. It's got one of the largest amphitheatres in the Empire, famous for its gladiator shows. There's a huge *ludis* just outside the city which sources their fighters directly from the lands of the Marcomanni and Quadi."

He leaned in closer, as if wishing to share a secret. "I've heard that the amber caravans are now bringing in fighters captured on the Ice Islands in the north. If I were a betting man, I would wager that Gallienus will insist on seeing those white-haired giants in action."

He took a sip from his cup. "They have races as well", he said, "or so I've heard anyway."

Hostilius reflected for a moment. "Come to think of it, I wouldn't mind spending a few days in Carnuntum myself. I haven't been to the theatre in years."

I reined in close to where a Roman barge was anchored, its wooden deck level with the wharf of Vindobona. With a nod I acknowledged the captain, who had been expecting us. We dismounted and led our horses onto the flat deck.

Less than a third of a watch later the barge was poled away from the reed-covered northern bank of the Danube – the relief clearly visible on the faces of the crew whose eyes were pinned on the treeline. We walked our horses into the woods and changed into our barbarian garb, donning the rich clothes of noblemen. Aritê draped a red embroidered shawl, stitched with gold plaques, over her shoulders. She pinned it in place with a jewelled brooch fashioned in the form of a horse. Both items were gifts from Bradakos and matched the etched plaques on her broad red leather belt.

Gordas nodded his approval. "No warrior will even dare address you without kneeling, Princess", he said, "never mind harm you."

We rode north, deeper into the lands controlled by the Quadi, following a muddy track meandering through the greenwood. Farther from the river, where the woods thinned, we came across small farms and pastures where family groups of Germani eked out a living from the soil. Our group was not large enough to intimidate, so the farmers straightened from their back-breaking toil in the fields and waved as we passed.

"The Germani are a friendly people", I said as we rode past another farmer who smiled and waved at us.

"Don't be fooled by appearances, Domitius", Hostilius growled. Gordas grunted his agreement from behind.

The sight of farms became more regular, and eventually we came upon larger settlements. While attempting to pass through one of these villages, we found our path blocked by a group of spear-wielding warriors - a man seated on a horse at their centre.

"Who wishes to pass through the lands of Lord Gabinius?" he said.

"Who is asking?" I said.

"Lord Gabinius", he said, issuing a grin.

I removed my helmet and nudged my horse closer to the warriors as a sign that I did not fear them. I inclined my head in a show of respect. "I am Lord Eochar of the Roxolani", I said in the tongue of the Germani. "I come to these lands to visit with a friend, Prince Belimar of the Quadi."

"King Belimar", he corrected me. "His father, Gabin, has crossed the bridge of stars and feasts within the Hall of Donar."

"You are welcome in my hall, Lord Eochar of the Roxolani", he said. "Sup with me, and on the morrow I will escort you north to the great hall of the king."

We spent a pleasant evening in the company of Gabinius, who was a no-nonsense warrior. His grandfather had been given the rule of a portion of the borderlands by Belimar's father years before, and he was a staunch supporter of the new king.

The following morning we departed early, escorted by Gabinius and five of his men. By late afternoon we arrived at the fort of the Quadi - a large stronghold surrounded by a packed stone wall topped with a rough-hewn wooden palisade. It was no impregnable Roman fortress, but still formidable when measured against the standards of the Germani.

The stout oak doors stood wide open. Gabinius waved to the burly guards, who smiled and returned the gesture. Unmolested we continued along the main thoroughfare, crowded with vendors struggling with carts filled with wares ranging from vegetables to iron-tipped spears and anything in between.

"It is a market day", Gabinius explained.

I could not help but notice that more than a few of the traders appeared to be Roman – the pottery, glassware and other goods they carried seemed to be of Roman origin. After struggling against the current of merchants for a while, we eventually arrived at an enormous wooden hall raised on a foundation of thick oak posts.

We tied our horses to a hitching rail while Gabinius ascended the steps to a doorway guarded by two rough-looking Germani warriors clad in Roman mail. They exchanged words, and afterwards one of the guards entered the hall, our host remaining outside.

Heartbeats later a regal-looking Germani, flanked by guards, stepped through the doorway. It took a moment to recognize the gladiator I had befriended years before. His dark hair hung loose to his shoulders, his braided beard dark and full. He wore a sleeveless mail jerkin that extended to his knees. His green woollen braccae, embroidered with gold-coloured thread, were tucked into calf-length soft leather boots. Gold and silver bands adorned his thick, muscular arms. My eye caught the golden torque of the goddess Sandraudiga which I had gifted him that night in the *ludis* in Rome.

Belimar broke into a grin, skipped down the stairs, and embraced me in a bear hug. "By the gods, Lucius", he said, "it is good to see you."

He clasped arms with Hostilius, and I introduced him to Gordas and Diocles.

Arité still lingered beside her horse a few paces distant, catching my Quadi friend's eye. "Who is the Scythian noblewoman?" he asked. "Is she your bride?"

"She is my daughter", I said, "and next in line for the Roxolani throne."

"The granddaughter of Bradakos?" he asked.

I nodded in response.

Gabinius had business to attend to, so we bade him farewell. Belimar led us into his hall while issuing orders to his guards and servants. "We will feast tonight", he said, which came as no surprise.

He gestured for us to take seats at a large oak table close to the hearth, in which a roaring fire blazed. Slaves and servants appeared with horns of mead and ale. A silver pitcher filled with red wine was placed on the table near the king. He reached out, filled a fine Roman glass to the brim, and passed the pitcher to me.

"Once one has tasted the fruits of civilization", he said, and raised his glass, "it is difficult to return to the ways of old."

While I was filling my glass, a man of advanced years, but not yet an oldster, entered the hall, followed by a comely woman. He appeared strangely familiar.

"Do you remember my brother-in-law?" he asked and stood to show his guests to the table.

I clasped the arm of Centurion Ulpius Bacchius, whose life I had saved many years before. He, a retired Roman officer, had married a slave girl taken from the lands of the Germani. The slave turned out to be a high-born Quadi, none other than Brunhilde, the sister of Belimar.

Behind Brunhilde strode two strong young boys.

"The debt that I owe you, Lucius, can never be repaid", Belimar said. "My father's last years were filled with happiness. These boys carry the blood of the great kings of old. They have learned the ways of the Quadi around the hearth of their grandsire, a legacy they will pass on to generations to come."

In spite of Hostilius's barbarian garb, Centurion Ulpius immediately recognized the Primus Pilus for what he was, and soon they were engaged in sharing tales of the legions, with Diocles listening intently. Brunhilde was chattering away with Aritê, leaving me with Belimar.

"Did your father have a good death?" I asked.

"He died with a blade in his hand", Belimar said, but in the way he pursed his lips it was clear that there were other things at play.

I did not respond, but kept my counsel, allowing him the time to compose his thoughts.

"To the north of the Quadi, across the mountains, lie the vast lands of the Semnones, the most ancient and numerous of the Germani tribes. Legend tells that in days immemorial a terrible people from the east spilled across the northern lands, conquering all in their path. The invaders were the ancestors of the Semnones, who still revere only one god, Wodanaz - Lord of the Terrible Horde. They are rumoured to perform atrocities within their sacred groves where none can enter unless restrained by chains – to show that they are slaves to the will of their god."

He took a swig of wine from the glass and continued. "For many years we have lived in peace with them. But they are ruled by men of new blood who are rekindling the violent ways of old, insomuch that they have changed the name of the tribe. They call themselves the Descendants of the Titans. I have heard Roman merchants call them Juthungi."

"The Juthungi horde invaded the northern lands of our kin, the Marcomanni, whose war leader, Attalus, called upon long-standing oaths, which the Quadi honoured. We fought a bloody battle in the north, one that ended in a stalemate. There, my father fell to a Juthungi spear."

"But the Juthungi are numerous and they are assembling an army for a second invasion. We have lost many warriors, Lucius, too many to be able to stall the Juthungi a second time."

"The people know that their lands will be taken and have no choice but to cross the Danube and find sanctuary in Roman lands."

"Why did the Marcomanni not speak with the Romans first?" I asked.

"You of all people should know the answer to that question, Lucius", he replied. "You, who fought to save your sword brother, Bradakos, while hunted by a corrupt emperor. You know the haughty nature of the Romans - the way they make deals that favour them, the way they look to exploit the Germani who they view as inferior and stupid."

I raised an open palm. "I spoke in haste", I said. "Your words are true."

He accepted my apology with a nod and said, "But Rome needs to be careful. The Quadi and the Marcomanni have seen and tasted the luxuries of Rome. We drink Roman wine, use Roman iron and sell slaves and cattle to them. We take taxes on the amber trade and grow rich in coin. But the Juthungi do not know the way of trade. They only know the way of the spear and the sword. If we do not shield the Roman lands of Pannonia from these savages, Rome will bleed. Rome needs us as much as we need them."

"There might be a way", I said and felt the familiar sensation as the god whispered into my ear.

Chapter 10 – Zubr

Belimar pleaded with us to remain in the lands of the Quadi for a few days. To refuse his offer of hospitality would have been tantamount to an insult.

Hostilius woke me early on the morrow, wearing a broad smile. "Get up, Domitius", he said. "If we don't get going before first light, we might as well start drinking."

Although I preferred the suggested alternative, I did as he asked.

I found Aritê and Gordas warming themselves beside the hearth, arguing over the choice of arrows for the hunt. Diocles sat to one side, disinterested, sipping on a mug of heated wine.

While I filled my belly with bread, cheese and ale, Hostilius ran a whetstone along the blade of his pride and joy – the brand-new spear with the magic markings. "Can't wait to see if this works", he said, and showed me the engravings made by the rune master.

I held out my hand to accept the weapon.

"It's bad luck for someone else to touch it", he said, and moved it from my reach.

"The spear has a name", he added proudly. "Target Finder", he whispered. "It gets used to the hand of the one who wields it."

"It is true", Gordas said from beside the hearth. "The men who carve the markings commune with the gods, who guide their hands."

I was not convinced, but nodded. "Maybe you can show me later, Primus Pilus", I said.

Belimar, Centurion Bacchius, and three of the king's oathsworn were waiting outside the hall. We shared a horn of mead to dispel the worst of the early-morning chill while we acquainted ourselves with the borrowed Germani mounts. When the grey pre-dawn light finally arrived, Belimar signalled to two of his men, who turned their horses towards the dark forest.

The path was narrow. Hostilius and Bacchius followed the oathsworn while Diocles and Aritê, who rode behind them, were watched over by Gordas. Strictly speaking, the Hun was supposed to be my bodyguard, but I had long ago made peace with the fact that somehow in Gordas's eyes my daughter had surpassed me in importance. I did not complain - she was a princess after all.

I rode abreast of Belimar, with one of his guards trailing thirty paces behind.

"There is something else", he said. "I am about to strengthen the ancient bonds between the Marcomanni and the Quadi."

It was not hard to figure out what he was referring to.

"What is her name?" I said.

"Pipara", he replied. "She is a comely woman with a head on her shoulders. Her father, Attalus, the war leader of the Marcomanni, supports our union."

"Good", I said. "But let me warn you, Germani women have minds of their own."

Belimar issued a grin in reply, clearly looking forward to the betrothal.

"By the way, what are we hunting today?" I asked.

"Zubr", he said.

He must have noticed my confusion. "Forest buffalo", he explained and handed me a heavy spear with a long, thin iron head. "If the heart is not pierced, bad things happen."

Hunting has never been my favourite pastime. I accepted the proffered weapon, intent on remaining a spectator.

"My oathsworn are experienced huntsmen", Belimar said. "They will signal when the animals are near."

Belimar had hardly issued the words when a strange, unearthly roar emanated from the left of the track, causing Diocles's horse to rear. Then the forest seemed to take on a life of its own. Three enormous horned monsters streaked across the path. One of the animals ran straight into Diocles's mount, throwing the young Greek from the saddle as his horse collapsed from under him.

My aide displayed his god-given adroitness by rolling out of the way at the last moment, causing the buffalo to viciously maul the unfortunate horse.

Hostilius's magic spear sang as it streaked through the air. But rather than impaling the buffalo, it struck the mutilated horse in the neck, killing it instantly. Belimar's spear entered the beast's flank a heartbeat later. I expected the animal to drop dead, but somehow the iron point had failed to pierce its heart.

The animal lowered its enormous head, snorted, and pawed the mud. In that moment I realised that its ire was directed at me. I raised my spear to strike, but an arrow slammed into the beast's eye socket, and its legs buckled. Aritê lowered her horn bow, removed the string, and slipped the weapon back into its case.

* * *

"Maybe you should call the spear Horse Slayer, Primus Pilus", I suggested.

"Nobody's laughing, Domitius", he growled. "That spear is bad luck. It's been tainted by dark magic."

"Where is it?" I asked.

"I cast it into the woods", he said. "Cursed bloody thing."

Hostilius brooded for the following two days, preferring a cup of wine to human company. I spent most of my time with Belimar discussing our plans.

We departed two days later, heading south toward the Pannonian Plain, the home of the Roxolani, accompanied by an escort of mounted Quadi warriors.

* * *

The king of the Roxolani had seen more than fifty summers. Although his hair and beard were mostly grey, he was still an imposing figure with an erect posture and a determined set to his jaw. He ushered us into his spacious tent, clearly pleased at our arrival.

Bradakos waved his guards and servants from his presence and clasped arms with Hostilius and Diocles before he embraced Aritê and me in turn.

He held his granddaughter for long. "I have prayed to the gods to keep you safe until you are ready to return to your people", he said. "I will sacrifice to Arash for answering my pleas."

Bradakos had big plans for my daughter. Wisely, I realised that it was something that he would take up with her in person. My opinion had no place in the matter.

There were, however, other things that I needed to discuss with the king of the Roxolani. The opportunity presented itself that evening at the feast.

"Know you of the Juthungi?" I asked.

He nodded. "They are a numerous and ancient people", he said. "Unlike most Germani tribes, many of their warriors fight from horseback. The Juthungi raid our northern lands, but as soon as our warriors show themselves, they melt into the forest with their loot. They are good riders but they fear our arrows and our armoured horses."

Bradakos listened to my proposal, nodding often while I spoke.

"Did the god of war and fire come to you?" he asked.

"I felt his presence", I confirmed.

He thought on my words for a span of heartbeats. Eventually he said, "The tribe prospers in these new lands. I will commit two thousand heavy riders and three thousand mounted archers."

"And what do the Roxolani wish for in return?" I asked.

Bradakos grinned, and gave me his answer.

* * *

The following morning Aritê woke me. She placed a neatly folded stack of robes beside my sleeping mat. "The king is waiting", she said.

I washed, using the bucket of fresh water provided by a slave, then donned the loose-fitting yellow silk trousers, richly embroidered with blue animal motifs. Bradakos had also gifted me a magnificent knee-length blue robe, the stitching matching the colour of the trousers. I fastened the robe with a yellow silk sash and slipped my feet into ankle-length riding boots of soft, undyed leather.

I revelled in the comfort of the clothes of my people compared to the impractical garb of the Roman nobility.

Bradakos was waiting with Kasirga outside the tent. What I saw took my breath away. My horse's saddlecloth was of blue woven wool, with yellow embroidery and matching tousles along the bottom edges. But that was not all. Kasirga's tack was replaced with gear fit for the horse of a king. The face piece, cheek pieces and rosettes on his harness were all adorned with golden plates, decorated with intricate etching.

The saddle, made in the Scythian style, was something to behold - crafted from soft, red leather, lined with felt and adorned with matching gold plaques. There was no doubt in my mind that it was padded with reindeer wool of the highest quality.

"I feel like a prince of the Sea of Grass", I said and vaulted onto Kasirga's back.

Ignoring the protests of his guards, Bradakos, Aritê and I soon thundered north without an escort, leaving the tented settlement far behind.

The change in my daughter's demeanour was immediately noticeable. She smiled and chatted excitedly while pointing out some item of interest or other. I knew then that she would never be content in the lands of Rome – there was just too much Scythian blood coursing through her veins.

We flew across the plains with the wind in our faces and watered our horses at crystal-clear streams. When we eventually returned to the camp, it was nearly dark. I was tired, but felt alive and invigorated. I longed to remain with the Scythians, but Arash had shown me that my destiny lay elsewhere.

We remained at the camp of the Roxolani for a week, spending our days in the saddle. In the evenings we gathered around the fire, drank Roman wine, and retold tales of heroic deeds.

When the time of our departure arrived, I hugged my daughter for long, but knew that she was where she was meant to be. Before I mounted Kasirga, Little Nik uncharacteristically approached and muzzled me. I bent down and placed a hand on his head, ruffling his ears. He licked my cheek and retook his place beside Aritê.

"The wolf has bidden you farewell", Gordas said as we rode away. "You will not see him again in this life."

I was never close to the animal, but was still overcome with grief.

"I know what it feels like, Domitius", Hostilius comforted me. "When my new spear turned out to be cursed, it hurt deep inside. But don't be concerned", he added, revealing his tender side, "slaying one's enemies works wonders for healing open wounds."

The Quadi warriors were waiting for us at the border of the Roxolani lands. Three days later we arrived at the hall of Belimar.

"The king of the Roxolani has agreed", I said.

"So has Attalus, the Marcomanni war leader", Belimar said.

"All depends on the Roman Emperor", I said.

"Then make sure he makes the right decision", he replied.

* * *

"I do not believe that it is of any benefit to Rome to get involved in disagreements between base savages", Gallienus said in a haughty tone. He took another deep swallow from his jewelled chalice and dismissed me with a flick of his wrist.

"I will think on it tonight while I am at the theatre, Tribune Domitius", he said. "It is a pity you do not appreciate the finer things in life. There is nothing like art to elevate one's being."

Back at the officer's accommodation at Carnuntum, twenty-five miles east of Vindobona, I recounted the story to my friends.

"He'll talk differently when a hundred thousand Juthungi flood into Roman lands", Hostilius said. "You had better think of a way to convince him."

"We could join him at the theatre tonight", I said. "Apparently a local playwright has written a comedy for the emperor's enjoyment. It will be an ideal opportunity to influence him."

Hostilius's expression morphed into one of disgust. "Have you taken leave of your senses?" he sneered. "If the boys in the legions find out you spend your time debauching with actors and jesters, they will lose all their respect for you."

Hostilius took a swig from his cup and wiped his mouth with the back of his hand. "Maybe we could accompany him to the races", the Primus Pilus suggested. "That's manly entertainment – something that will boost your esteem in the eyes of the soldiers."

Chapter 11 – Pipara (June 255 AD)

Gallienus held up his open palm, stopping me midway through a sentence.

"The comedy at the theatre was truly inspiring", he said. "There was one scene that reminded me of our current discussion", he added, and snickered into his cup as he recalled the jest before savouring another swallow of the priceless wine.

"I can see that it is an issue of great importance to you. For that reason, and for that reason alone, I will accompany you to the barbarian lands to evaluate the threat from an unbiased perspective."

He suddenly frowned, as if recalling an important point. "We will be safe from the whims of our barbarian allies, won't we?"

"I have their oaths that Caesar will not be harmed", I said.

* * *

Hostilius, Gordas, Diocles and I rode west the following morning, returning to Vindobona where our men were billeted.

Ten days later a thousand Illyrians were arrayed on the northern bank of the Danube, awaiting the arrival of the emperor. Belimar had arranged for Gabinius, one of his southern lords whom we had previously met, to escort us north.

The Germani lord sat on his horse as we watched the bend in the river for the appearance of the emperor. His men, a motley group of hard-looking warriors, sat on their horses a hundred paces behind us, at the left of the Illyrians.

"Your king must be a great warrior", Gabinius mused.

"Don't confuse Rome with Germania", I replied. "We do not get to choose our emperor like the Germani get to choose their war leaders."

"Why not just kill him?" Gabinius asked, perplexed by the strange customs of our lands.

"It happens", I said. "Regularly."

Gabinius nodded knowingly and pointed at the river where three large imperial barges had appeared from around the bend. "Here he comes."

With much aplomb, Gallienus and his escort of a hundred mounted praetorians disembarked. The emperor acknowledged me with a curt nod, and signalled for us to lead the way. He glanced over Gabinius with disdain.

The Quadi lord and I led the way, with Hostilius, Gordas and Diocles following close behind. Gallienus was mounted on a pure white stallion, surrounded by the immaculately attired praetorians in their red tunics and polished mail.

The Illyrians wore plain tunics and red cloaks - their armour and weapons carried on spare horses at the rear of the column.

Gabinius had remained silent ever since he had laid eyes on Gallienus.

"You should reconsider killing him", he advised.

"I owe his father much", I said.

Gabinius thought on my words for a span of heartbeats, then asked, "Have you given your oath?"

"No", I said.

"Good", he replied, and clicked his tongue to bring his horse to a canter.

A third of a watch before nightfall we arrived at the stronghold of Attalus, great lord and war leader of the Marcomanni.

Gallienus and his praetorians halted outside the hall, remaining atop their horses. Gabinius and I were led up the wooden steps to a walkway outside the carved wooden doors. Not long after, a man appeared, ducking through the doorway. It was immediately evident why Attalus was the leader of his people. His dark hair hung to his shoulders and his beard was cropped short. The mail he wore appeared Roman. I was sure that it had been forged from two sets of looted armour as I had never seen Roman mail made to his proportions.

"Lord", I said in the tongue of the Germani, and inclined my head. "I am the Roman with the blood of the Scythians - friend of Belimar of the Quadi, sword brother of King Bradakos of the Roxolani."

He clasped my arm in the way of the warrior. "I am Attalus of the Marcomanni", he said. "I have heard the tales of your deeds, Lord Eochar."

He gestured with his head towards Gallienus. "Is that man your king?" he asked.

"He is the Roman king, the ruler of our lands", I said.

"You are all welcome at my hearth, Roxolani", he said.

I left him outside the door and came to a halt in front of Gallienus. "The warrior I spoke with is Attalus, war leader of the Marcomanni", I said. "He is honoured to meet the emperor of Rome, and he wishes to bid you welcome to his hall."

Gallienus sighed. "Very well, Tribune Domitius", he said. "What does decorum dictate?"

"Take only one man with you, Caesar", I said, "and clasp arms with the war leader."

He turned to the commander of his guards, but seemed to reconsider. "Come, Tribune Domitius", he said, "you will accompany me."

The Marcomanni had been living in close proximity to Rome for years, therefore Attalus had a rudimentary command of Latin, yet failed to follow Gallienus's haughty words.

The Marcomanni gestured for an oathsworn to attend him. "Call for Pipara", he said.

I could have translated Gallienus's words, but that would have robbed the Marcomanni king of the opportunity to show off his educated daughter.

While Gallienus forced down another sip of mead, the daughter of Attalus arrived. The Marcomanni lord, who sat with his back to the door, turned around to greet her. Gallienus's jaw dropped when the woman entered the hall.

She was comely, with long blonde hair and intelligent, dark blue eyes. But most of all, she held herself with the grace of a Roman noble.

Pipara curtsied to Gallienus. "Welcome to our humble hall Lord Caesar Augustus", she said in near perfect Latin. "It is an honour to make your acquaintance."

"Translate for us, daughter", the Marcomanni said.

I thanked the gods that Gallienus managed to close his maw before Attalus turned to face him.

"She is my pride and joy, Lord Caesar", Attalus said in his broken Latin. "She was tutored by a Roman", he added.

Gallienus inclined his head to Pipara. "It is a pleasure to meet the princess of the Marcomanni", he said.

A sinking feeling overcame me when I saw the way they looked at each other. Gallienus must have noticed my scrutiny.

"Thank you, tribune", he said. "That will be all. You may leave us."

I inclined my head and left the hall, a feeling of dread accompanying me.

"Gods", Hostilius said after he had listened to my tale. "This won't end well."

"It's not too late to slit his throat", Gordas suggested.

I ignored the Hun.

"Maybe you should warn him", Diocles suggested. "He is ignorant of the ways of the Germani."

I shook my head. "He can be capricious when it suits him", I replied. "I cannot endanger our plans just because we think that the emperor has looked at a Germani girl in the wrong way."

Hostilius scowled. "Have it your way, Domitius", he said, "but don't say I didn't warn you."

"Tomorrow we ride north", I said. "He will soon forget the girl."

On the morrow we departed early. Gallienus and Attalus rode at the head of the column, followed by the praetorians and the war leader's oathsworn. A thousand Marcomanni, the warriors from the canton of Attalus, followed in our wake.

"Where are we heading?" Diocles asked.

"The hill country of the Marcomanni lies to the west", I said. "To the east live the Quadi. Both lands are protected by the high peaks to the north – impassable mountains which do not shed their snow even in high summer. Seventy miles to the north, the gods have created a passage. The barbarians call it the Gate of the River. There the Juthungi are amassing to invade and conquer the fertile lands to the south."

"If we do not defeat them, they will conquer the Marcomanni and Quadi and assimilate their warriors", I said. "Soon the bolstered horde will spill into Roman lands."

"Will we be able to stop the invaders?" Diocles asked with concern in his voice.

"That", I replied, "is a question only the gods are able to answer."

Chapter 12 – Price

It took five days to reach the place where Belimar was camped with the Quadi. We arrived late in the afternoon, tired after a long day. Gallienus was not accustomed to spending his days in the saddle and retired to his tent after mumbling some excuse or other.

When darkness fell, I went in search of Belimar and found him sharing wine with Attalus beside the fire in front of his tent.

"How many warriors are the Quadi able to field?" Attalus asked.

"Eight thousand are fit to fight", Belimar said. "We have lost four thousand in the recent battle with the Juthungi. More than a thousand of my men are little older than boys."

"Warriors are still arriving", Attalus said, "but our numbers will not be more than twelve thousand. After the previous clash with the horde, thousands of Marcomanni feast in Donar's hall. Many of my men are young warriors, boys who inherited a spear and a shield from a slain father."

"Rome has sent a thousand horsemen", I said. "The Roxolani are on their way with five thousand mounted warriors. Two thousand are heavily armoured riders."

"My scouts have sighted the Juthungi", Belimar said. "Ten thousand riders and twenty-five thousand warriors on foot. All appear to be battle-hardened men, veterans of their wars with the northern tribes."

"We have fewer horsemen than the enemy", Belimar said, "and fewer foot soldiers."

"There is something that we have that they do not", I said.

The two men stared at me blankly.

"I have read the Roman scrolls", I said. "They give an account of every battle Rome has fought during the past thousand years. Every victory is described. Every defeat is written about in much detail. And I have read them all."

Attalus stared at me incredulously. "It is akin to possessing the knowledge of the gods."

"Tell me", I said. "Are the Juthungi easily insulted?"

"The fact that we still draw breath annoys them beyond what you are able to comprehend", Belimar replied.

"Good", I said. "Then we possess another weapon that is far superior to what our enemies will ever be able to field. His name is Caesar Gallienus."

* * *

Halfway between the two armies, Gallienus, Belimar, Attalus and I waited for the delegation of the Juthungi. The two-mile wide valley was bordered by forested hills to the west. The tree-lined banks of the Bečva River formed the eastern boundary. Four hundred paces distant, the milling, chanting horde of the Juthungi were working themselves into a frenzy for the coming battle. It was too far away to discern individuals, but I did notice that the enemy had deployed their cavalry on the flanks – five thousand horsemen on each side.

A nervous twitch settled around the corners of Gallienus's mouth. I shared his concerns, but could not afford to display it.

"May I remind you, lord", I said, using a neverminded tone, "that they are but base savages."

"It is a valid point, Tribune Domitius", he replied. "One tends to forget that they are an inferior race."

Four mounted warriors separated from the milling enemy and approached at a walk.

The Juthungi reined in a few paces from us. They wore leather braccae and embroidered woollen tunics. Their armour and helmets were a motley collection of chain and scale of Scythian, Roman and maybe even Greek origin. Bearskin cloaks were draped over their muscular shoulders. By the way they carried themselves it was clear that they were of the nobility. Judging by the variety of scars that adorned every inch of exposed flesh, and the silver warrior bands clamped around their arms, they were no strangers to war.

Gallienus wrinkled his nose and an expression of utter disgust settled on his face. He leaned towards me. "Gods, Domitius, but these savages carry a revolting odour."

"What did the hairless one say?" a grey-bearded Juthungi growled.

I understood the meaning of his words, yet it sounded strangely guttural, even ancient.

"He says that you smell like a man from his village", I said, "whose maggot-ridden corpse was discovered after it had festered for ten days in the summer sun."

A sneer formed on his bearded face and his hand moved to the hilt of his sword. He started to speak, but the haughty Gallienus raised an open hand to stall a response. The

Juthungi stopped mid-sentence, either due to utter surprise at the arrogance of Caesar, or mayhap he was angered to such a degree that he had trouble speaking.

"Tell the, er…, whatever he is, that if they submit to us as slaves, that we will spare them", Gallienus said. Then he grinned at me and added, "Surely being a Roman slave is far more alluring than wallowing in some putrid Germani bog or other?"

This time I translated the emperor's words without altering them. Although I believe Gallienus's facial expression would have been enough to initiate what followed.

The Juthungi drew his blade and kicked his horse forward, intent on slaughtering the emperor. Kasirga, who had picked up on the tension of his master, was like an arrow held at full draw. I touched his sides with my feet and my enormous warhorse powered forward. He slammed into the side of the smaller Juthungi animal, launching the grey-bearded warrior from the saddle.

"Go", I said to the other three, and pointed at the noble lying in the dust. "He has dishonoured himself by drawing a blade during a parley."

They growled some inaudible insults, waited for their comrade to gain his mount, and galloped towards the milling mass of barbarians. A heartbeat later the enraged horde charged, screaming for blood.

We cantered back the way we had come, but did not close with our line, as they had started to retreat at a jog, nearly matching the pace of the charging Juthungi.

"It was a good decision to place the boys in the front line", Belimar said. "They will soon tire the enemy."

We drew level with the line of young warriors and noticed Hostilius approaching at a gallop. He fell in beside Gallienus and escorted him to where the praetorians were waiting to whisk the emperor away to safety.

At first the enemy cavalry kept pace with their slower infantry. But their discipline did not hold for long. The lure of riding down the fleeing warriors was too much and they surged forward from the flanks. Within twenty heartbeats the horsemen drew away from the horde, gaining on their prey.

I put an arrow to the string and released it into the clear blue sky. In response to my signal, thousands of Roxolani mounted archers spilled from the cover of the trees at the sides of the valley, darkening the sky with wave upon wave of arrows.

Hundreds of Juthungi riders fell to the storm of arrows, which abruptly stopped as the ground began to shudder. Our retreating young warriors parted their ranks and two thousand heavy riders thundered down upon the northern horsemen. The Roxolani rode boot to boot, the riders and horses clad with near impervious scale and chain.

The Juthungi were unaccustomed to the ways of the Scythians and reined in – a fatal mistake. Their front ranks attempted to retreat, but the rear ranks were still advancing, resulting in a milling mass of panicked horsemen. The Roxolani went to a gallop and lowered their heavy two-handed spears tipped with armour-piercing iron. I watched as the wall of metal and flesh spilled over the Juthungi cavalry, pulverising all in its path. When the momentum of the charge was spent, the Roxolani iron-clad monsters drew their flanged maces, crushing most of what remained of the stunned enemy.

Having dealt the Juthungi a debilitating blow, the heavy cavalry disengaged, allowing the mounted archers to swarm around the remaining horsemen, picking their targets at will. Before the tiring enemy foot reached them, the Scythians grabbed the reins of thousands of riderless horses and retreated, pouring arrows into the unprotected flanks of the horde of footmen.

The fleeing young warriors of the Marcomanni and Quadi finally reached the safety of the shield wall of their comrades. As soon as the last of the boys had passed through, the veterans locked their shields, ready for the Juthungi horde to arrive.

But the battle was far from over. Although we had robbed the enemy of their horsemen, their footmen still outnumbered us by far.

From the right flank of the alliance, a column of black-clad riders appeared, led by none other than Gordas. I fell in beside him.

The Hun issued a grin. "Let us show them why it is foolish for Germani to stray from the forests."

We led the column to the left, wheeled, and formed a line, thundering down on the innumerable horde which had slowed down to a tired jog.

Hundreds of plumbatae arced into the air. Wave after wave rained down on the horde, barely slowing them down. On my signal, each rider took a leather pouch from his saddle. The column wheeled, spread out over the width of the field, and seeded the ankle-high grass behind them with twenty thousand razor-sharp caltrops.

As the Illyrians wheeled to the east to retreat behind the shield wall of the alliance, I turned to glance over my shoulder.

Even if the Juthungi had wished to halt, it would not have been possible. They did not advance in ordered ranks - the mile-wide column of screaming, chanting warriors was more than eighty paces deep. Thousands impaled their feet on the barbed, two-inch spikes, and went to ground in the process. They were trampled by the warriors at the rear, who in turn were pierced by the jagged iron as they, too, tumbled to the ground.

It was the moment that Belimar and Attalus had been waiting for. They led the shield wall forward at a run to engage the chaotic ranks of the enemy. Hundreds of exhausted, disorganized Juthungi warriors were slain, but most fled the field, with the Marcomanni and Quadi unable to pursue across the barrier of caltrops.

* * *

"Has the threat to the Marcomanni been eliminated?" he asked.

"No, Lord Caesar", I said. "We have destroyed but a fraction of the warriors that the Juthungi are able to call upon. They will attack again, and this time they will be forewarned."

He dismissed my words with a wave of his hand. "You give the savages too much credit, Tribune Domitius", he said. "We defeated the Juthungi with ease."

He swatted at a troublesome fly and continued. "But the Marcomanni still believe that the Juthungi pose a threat?"

"Yes, lord, they do", I confirmed.

Gallienus's question should have served as a warning, but the words he uttered next made me forget all about it.

"I am in favour of the idea to provide the Marcomanni with lands in Pannonia Superior", he said. "They will act as a shield. We already have to deal with the Franks and the Alemanni on the Rhine frontier, the Scythians on the Danube and the Sasanians in the East. It will serve the Empire well to turn a potential enemy into an ally. We cannot afford more enemies – especially not now."

I was speechless, of course. They were not the words I had expected.

"I can see that my strategic suggestion has taken you by surprise, Tribune Domitius", Gallienus said. "I forget that you are but a soldier who comprehends little of politics."

"I wish to negotiate the terms with Attalus before we return to Roman lands. Is it not best to strike while the iron is hot? I trust that you will make the necessary arrangements", he said, and dismissed me.

* * *

Bradakos led the Roxolani back to the plains to the east. He was content, as the tribe had gained six thousand horses with a minimal loss of warriors.

Belimar returned to the lands of the Quadi with much loot and an enhanced reputation as the victorious king, destroyer of the Juthungi.

The Marcomanni had taken cartloads of weapons, armour and other spoils from the dead and the abandoned camp of the enemy, strengthening Attalus's influence over the tribe.

To give effect to Gallienus's wish, I arranged that we accompany Attalus to his hall to allow the negotiations to take place in a safe and comfortable environment. It suited us, as it was on our way home.

* * *

Three days later we arrived at the stronghold of the Marcomanni where Gallienus entered into negotiations with Attalus.

While the Roman emperor spoke with the Marcomanni war leader, Hostilius, Gordas, Diocles and I whiled away the watches in front of the fire outside the warrior hall assigned to us.

"There is something he desires in return", Diocles said. "Something sinister."

"Why sinister?" I asked.

"Because he is speaking to Attalus alone", he said. "With only Pipara to translate his words."

"You read too much into it", I said.

"I agree with the Greek", Hostilius said, and took a swallow of wine from his cup.

"What could he possibly want?" I said. "Apart from maybe Marcomanni warriors to serve as auxiliaries."

"He wants Attalus's daughter", Gordas stated casually.

"For a slave?" Hostilius asked.

"For his woman", Gordas corrected him.

I dismissed the Hun's words. "You don't understand Roman culture, Gordas", I said. "Gallienus is a married man. It would be highly irregular for him to take a concubine or a second wife. The Roman Senate has ostracised their own for lesser transgressions."

"I have seen the look in his eyes", he said. "And in hers. She will come willingly."

"And", Hostilius said, lowering his voice, "he will probably say that Rome is taking her as a hostage."

I drained my cup. "I hope that you are wrong", I said, but I experienced a growing feeling of dread.

* * *

"I have reached an agreement with Attalus", Gallienus announced. "The Marcomanni will be allowed to settle their displaced people south of the Danube in Pannonia Superior. In return for the land they will shield the empire from attack by the northern barbarians."

I felt a heavy weight lift from my shoulders.

"And", he added, "Attalus has bent my arm to take his daughter as a concubine. The Germani have strange customs, eh?"

"You are aware that she is betrothed to the Quadi king, lord?" I asked.

Gallienus chuckled. "He is but a minor chieftain", he said. "It is of no consequence."

For a heartbeat I considered undoing the scheme that Gallienus had concocted. I could have sent him to the far bank of the Styx, but realised that it would come at a great cost – the stability of the Empire. It was a bill I was unwilling to foot.

Needless to say, I rode east the same day, heading for the hall of Belimar. Hostilius and Gordas insisted on accompanying me.

We arrived at the stronghold of the Quadi two days later.

"You look as if you bear tidings of death", Belimar said as he clasped my arm.

When I had told all, it was clear that the Germani had difficulty controlling his anger.

"You are of the blood of the Scythians", he seethed through clenched teeth. "But you have chosen the path of your Roman father. I will allow you to leave the lands of the Quadi with your life, but you are not welcome to return."

I wished to placate my friend, but he held up an open hand. "Leave now, Roman", he said without meeting my gaze, "before I change my mind. And remember", he added, "it is the path you chose."

I offered no explanation to my friends, but mounted and rode from the Quadi settlement.

The words of Valerian milled around in my mind as we thundered south, towards the lands of my father.

I had made another sacrifice for the Empire.

Chapter 13 – Ursa (July 255 AD)

My large friend buried his head in his massive paws. For the first time Ursa appeared weary, even old. He drank from his cup and rubbed his brow with his left hand, pinching the bridge of his nose between his thumb and forefinger while keeping his eyes closed.

"Umbra", he sighed.

"For the sake of the gods, Ursa", Hostilius said, "just say it. If I didn't know better, I would have thought that you are about to tell us that you are with child."

Ursa scowled in reply. "I'm not travelling east with you tomorrow", he said. "I've decided to join Pumilio and Silentus in Rome. They need me there, they do."

Hostilius and I stared at him in anticipation.

Ursa returned our stares.

"And what?" Hostilius said.

"And nothing", Ursa said. "It's just that goodbyes make me sad", he added and wiped his eyes with his sleeve.

Hostilius clasped the big man's shoulder – there was no need for words.

Ursa nodded his appreciation and swallowed away the emotions with two huge gulps from his cup. "That's better", he said, sighing contently. "Wine sure is a balm for the soul."

Marcus and Vibius arrived soon after Ursa had left to pack his belongings.

On account of his knowledge of the East, Valerian had requested that Vibius accompany us. Marcus would remain in Mogantiacum, or rather, that was what I thought.

"Ursa can travel with me and my retinue", Marcus said after I told him of our friend's plans.

"What in Hades are you going to do in Rome?" Hostilius asked.

"Not Rome, Centurion", Marcus said. "I am travelling to Mediolanum."

It was my turn to frown. "Mediolanum?" I asked.

"I have been reassigned to the Illyrian cavalry", Marcus said with a smile. "In my absence, Gallienus will personally take on the responsibility of defending Germania Superior."

My friend's reaction puzzled me, as I believed it to be a demotion.

"It is not what you think, Lucius", he said. "Gallienus knows what the Illyrians are capable of, and has convinced Valerian to make them a priority. Enough gold will be made available to increase their numbers to ten thousand."

I could not even begin to imagine the power such a force would wield.

"Whoever controls the Illyrians controls the western portion of the Empire", Hostilius said. "Ten thousand Illyrians would wipe a legion from their path without slowing to a canter."

"I believe it is the reason why he does not wish to base the Illyrians near Mogantiacum in Germania. A usurper can only be legitimate once he has come to Rome to intimidate the senate into supporting him. With the Illyrians in Mediolanum in Northern Italia, they would discourage any would-be claimant to the purple to enter Italia."

Marcus held out his cup for a refill.

Vibius continued, "And the Illyrians are mobile. If anyone gets an idea above his station, Gallienus's cavalry could be at his front door within days, without weakening the border defences."

"What's to stop the commander of the Illyrians to take the purple for himself?" I asked.

"Nothing", Marcus replied and took a deep swallow from his refilled cup. "That is why they will have two commanders."

"You and the bootlicking toad?" Hostilius asked.

"I have come to know Aureolus better over the weeks that you were absent", Marcus said. "I prefer him to Gallienus."

"I would prefer Hades to Gallienus", Hostilius countered.

Marcus ignored the jibe. "Aureolus will have nominal command", he said and leaned in, "but we all know who is going to command the men's loyalty."

* * *

The following morning a four-horse coach, driven by two legionaries, arrived at the gate of our villa. It was considered unseemly for Roman matrons to travel on horseback. Since we were on official imperial business, Marcus had insisted to provide Segelinde, Adelgunde and the young Maximian with an appropriate method of transport.

Gordas, Vibius, Cai, Diocles and I followed on horseback, our spare mounts secured to the rear of the coach.

"What is to stop the Franks and the Alemanni from overrunning Germania and Gaul?" Diocles asked.

"The Franks have been dealt many defeats", I said. "It will be some time until they have the courage to cross the limes again. But the Alemanni will no doubt invade soon. Postumus is a competent general. I am confident that he will assist Gallienus to keep the Alemanni at bay."

"And if they struggle, the Illyrians will be called upon", Vibius said. "Chrocus and his men would have heard about the black riders from Hades."

Diocles still suspected Postumus of instigating the attack on the fort at Niederbieber. The young Greek always seemed to view things from a different angle and said, "That is if Postumus wishes to keep the Alemanni out of Germania and Raetia."

"Why would he allow the savages to claim the *Agri Decumates* north of the rivers?" Hostilius asked.

"Rome occupies the territory north of the Rhine and Danube for one reason alone", Diocles said. "And that is because it links Germania Superior with Raetia and Pannonia to the east. If that link is broken, Gallia and Germania will be all but cut off from the rest of the Empire."

132

"How will that aid a usurper?" Vibius asked, now interested.

"He only has to defend the passes through the Alps", Diocles explained.

"Rome could land the Italian legions in Gallia", Vibius countered.

"Which would leave the path wide open for the usurper to move south through the passes and claim Rome for himself", Diocles said.

"Gods, Diocles", Vibius said. "You've considered everything. When do you get the time to dream up all these schemes?"

"I suffer from insomnia, tribune", he said, and took a swig from his wineskin.

* * *

We continued our trek south along the Via Agrippa, through the beautiful green province of Gaul along the banks of the Rhodanus. Three weeks later we arrived at our destination, the Roman port of Arelate.

The city was close to twenty miles from the sea, but the wide, deep river made it ideal as a natural harbour for sea-going vessels.

Our old friend, Master Herminius, was waiting on our arrival - his trusted liburnian moored alongside a section of the wharf reserved for military ships on imperial business.

"Welcome, tribune", he said, and greeted the rest of the party. "Thank you for the advance warning of your arrival. We replenished our stocks this morning, and are ready to cast off. The boys had time to put away a good square meal as well."

We assisted the crew to load our horses while the captain arranged for our baggage to be stowed in the bilge.

"Untie the moorings", the master shouted once all were on board. "And for the sake of the gods store the kedge, Scaevola." Herminius shook his head, muttering to himself, "Don't think that bastard is ever going to get to know the ropes."

"I remember Scaevola", Hostilius said, lowering his voice. "He seems to be a shirker. Why haven't you given him the boot?"

"He's related to me", Herminius sighed. "But not by blood, if you know what I mean", he added, drawing a sympathetic nod from the Primus Pilus.

"My wife's sister's son", he explained. "If I don't watch him, he stands around chewing the fat all day long. Makes me want to comb the cat every time I lay eyes on him."

* * *

The ship's master waited until we reached the open sea before pouring a libation of wine into the water. "May Salacia bless our journey", he said.

He noticed a pair of dolphins playing around the prow and poured another to appease Neptune, the violent one.

The goddess of the sea blessed us with calm waters, clear skies and a gentle wind. During the day we spent our time training with the sword, spear and bow, or lounging underneath the canvas canopy that the women used as sleeping quarters.

The liburnian mostly hugged the coast, but crossed the open ocean from time to time. Ten days after departing from Arelate we entered the narrow Strait between Italia and Sicilia.

We docked at the port of Messana where the presentation of the scroll carrying the orders of the emperor saw us restocked within less than a watch.

Before the sun set, we exited the strait. Master Herminius set a course due east, across the Ionian Sea, heading for Corinth.

It was a glorious late summer evening. Hostilius and Adelgunde were playing with Maximian while a few paces away, Gordas and Vibius imparted their knowledge of the finer points of blade craft to Diocles.

Segelinde and I sipped wine while reclining on the soft cushions underneath the canopy.

"Do you ever think of Kniva?" she asked.

"I think of him every day", I replied truthfully.

"Yet you have not tried to exact revenge on Cannabaudes?" she said, her words tainted with a hint of bitterness.

"I have asked the gods to preserve The Crow's life", I said, drawing a frown from my wife, "so I may have my vengeance. But I will not chase after him like a fool – I will bide my time until Arash deems it appropriate. The god will choose the perfect time and place."

Segelinde was placated by my words. "Have you had any news of the Goths?" she asked.

"Traders say that Octar of the Huns has broken the fragile peace with the Goths", I said.

Just then Gordas joined us underneath the canopy. I handed him a brimming cup. "Any news of your people?" I asked

"The Huns slowly creep west, subjugating all in their path. The Goths are trying to halt their advance", he said, and grinned like a predator. "But we all know they cannot stop the wolves."

"There have been no raids into Roman lands recently?" Segelinde asked.

"The Goths will be pushed towards Roman lands", Gordas said, "with the Huns nipping at their heels."

"For the first time in years there is no internal strife in the Empire", I said. "The Goths will find it difficult to breach the Danubian Limes. General Ingenuus, who protects the frontier, is a hard and capable soldier."

Diocles and Vibius, having finished their training, joined us.

"How long until we arrive in Byzantium?" Diocles asked.

"Three weeks", I said, "according to Master Herminius."

"In the old days, when the Greeks were in charge, it would have taken three days less", Diocles said, and took a sip from his cup.

"The Diolkos?" I asked.

"What in Hades is a Diolkos?" Hostilius asked, arriving at the tail-end of the conversation.

Diocles explained while he filled the Primus Pilus's cup. "Seven hundred years ago the tyrant of Corinth built a five-mile long road across the narrowest point of the peninsula. Slaves dragged ships onto wheeled platforms and pulled them across the strip of land in less than a watch. It saved days of sailing through treacherous waters."

Hostilius narrowed his eyes. "And my father was the emperor", he guffawed.

"Your Augustus Caesar moved more than a hundred of his liburnians this way in the war with Marc Anthony", Diocles continued.

Hostilius looked in my direction for assistance. I nodded in confirmation of Diocles's words.

"Bloody Greeks", Hostilius said and took a deep swallow from his cup. "They were too busy inventing useless things to realise that Rome was about to conquer them. When the legions arrived at the front door their Diolkos helped them naught."

Chapter 14 – Byzantium

I found the emperor stooped over a large vellum map, spread out on an even larger marble-topped table.

Valerian frowned at the disturbance, but broke into a grin when he noticed me outside the doorway behind the hulking praetorians. He walked towards the door and gestured for me to enter. The guards immediately stepped to the side. "Leave us", he said, "and bring more wine."

"I trust that the needs of your family and retinue have been tended to?" he asked.

"Caesar is most kind", I said, referring to the comfortable villa that had been assigned to us as temporary accommodation.

He beckoned to me to join him at a large window overlooking the northern estuary where the setting sun made the water take on the appearance of molten gold.

"They call it the Golden Horn", Valerian said and inhaled the salty breeze blowing in from the north.

The emperor gestured to the multitude of ships laying at anchor. "Every day they arrive", he said. "Ships laden with soldiers. Vexillations from every legion in the empire.

Auxiliaries from Germania, Gaul and Hispania - even as far as Britannia."

"How many?" I asked.

"They will number seventy thousand once all have arrived", he said, and issued a grim smile. "About the same number of men who lost their lives or their freedom at Barbalissos."

When the moment had passed, he strolled towards the map. Using a blunted, gilded arrow he pointed at a harbour near the southeasterly corner of the Dark Sea, the *Pontus Euxinus* as the Romans called it. "All the ships are on their way to the Port of Trapezus, where the army will gather."

Although I had used the many days at sea to discuss the upcoming campaign with Vibius, Hostilius and Cai, it was not my place to give advice unless prompted.

"I have not asked you to come halfway across the breadth of the Empire to listen to the ramblings of an old man", he said. "Tell me what you think."

"Trapezus is a good choice, lord", I said and pointed to the Roman forts arranged in a near straight line south of the port - first along the mountain passes of Cappadocia, then following the western bank of the Euphrates.

141

"Our first step should be to expel the Sasanians from Cappadocia and Syria", I continued. "That means that we have to liberate the Roman forts and cities which they still hold. It would be a fool's errand to try and win back Mesopotamia, east of the Euphrates, with the enemy at our backs."

Valerian nodded his agreement. "And what of Antioch?" he asked. "Sasanian spearmen still patrol the walls."

"Eventually, Antioch needs to return to the fold of the Empire", I said.

"I agree", Valerian said, "but it is easier said than done – the walls of Antioch are formidable. What do you suggest?"

"We retake the lost lands in the same way the Easterners eat an elephant", I said, drawing a frown from Valerian.

"One bite at a time, lord", I said, and drained the last swallow from my goblet.

* * *

When the master of the imperial galley gave the signal, the steersman pulled on the tiller and the large vessel veered to the

142

south, heading for the port of Trapezus. Rhythmically the rowers pulled at the oars, propelling the oversized liburnian across the surface of the grey water.

Segelinde and Cai were in conversation with Valerian and Adelgunde entertained Maximian. Hostilius, Vibius, Gordas, Diocles and I stood at the railing close to the prow.

"My people named it *Trapezous*, which is Greek for table", Diocles said, and pointed at the flat expanse of the city, protected by cliffs rising steeply from three sides. From afar, the fortress appeared small against the backdrop of the Pontic Mountains.

As we drew closer, Hostilius gestured at the battlements atop the cliffs. The towering stone walls were interspersed with massive protruding towers. "If the water cisterns and the stores are filled, give me three veteran cohorts, and I will hold out against the whole of the Sasanian army for a year", he said.

"It is no surprise that the Sasanians did not even attempt to take it", I said. "But the fort at Satala, eighty miles to the south, is still in the hands of the enemy."

"I've heard that Hormizd, the second son of Shahanshah Shapur, personally led the attack", Vibius said. "And the word amongst the merchants is that he has been tasked to hold it."

"Why would the son of the king wish to defend some godforsaken place in the middle of the passes?" Hostilius asked. "The Sasanians are spread too thin to hold on to their gains. He is a fool to think that he can hold Syria."

Vibius held up a hand to stall the Primus Pilus. "There is more Centurion", he said. "King Tiridates's son, the one who was wooed by the Sasanians, was assassinated by an Armenian nobleman, no doubt instigated by Shapur."

"Thank the gods that we helped the old king and his grandson to reach the safety of Rome", Diocles said, "or they would have shared the same fate."

Vibius nodded his agreement. "The Armenians did not take kindly to the treachery of one of their own, and they slit the murderer's throat in the night."

"So, who's the king of Armenia nowadays?" Hostilius asked.

"This is where it gets interesting", Vibius continued. "Shapur came to the rescue and placed his son, Hormizd, on the Armenian throne."

"I thought the Armenians were loath to accept a Sasanian as king", Hostilius said.

"They are", Vibius said, "but Hormizd's mother is a noblewoman with the blood of the old kings of legend - the ones who conquered the land centuries ago when they came from the Sea of Grass. The Armenians will endure Hormizd only because he has a claim to the throne via his mother."

"And Satala guards the road to Armenia", Diocles finished for Vibius. "That is why it so important to Hormizd. Syria does not concern him - he cares only to keep the armies of Rome from entering Armenia."

An idea started to form in my mind as the large ship came to a halt alongside a portion of the wharf reserved for dignitaries. "What do Sasanian nobles do to keep themselves busy?" I asked.

"They hunt", Vibius said.

Judging by the grin on Gordas's face, it was clear that the Hun had divined my thoughts.

* * *

The arrival of the emperor in Trapezus was no minor occurrence.

Valerian led the procession, resplendent in gilded armour, his rich purple cloak fluttering in the breeze. He rode a pure white stallion which he had brought all the way from Rome. Mounted praetorians clustered around their lord to ensure that none approached close enough to threaten his person.

Thousands of soldiers, neatly arrayed and all immaculately attired, lined the cobbled road leading up the hill to the main gates of the city. They craned their necks to catch a glimpse of the ruler of the world - the one they had vowed to defend with their lives. It was a memory to treasure, one they could share with their children and grandchildren.

Once we had dispensed with our duties, we retired to our appointed quarters. Trapezus was a near impregnable fortress, and I felt at ease with our decision to leave Segelinde and Hostilius's family within the safety of the walls while we were on campaign. The fact that the city was a bustling centre of trade, and as close as one could get to Elysium for a woman with coin in her purse, played no small part in the decision.

Once our baggage had been delivered and all had settled down, my friends and I retired to the dining room. From the comfort of couches, we were afforded a panoramic view across the city, the dark blue of the sea beyond the far walls completing the picture.

Gordas, who had been strangely quiet ever since we had entered the city, spoke up for the first time. "Have you heard of a tribe called the Borani?" he asked.

Even Diocles, who had read most of the Greek scrolls ever penned, shook his head.

"To the north of the Greuthungi Goths, on the edge of the great forest, lives a vicious breed of people. Their origins are shrouded in myth, but it is said that their founding fathers were outcasts and criminals - Huns, Goths, Celts and even Greeks."

Hostilius took a swig from his cup. "Interesting", he said, "but what has it got to do with us?"

"I noticed three Borani warriors in the city today", he said. "They were dressed as traders", he added with a sneer. "The Borani are killers. They do not trade."

"How can you be sure?" Vibius asked.

"Warriors of the Borani display the number of men they have slain with tattoos on their necks below the ear", the Hun said. "The men I saw today have killed many."

Gordas drank from his cup and held it out to Diocles for a refill. "The Borani are here for one reason only – they covet the wealth of Trapezus."

147

"They live hundreds of miles to the north", Diocles said. "How will they reach the far shores of the Pontus? Do they use boats?"

"I simply recount what I have seen", Gordas replied. "I do not attempt to prescribe to the gods what is possible and what is not, Greek."

I had come to appreciate the value of my Hun friend, who would not have spoken unless the threat was real.

"A large garrison protects the city", I said, "but I will ask the emperor to bolster it. Even the Borani will not be able to take these walls when they are defended by thousands of veterans."

Chapter 15 – Cats (September 255 AD)

A patrol of Sasanian horse archers thundered north along the Roman road, unaware of our presence.

Hostilius, Vibius, Gordas, Cai and I watched from the cover provided by an overgrown ravine. Our guide, Quintus Atilius, a decurion attached to the XV Apollinaris, stared at the horsemen with undisguised hatred – his knuckles white as his sword hand throttled the hilt of his spatha. Three cohorts of the Apollinaris, Atilius's brothers, were slain to a man when the Sasanians captured Satala. The decurion escaped the same fate only because his turma had been patrolling the road to Trapezus.

The grass-covered slopes provided little concealment to men who wished not to be noticed, so we were forced to keep to the ravines and lesser paths. When the sun dipped behind the faraway peaks on the third day on the road, the stone walls of Satala were visible in the distance.

We were too close to the enemy to light a fire, but the quality of the cold fare that we carried made up for the lack of warm food. The emperor's cook had filled our leather pouches with wheat bread, cheese, olives, beech smoked pork, dates and figs. Similarly, on Valerian's insistence, our wineskins had been replenished from the imperial cellar.

Summer was long gone and the night cold. We made camp in a thicket behind a rocky outcrop, eating by the light of a waxing moon.

"What does an Armenian king like to hunt anyway?" Hostilius asked, and used his dagger to cut a thick slice from a haunch of smoked pork.

"Lion", Vibius said, struggling with a mouthful of cheese and olives. He swallowed it down with a gulp of wine. "In Sasanian lands, hunting of lions is reserved for men of royal blood. Beaters chase the lions into a valley. There, the king spears the trapped beast with two of his most capable warriors at his side to protect him. A group of the king's men makes sure that no one enters or leaves the valley."

"The king will hunt to honour the Armenian lion-slaying god, the one the Romans call Hercules", Vibius added. "Hormizd will surely choose an auspicious time - the day before the night of the full moon, two days hence."

"Is there a suitable valley nearby?" I asked our guide.

The decurion had been stationed at Satala for sixteen years and knew the surrounding area like the back of his hand. He contemplated my question for a span of heartbeats. "There is, tribune", he said. "Less than twelve miles to the west of the fort." He gestured to the low mountains surrounding us. "These hills are infested with lions, sir. They regularly take a goat or a sheep from the locals' flocks during the night."

I heard a rustling behind us and turned to make sure I wasn't being stalked.

"They rarely attack men", Atilius said. "In all my years at Satala only a double handful of goatherds have been taken." He pondered the wisdom of his own words for a moment. "Of course, it's the campfire which keeps the beasts at bay", he added, and stole a glance over his shoulder.

* * *

On the morrow, long before the sun appeared, Atilius led us to the valley west of the Roman fort. It did not take long to find an ideal refuge – a ravine, bordered by a meltwater stream to the east. We had hardly entered the cover of the shrubs when the noise started.

"Beaters", Hostilius said. "I've seen it done many times. If there are lions in these hills, they will flee the open ground and take refuge in the valley."

By late afternoon a multitude of soldiers doing duty as beaters appeared on the crests of the hills. Having completed their task of herding the king's quarry into the valley, they ceased their interminable raucous that had put all, including our horses, on edge. Many large fires were lit along the surrounding ridges in an obvious attempt to discourage the trapped animals from fleeing the valley prior to the king's imminent arrival.

We took turns to keep watch during the night, more out of concern of being mauled by a cornered lion than being discovered by the Sasanians. Although we were tired, we enjoyed precious little sleep due to the baying of the beaters' hounds.

While Cai and Gordas unpacked our morning rations onto a worn fur, Hostilius and I walked to the stream. He crouched down low, scooped a handful of ice-cold water into his hands, and rubbed his red eyes.

"Bloody dogs", he mumbled and dried his face with his tunic. "If I had a watch of sleep, it's a lot. I prefer cats to dogs."

We broke our fast on cheese, olives and ham, all swallowed down with white wine.

"The king will have to pass through here", Atilius said, and gestured with his chin towards the hundred-paces wide valley floor which lay just beyond the shrubs. On the far side, rock-strewn slopes rose at a steep angle towards the north.

While we waited for the king to appear, we made sure that our equipment was in good repair. It provided us with much needed distraction, and would increase our chance of success.

I was testing the straps of Kasirga's saddle when I noticed his ears prick up. He pulled on the reins as if he wished to retreat further into the bush. After securing the leather to a sturdy tree I stroked his neck to comfort him, but it helped naught. I noticed that my friends were experiencing the same issues.

Cautiously we advanced towards the edge of the shrubs from where the valley floor was visible. An enormous male lion slowly made its way towards our hiding place - its head extended and its body close to the ground, in the typical way felines stalk their prey.

Gordas and I both placed hunting arrows to the strings of our bows. Cai and Hostilius readied their spears. Atilius and Vibius drew their longswords.

A thundering roar split the air right behind us, and in that moment, I believed that we were doomed. A yellow and black streak tore through the underbrush, moving at a pace that was difficult to comprehend. The beast was upon us before we could bring our weapons to bear.

But we were not its prey. The lion powered past, knocking Hostilius into the undergrowth. The two huge males met in an embrace of fury, rolling through the dust, snarling, clawing and biting. Spellbound, we watched from the shadows as the monstrous beasts fought for supremacy.

We were so distracted by the scene that we did not notice the arrival of a third lion – the lion of Armenia. Hormizd, mounted on a magnificent stallion, thundered towards the fighting animals. Two warriors accompanied him – one wore the garb of the Armenians, the other clearly a Sasanian dressed in the way of the immortal guards.

The king launched a spear thirty paces from the beasts, that seemed oblivious to the arrival of the horsemen. The weapon slammed into the side of the nearest lion, causing it to emit a primal roar of pain.

The injured animal launched itself at Hormizd, but in a display of self-sacrificing bravery, the immortal pushed his horse in between the beast and the king. The lion attacked, bowling

154

over the horse and leaving the rider in the dust, motionless.
The beast pounced onto the prone man and viciously mauled
him, shaking him as if he were a rag. Were it not for the thick
scale and chain favoured by the immortals, he would have died
instantly.

The king cast his spear at the second lion. But the animal had
its sights on the remaining guardsman, and at that moment, it
attacked - Hormizd's weapon missed, scoring a line along the
flank of the beast.

The Armenian guard had waited for his king to spear the
animal, leaving his own throw too late. His fate was sealed. A
heartbeat later he was unhorsed and mauled.

The king drew his sword.

The second lion's attention was focused on mauling the
screaming Armenian. I could not help but notice the look of
satisfaction on Atilius's face, like a man watching his favourite
moment of a play in the theatre.

Meanwhile, the first lion had lost interest in the immortal. It
still had fight left in it and turned its attention on Hormizd,
whose whole demeanour had made the shift from hunter to
prey. The injured beast sprang forward, reared up on its hind
legs, and slapped the king's stallion with a massive paw. The

horse's skull was crushed by the blow. It staggered to the side and the king fell from the saddle as the horse collapsed.

The lion lowered its massive, black-maned head and limped towards Hormizd, its lifeblood dripping from its side.

We could not wait any longer.

Hostilius rushed forward, his favourite hunting spear drawn back. The heavy weapon whistled through the air and struck the lion in the flank, piercing its heart and bowling it over onto its side.

The second lion, having finished off the unfortunate Armenian, issued a blood-chilling roar, snarled, and trotted off into the hills.

"I thought you liked cats, Primus Pilus?" I said.

"Not the big yellow ones", he replied, and walked to retrieve his pride and joy.

Chapter 16 – Hormizd

Atilius raised his sword to strike the prone immortal guard who had sacrificed himself for his king.

I grabbed his wrist in a grip of iron. "No", I said. "I have seen few braver deeds. And someone needs to tell the story."

For a heartbeat the decurion stared at me defiantly, then lowered his sword.

"They slaughtered my brothers", he whispered.

"It is the way of war", I said. "Come, we have much to do."

We relieved the injured immortal of his garb.

Gordas walked towards the king, who was moaning incoherently. He bent down and struck Hormizd against the temple with the hilt of his dagger. "Help me bind him", the Hun said.

While Hostilius and I assisted Vibius to don the immortal guard's clothes and armour, Gordas wrapped the naked Sasanian in a sheet and draped him over the neck of his horse.

Vibius was a sight for sore eyes when we were done. He sat atop the Sasanian's horse, his armour torn, his face and clothes covered with the blood of the dead lion. He spoke words in the tongue of the Persians, and even I had to remind myself that he was not a Sasanian.

I nodded, and Vibius galloped off on the Sasanian horse, heading for the troops who guarded the entrance to the valley.

We then dressed the body of the dead Armenian guard in Hormizd's garb and soaked the mauled corpse with the lion's blood, taking care to shred the guard's face with the claws of the expired lion. Finally, we heaved the lion onto the corpse.

Hostilius retreated a step to admire his handiwork. "Looks like a scene straight out of Hades", he said. "They will never know that it is not the corpse of the king."

"They come", Gordas said, and mounted.

We draped the unconscious king over Vibius's horse and walked into the cover provided by the shrubs, mounted, and made our way to the entrance of the valley, using the path at the far side of the stream.

A bloodied Vibius lay still in the dust beside the borrowed horse.

He opened his eyes when he noticed our approach. "Are they gone yet?" he asked.

I nodded.

"They took one look at me and rode to help their king", he said. "I had to fall from my horse to make it look believable", he added, and winced as he flexed his shoulder.

"You should consider a career in theatre", I said.

While Cai and I assisted Vibius to fit his own clothes and armour, Gordas and Hostilius extended the same courtesy to the injured Sasanian immortal.

"The Sasanian guard will not remember riding for help", Vibius said. "But he will be rewarded for risking his life for his king."

"Will they not think it strange that the Armenian guard has disappeared?" Atilius asked, and gestured to the corpse draped over his horse's back.

Vibius shook his head. "The disappearance of a warrior is insignificant compared to the passing of the king", he said. "The Sasanians will believe that the second lion took the corpse of the Armenian. They will give it no more thought."

* * *

While on our way to where we had left the spare horses, Hostilius said little – it was clear that he was in a reflective mood.

"What is the matter, Primus Pilus?" I asked.

"Something has been bothering me, Domitius", he said. "But I believe I've figured it out."

I remained silent to allow him to speak his mind.

"The second lion, the one that appeared from behind us, that's what's been bothering me. It was no accident", he said. "It was divine intervention."

"Why do you think that?" I asked.

"The lion had two chances to attack us, but it didn't. That", he said, "is not normal. And, what is more, the lion survived with barely a scratch."

Hostilius's reasoning was sound. "I believe that you are right, Primus Pilus", I replied.

"Wise man from Serica said that when lion chase man up tree, best is to enjoy view", Cai said from behind us.

* * *

A full watch after we had taken the king, there was still no sign of pursuit.

Hormizd was showing the telltale signs of coming to, and Cai warned us of the inevitable. "Go now", he said. "The Hun and I will take care of king. It no use if he sees you."

"Keep to the greenways and the back roads for the next twenty miles", I said. "Then follow the Roman road. We will meet you there."

* * *

Two days later Hostilius and Vibius rode beside me at the head of five hundred Roman horsemen.

We thundered down the cobbled road in pursuit of three men – one, clearly a prisoner, was tied to the saddle.

Slowly we closed the gap, until only a hundred paces separated us from our quarry. I took two blunted, broad-headed arrows from my quiver, drew, and released. The arrow flew true, striking the wild-looking barbarian in the low of his back. A

161

heartbeat later my second arrow struck the second small-framed bandit.

The first barbarian's horse slowed down and the rider slumped in the saddle before he toppled onto the stones. The second man veered off the road in an attempt to escape.

I held up my hand and the neatly dressed ranks of horsemen came to a halt. Hostilius, Vibius and I walked our horses towards the captive who took turns in staring at us and the barbarian lying facedown in the road.

"At least we have another slave for the galleys", Vibius chuckled in Greek. He turned to an underling. "Take him away."

The bound man was clearly terrified, judging by the look of horror he wore. Decurion Atilius, who stared at Hormizd with hatred, roughly led him away. When the column had disappeared in the distance, Gordas stood and plucked the arrow from his mail. Moments later Cai appeared from the shadows of the trees.

"Well done", I said.

Gordas waved away my praise. "Thank the Easterner", he said. "If it were up to me, I would have opened Hormizd's throat two days ago to stop his whining."

"Make sure he does not lay eyes on you again", I said, passed them a packhorse loaded with appropriate garb, and turned my horse to follow the Romans.

Kasirga soon caught up with the horsemen, who were riding at a slow canter.

I fell in beside Hostilius and Vibius.

"Come", I said, calling a halt. "Let us go speak with our prisoner."

Hostilius, Vibius and I found the king of Armenia in Atilius's care. Hormizd slumped in the saddle, wearing a resigned expression.

"Leave us", I said and waved away Atilius and his troops. Hostilius cut the ropes that secured the prisoner's wrists.

"Before we ended his suffering, one of the bandits told us that you are of royal blood", I said to the prisoner.

A flicker of hope appeared in his eyes and he sat up straight in the saddle. "I am Hormizd-Ardashir", he said, "the king of Armenia, the one whose reign is sanctioned by the gods."

I inclined my head. "Lord", I said, "forgive us, we did not know that it was you. Your name and deeds are known even in the lands of Rome."

My words and submissive behaviour pleased the king. "I am grateful for your intervention, Roman", he said. "I wish to be returned to my lands immediately."

"That, Lord", I said, "I cannot do. Your release is the decision of Lord Valerian Augustus, the Roman emperor."

* * *

Two days later I was summoned to the quarters of the emperor.

I found Valerian in conversation with Hormizd, who once again resembled a king. He was attired in expensive embroidered clothes and his hair and beard were curled and oiled in the way of the Easterners.

"Tribune", the emperor said. "Our honoured guest has given his word that the fort of Satala and the city of Antioch will be returned to Roman control. But his father, the great king, needs to confirm it. Tribune Domitius, you will travel to Ctesiphon, to meet with Shahanshah Shapur."

"It will be an honour", I said. "I have not seen him in many years."

Chapter 17 – Brothers

The decision we were faced with was whether to leave Hormizd at Trapezus, or alternatively, take him along on the journey to Ctesiphon.

"What will prevent Shapur from simply thanking us for returning his son and then slitting our throats in gratitude before throwing our corpses into the Tigris?" Hostilius said.

"Nothing", I said, "except the high king's sense of honour."

"The Sasanians have little honour", Vibius said, "but more than the Romans do."

Before Hostilius could retort, I said, "I will let Hormizd make the decision. If he is willing to surrender the fort at Satala as a gesture of good faith, I will allow him to accompany us."

"At least our deaths won't be in vain then", Hostilius scowled.

Hormizd made the obvious choice.

Three days later we rode south, leading a force of three thousand Roman infantry – a collection of vexillations drawn from all around the Empire. It took a handful of days to complete the trek across the Zigana Pass and reach the outskirts of Satala.

The Sasanian garrison was aware of our approach. It came as no surprise when we were met by hundreds of enemy spearmen and archers lining the battlements along the wall walk of the Roman fort.

Hormizd sat beside me, on the white stallion that Valerian had gifted him. With pride in his eyes he studied the fort.

"They are a formidable force", he said. "You would have found Satala a tough nut to crack."

"That's because it was built by Romans", I heard Hostilius mumble from behind.

I thanked the gods that Hormizd did not speak Latin.

"He echoes your thoughts, lord", I said in answer to the Sasanian's enquiring glance.

"How do we proceed?" I asked.

Hormizd removed his helmet to make sure that he would be recognized. "Let me show my men that I still live", he said. "You may accompany me, tribune."

I turned in the saddle to tell Hostilius that there was no need for him at my side.

"You're wasting your breath, Domitius", he said. "I'm not allowing you to go on your own. When they turn on you, you'll thank me."

Hormizd could not understand the Primus Pilus's words, but picked up on the defiant tone. "You are too lenient with your underlings", he said in Greek. "That is why you lost at Barbalissos. There is no discipline."

I kept my counsel.

The prince did not seem to mind the escort. We trotted down the gentle slope and came to a halt four hundred paces from the wall.

I raised a leafy branch which I had picked earlier.

Thirty heartbeats later the enormous, iron-studded gates opened a crack and three riders spilled from the fort. They approached at a trot, displaying their disregard for the enemy.

When they were a hundred paces from us, their demeanour suddenly changed. They approached with eyes wide, vaulted from their saddles, and prostrated themselves on the cobbles in front of the prince.

"Lord", the leader said. "You have returned from the dead."

Hormizd ignored the words of the Sasanian commander. He spoke in Greek, the language of the nobility. "Ready the men", he said. "We travel south tomorrow at first light. I have decided to abandon the fort."

A Roman commander might have hesitated given the same situation, but from the viewpoint of the Sasanian, he was not speaking with a man, but rather listening to the commands of a god.

"It will be as you wish, lord", the warrior said.

Hormizd issued a curt nod. "I need my clothes and a spare horse. Make sure it is delivered to the Roman camp without delay."

"I will personally see to it, lord", he said, and pressed his forehead onto the cobbles.

The prince turned his horse and galloped away without another word. "Did you take note of how it should be done?" he asked.

* * *

Their lord and commander had spoken.

168

While we dined with the prince, the sounds of men preparing to depart carried on the east wind blowing from the direction of Satala.

Hormizd took another ball of saffron-spiced minced lamb and swallowed it down with a mouthful of red from Valerian's cellar.

"Acceptable, but not of the same standard as Sasanian wine", he said, but held out his cup for a refill nonetheless. "Tomorrow", he added, "I will send the garrison east, to Armenia. Ten of my best men will remain at my side. We will ride south along the Euphrates, through the passes. At Zeugma we will cross the river and head east."

He contemplated his plans for a handspan of heartbeats. "Ready yourself, tribune. Few Romans are able to keep up with Sasanian horsemen."

The following morning at first light, the garrison was arrayed on the flat ground in front of the Roman fort. Not long after, their commander arrived, seeking the orders of his lord and prince.

When the last of the Sasanians had crossed into Armenia, Hormizd nodded and we kicked our horses to a canter, heading south along the Roman road.

Hostilius, Vibius and I allowed the prince and his ten oathsworn to take the lead. We powered up the Sipikor Pass, crossed the ridges, and a third of a watch later descended along the slopes onto the plain of Erzincan.

The Sasanians had been riding hard and I suspected that Hormizd wished to prove a point. But in the veins of our horses coursed the blood of Simsek, my Hun stallion. The horses of the prince and his retinue were no match. The surprise was evident on Hormizd's face when he glanced over his shoulder – not expecting to find us trailing only twenty paces behind.

When we stopped to rest and water the horses, the prince beckoned me to approach. He eyed me warily. "You are no Roman, tribune", he said.

"My mother was a princess of the Roxolani", I said. "I was raised in the land of the Scythians."

"You have the blood of the Royal Scythians?" he asked.

"Mixed with the blood of the Romans", I confirmed.

"My mother's line can be traced back to the Royal Scythian kings of old", he said. "Now I understand why you ride like a Sasanian. We share the blood of the kings of the Sea of Grass."

Our conversation marked a subtle change in Hormizd's attitude towards me. From then on, he seemed to regard me as an acquaintance, rather than an inferior, as he had before.

Two days of hard riding brought us to the Roman fort at Zimara, in sight of the western bank of the Euphrates. As senior officers bearing the personal orders of the emperor, we enjoyed the hospitality at the fort. It was clear to all that our companions were Sasanians, but we did not disclose Hormizd's identity, only referring to him as a Sasanian ambassador.

For two more days we traversed the high peaks and deep-cut valleys of the Antitaurus Mountains before arriving at the gates of the last Roman outpost in the Province of Cappadocia, where we spent the night within the safety of the walls. The following morning we departed from the fort at Melitene, again heading south.

Before the end of the first watch of the day, we passed by a group of peasants struggling with a cart filled with produce destined for some local market. They left the road when they noticed our approach, jabbering in their local tongue.

"We've entered Syria", Vibius announced.

"How do you know?" Hostilius asked. "We haven't passed a marker in the road."

Vibius gestured with his thumb over his shoulder. "Those peasants spoke Aramaic", he said. "The Cappadocians are a proud people. The upper classes speak bastardised Greek and the peasants still jabber in Phrygian, but they wouldn't be caught dead speaking in the Syrian tongue. If you hear Aramaic, you are in Syria."

We continued along the road, ascending the foothills of the Taurus Mountains, slowly making our way towards the legionary fort at Samosata.

By late afternoon we travelled along a cutting on the eastern slope of a steep hill. Rounding a bend in the road, a wide, gravelly floodplain came into view to our left. At the far side of the flat expanse, a bubbling, fast-flowing meltwater river cut through the landscape.

Vibius pointed to a stone bridge spanning the creek. "It is the famous bridge of Septimius Severus", he said. "He had it built when he invaded Parthia nearly sixty years ago." A frown creased my friend's brow. "Come to think of it", he said, "Just like us, Severus was also on his way to Ctesiphon. The only difference is that he sacked the city, which I think will be difficult seeing that there are only three of us."

"Maybe we should try", Hostilius said, and we all broke into laughter.

It was late in the day, so we decided to make camp on the northern bank of the Chabinas River. Once we had set up our tents, Hormizd and four of his guards approached.

"Join me, tribune", he said. "I wish to inspect the Roman bridge."

Hostilius, who was getting a fire started, spoke without looking up from his toil with the flint. "Everyone knows it's bad luck to cross a bridge without a proper reason", he mumbled to himself while blowing into the smoke.

Vibius shrugged at the Primus Pilus's words and we continued towards the stone structure, which was less than two hundred paces from our overnight camp. At the far side of the arched bridge, two marble pillars were placed. It appeared that they were once mirrored by two similar columns at the northern approach to the bridge, but one column had been removed.

Hormizd shared my confusion. "Why despoil such a masterpiece of architecture?" he said. "This is not the work of the Sasanians. It is not our way."

Vibius grew up in Syria and knew the history. "After his victory over the Parthians, four cities of the surrounding area

173

honoured Emperor Septimius Severus, his wife and his two sons by erecting a column for each one at the four corners of the bridge", Vibius explained. "After Severus's death, his son, Caracalla, had his brother, Geta, killed. Caracalla decreed it a capital offence to speak or write Geta's name", he added with a chuckle. "So, naturally, his column was destroyed."

The story seemed to resonate with the Sasanian prince, who took me by the arm and stepped to the side. "Brothers", he said in a low voice and shook his head in resignation. "Most of them, especially my eldest brother, Bahram, would like to see me dead", he confided.

It was no secret why princes had little affection for their siblings. Yet, it was strange why the older brother, who would normally be first in line for the throne, would wish his younger brother dead.

"I am first in line for the Sasanian throne", Hormizd revealed with pride. "My mother has the blood of the old kings, as you know. Bahram's mother is but a lowly whore."

I imagined that a noble concubine lacking royal blood would count as a whore from Hormizd's perspective.

"Some people don't know their place", I replied.

My answer pleased the prince, who spat, "Bahram is poison. He would kill me if given half a chance."

I believe that Hormizd challenged the gods with his statement, because in that moment, Bahram did just what his brother had prophesied.

Chapter 18 – Lion's Den

One of the royal guards screamed in pain and collapsed with a dagger embedded at the base of his neck. The culprit, one of the other guards, approached Hormizd with a sword in his hand. He lunged at the prince, who staggered backwards in surprise. The well-aimed blade would have split his armour and pierced his heart, but ironically Hormizd tripped over a rutted Roman paving stone. With a dull thud his head struck the cobbled surface.

The remaining two guards were accomplices of the traitor. They drew their blades and advanced on Vibius and me.

I slid my blade from its scabbard. Vibius followed suit.

Rather than waste time to block the downward strike of the first guard, I lunged in an attempt to breach the two paces separating us. The attacker's attention was fixed on his helpless prey – his sword drawn back to claim his prize. The tip of my weapon entered his throat, piercing the bone and marrow at the back of his neck. He dropped like a stone, falling on top of the future king.

"Today you die, Roman", one of the two remaining guards hissed in Greek and stepped in, slashing with his longsword from above his shoulder. I moved to the side, across his line of attack. The blade missed my shoulder by the breadth of a finger. I rotated my weapon using a double-handed grip, stepped in, and with a powerful vertical cut severed his sword hand at the wrist. He grabbed at the stump in desperation, exposing his throat. A heartbeat later he lay beside his comrade, his lifeblood trickling along the joints between the cobbles.

Vibius was no fool with a sword. The guard who had attacked him lay at his feet, clutching his pierced stomach.

Hormizd, who had regained his senses, managed to crawl from underneath the corpse of his attacker. He slowly came to his feet, displaying a face and torso stained red with the blood of the man who had tried to kill him.

The prince walked over to the dying guard at Vibius's feet.

"You know I am a priest of Ahura Mazda", he said to the man, and placed the tip of his blade against the prone guard's neck. "Give me a name, or I will beseech the Lord of Wisdom to condemn your shade to the realm of the one whose name is written upside down, the one whose name should not be spoken."

The dying man's eyes widened in anguish. He hesitated for a heartbeat, but must have realised that he had much to lose should he defy Hormizd.

"Bahram", the man spat.

Hormizd's expression morphed into a sneer as he pushed down on the sword. "Family", he sighed, and gave the blade a vicious twist.

* * *

The following morning we struck camp early and continued our journey.

"Bahram knows that the blood of his mother makes it almost impossible for him to be the high king of the land", Hormizd explained while riding alongside me.

"Almost?" I asked.

The prince nodded. "For that reason, he has turned to the one thing that transcends blood", he said.

"Religion", I surmised.

Hormizd nodded. "He has aligned himself with a powerful priest, Kartir - a fanatic who wishes to eradicate all who do not serve Ahura Mazda, The Lord of Wisdom. My father, Shapur, on the other hand, is tolerant towards all the religions of the lands he has conquered - Jews, the ones who follow Jesus, Hindus and Buddhists. Shapur and Kartir endure each other, but I suspect that the priest is trying to ensure that my father's successor is a man of the same mind as he."

I was not overly concerned with the machinations of the Sasanians, but it was imperative to ensure that Hormizd arrived in Ctesiphon in one piece.

Two thirds of a watch before nightfall, after a day of hard riding, we approached the greatest of the Roman strongholds in the province of Syria.

"You do realise that we are still enemies?" Hormizd said.

"I do, lord", I replied.

"Then why are you willing to allow me to enter the impregnable Samosata?" he asked, and gestured towards the massive walls of the city perched a hundred feet above the Euphrates.

"Because the spies of the great king have already told you all there is to know", I said.

A smile played around the corners of the prince's mouth. "If you say so, tribune", he replied.

The missive bearing the personal seal of the emperor ensured that Hostilius, Vibius and I soon found ourselves in the praetorium of the legionary fort. It was situated in the southwestern corner of the city, guarding the formidable, yet most vulnerable slope of the mound.

On the insistence of the legate of the XVI Flavia Firma, which garrisoned the city, the Sasanians were kept confined to their quarters.

Hostilius, Vibius and I, accompanied by the legate of the legion, used the last third of a watch of daylight to inspect the defences of Samosata. On our return we were invited to dinner.

Legate Marius Perpetuus took a handful of dates and reclined on the couch. "As you have seen", he said, "the problem is not the walls. The challenge is where to find two thousand five hundred men to man the three-mile long battlements."

"How many men do you have?" I asked.

"Less than half that number", he replied. "After the disaster at Barbalissos."

"The good news is that you will soon have the men you desire", I said, and handed him a scroll.

The legate's smile faded and he turned pale as he read the words of Valerian Augustus.

"Seventy thousand men", he whispered.

"It will be temporary", I said in an attempt to set his mind at ease. "The emperor will use Samosata as a base to re-establish Roman control over Syria. When the goal is achieved, he will relocate to Antioch."

We departed early the following morning.

It took two days to reach Zeugma, where a Roman pontoon bridge spanned the Euphrates. It was the same bridge we had used all those years before when we marched as part of the army of Gordian III. Our military rank ensured that we crossed into Roman Mesopotamia without incident and without paying the required toll.

Roman lands to the east of the Euphrates were largely unaffected by the Sasanian invasion as Shapur had travelled north along the river, invading Syria rather than Mesopotamia.

We made our way east along the ancient trade route that crossed the scorching Nineveh Plain, passing colourful caravans that had journeyed all the way from the Land of Silk. Despite the heat, merchants of every creed and colour greeted us with broad smiles, jabbering away in a thousand tongues.

On Hostilius's insistence, we entered the city of Carrhae to sacrifice at the famous temple of Sin, the ancient moon god. We spent a night at Resaina, close to where we had won the famous battle. From there we travelled east along the banks of the Khabur to the easternmost outpost of Rome – the fort at Singara.

We approached Singara from the west, riding along the foothills of the strange mountain rising from the flat expanse. From time to time we noticed goatherds on the slopes. They disappeared into overgrown gorges as soon as they laid eyes on us.

"Many peasant farmers make a living in these mountains", Vibius said. "They plant figs, lentils and even grapes which they sell to the quartermaster at the fort. They don't really care whether the Romans or the Sasanians are in control, as long as they can sell their produce."

"That's the benefit of being backward", Hostilius said. "You can sleep soundly because you're not worth conquering."

The following day we crossed the border into Sasanian lands, continuing our journey east through hilly country. Two days later we stood on the western bank of the Tigris.

Hormizd pointed at the ruins of massive stone and mudbrick walls on the eastern bank across the river. "Once, Nineveh was the greatest city on earth. The walls were fifty feet high and nearly as thick."

"Who were their enemies that they deemed it necessary to build such fortifications?" I asked.

"My forefathers, of course", he said.

"Let us ride south with haste", he added after a few heartbeats. "In a few days we will arrive at Ctesiphon – only then will you truly understand what greatness means."

* * *

Hostilius, Vibius and I walked along the paved path towards the palace complex of the king of the Sasanians.

It had taken many days to arrange an audience with Shapur.

On our arrival, ten days before, Hormizd had established that his conniving brother, Bahram, was present in the palace. The prince feared that he would be killed even before he was able to inform his father of the treachery of Bahram. Hormizd therefore remained in hiding west of the Tigris.

Armed with a scroll bearing the seal of the emperor, Hostilius, Vibius and I entered Ctesiphon as ambassadors of the Roman Empire. But I also carried a letter penned by Hormizd – a letter meant only for the eyes of his father.

The closer we came to the magnificent White Palace, the more the enormous scale of the structure became apparent. In the centre of the colossal building was a vaulted room – walled on three sides and open to the front. The top of the arch must have been more than a hundred feet high, surpassing anything I had laid eyes on before.

"Not too shabby", Hostilius whispered. "I wouldn't be surprised if a Roman builder had a hand in it."

"It is the audience hall of the shahanshah", Vibius said. "It is famous in all the land."

I estimated the room to be twenty-five paces wide and fifty paces deep. At the back, against the wall, was a beautifully crafted wooden podium with the jewelled throne of the high king. Behind the podium, against the rear wall, a magnificent painting depicted Ahura Mazda handing the crown of ultimate power to Shapur. It left no doubt in anyone's mind who had placed Shapur, the supreme ruler, on the throne. When the king dispensed justice it was not only backed by the gods, it was as if the Lord of Wisdom himself had spoken.

Hostilius gestured with his head at the fresco. "I'm sure he can trace his lineage directly to Ahura Mazda", he whispered.

Before the Primus Pilus could continue, the immortal guards, who protected the king, stamped the hafts of their spears three times. As one, the petitioners fell silent.

A man, strangely beardless, emerged from the doorway that led onto the podium.

"Shapur has changed a lot", Hostilius whispered.

"It is not Shapur", Vibius replied in a low voice. "That will be the eunuch priest Kartir – the keeper of the veil", he added, drawing a deep frown from Hostilius.

"It is an insult of the worst kind for a mere mortal to speak directly to the king, Centurion", he said. "Neither will the king disgrace himself by speaking to a subject directly. Only a priest of Ahura Mazda is worthy."

Servants strategically placed smoking incense burners, filling the air with a sweet aroma.

"Cedar and myrrh", Vibius explained, "to ensure the gods are in a pleasant mood."

Hostilius was still frowning by the time that the eunuch closed the sheer silk veils on the three exposed sides of the podium.

Again, the immortals stamped the hafts of their spears on the marble floor.

"All hail the king of the four corners of the world", the eunuch boomed. "May he be immortal."

From the doorway, visible through the silk veil, the king of kings appeared.

The assembled crowd echoed the words of the keeper. "May he be immortal", they all chanted.

Shapur wore the golden diadem of sovereignty. His hair and beard were immaculately oiled, curled and blackened with henna, and adorned with gold. The king's face did not appear human – it had been enhanced with kohl and antimony to lend it a godlike quality. Loose-fitting, gold-embroidered robes of yellow, purple and green contributed to his divine aura.

We were not first in line.

A scribe, seated at a table decorated with gold leaf, read names from a scroll.

"The embassy from Kangju", he said, followed by the jabbering of various interpreters.

Once the names were spoken and the ambassador and his entourage had stepped forward, the men were searched for concealed weapons. A group of immortals wearing full face helmets and brandishing whetted spears escorted the party, coming to a halt five paces from the dais, where they prostrated themselves before the shahanshah.

When the king was satisfied, he nodded. The keeper of the veil then instructed the men to rise.

The ambassador spoke for long and handed over gifts via the intermediary.

At long last the keeper disappeared behind the veil where the king whispered into his ear. The intermediary then spoke to the ambassador, who bowed low before reversing his steps until he had left the presence of the king.

"By the gods", Hostilius said. "We are going to be here for days. Now I know why Rome rarely treats for peace with these bastards. It would have been quicker to storm the walls of Antioch rather than to wait for an answer."

"And I'm not prostrating myself", he growled. "Not before that pansy."

"Would you rather prefer to see thousands of Roman farm boys skewered by Sasanian arrows while they storm the walls?" I asked.

I received a scowl in reply.

Less than a watch later the name of the ambassador from Rome, Lucius Domitius, was called out by the scribe.

Once we had been told to rise, and had handed over the customary gifts of ornate swords and daggers, it was my turn to speak. I realised that the words could doom us all. But I gambled that, like all men, even the god-king would have a desire to get even with enemies of old.

"I am Prince Eochar of the Royal Scythians", I said in Greek.

Shapur, who until moments before had worn a generally bored expression, suddenly sat upright on his dais.

"I wish to reconcile with Lord Shapur after parting ways under less than favourable circumstances", I continued.

I noticed a smile form around the corners of Shapur's mouth as recognition dawned in his eyes. He gestured to the keeper of the veil to enter the silk sanctuary and whispered to the man, who broke into a leer.

"Take them", Kartir said to the guards as he appeared from behind the veil. "They have affronted the gods."

Chapter 19 – Gift

I was taken to the private quarters of Shapur. He was without his diadem, makeup and embroidered robes, attired in a long-sleeved tunic with green embroidery and matching fluted pants in the eastern style.

"You are a fool, Scythian", he said. "I never forget an insult."

"May we converse in private, lord?" I asked.

"Bind him", he said to a guard, who immediately gave effect to his lord's desire.

I waited until only Shapur and I remained in the room. "Lord", I said, "your son, Hormizd, fears for his life."

"Then your message is too late, Scythian", he sneered. "My son died while hunting lion – an honourable death."

I struggled with my bound hands but managed to reach the letter concealed inside my robes. "He is not dead", I said, "although Bahram has tried to make it so."

Shapur's complexion turned ashen and he grabbed the folded parchment. With a trembling hand he read the words penned by his favourite son, the heir to the throne. He read the letter more than once – maybe even thrice.

"Perhaps you are a fool", he said, "but a coward you are not. First, I will deal with Bahram. Only then will it be safe for Hormizd to return."

"Until then, you are my guests", he added. Then his eyes narrowed. "I will honour you, whatever you are, Scythian or Roman. But do not make the mistake to believe that I have forgiven you. Remember, the vengeance of the great king walks with leaden feet but strikes with a fist of iron."

"May you be immortal, lord", I said, and bowed my head in supplication.

* * *

Shapur was not one who procrastinated. Not long after our meeting, he dispatched Bahram and his entourage to the province of Gilan, where he would become the king, the Gilanshah.

Three days later, I stood at the window of our room in the great palace beside Hostilius and Vibius and watched Bahram leave for Gilan. The people of Ctesiphon lined the streets and cheered the departing prince, unaware of the dark reason behind the decision of the king.

That night we were summoned.

It was more of a meeting than a celebration, but still, when the ruler of the East feasted, no expense was spared.

Shapur and Hormizd waited for us underneath a silk canopy erected in the centre of a courtyard ringed with ancient manicured olive trees. We sat on lush, hand-woven woollen carpets spread out on the ground beneath the awning, the light provided by gilded lamps. A few paces away a team of cooks prepared the royal feast above a blazing fire, their mouths covered as to not contaminate the food.

Dancers, jugglers and dagger-players performed to the tunes of musicians playing on flutes and lyres.

We told tales of war and hunting while we were served lamb, pheasant and peacock – all flavoured with exotic eastern spices. Dancing girls kept our glasses filled with the best vintages from Babylonia and Basarangia.

When we had finished our meal, Shapur clapped his hands. As if by magic servants appeared bearing plates of sweetmeats and chilled sweet wine. He nodded to a guard, and the cooks,

192

entertainers, slaves and servants vanished from his presence, leaving us with only a few guards watching out of earshot.

"You have done me a great service", Shapur said. "As you have saved the life of my son - not once, but twice. I have decided to accede to your emperor's request to withdraw my troops from Antioch. In addition, I ratify Prince Hormizd's decision concerning Satala."

"I will cease hostilities with Rome until the end of the year", he added. "But be warned. In time, I will retake all the lands that the Empire has stolen from my forebears."

"You honour us, lord", I said and bowed my head.

Again, the great king clapped his hands.

A servant appeared, carrying a large silver dish depicting a scene of horsemen engaged in a lion hunt. Moments later the large double-storey doors at the far end of the courtyard swung open. A strange-looking man appeared leading an enormous bull elephant – its massive head and tusks adorned with gold.

I heard Hostilius swear under his breath. "By the gods."

Shapur gestured to the silver dish and the elephant, which the handler kept at a safe distance. "These are my gifts to you,

Scythian. Although we are rivals, let the people say that
Shapur the Great is magnanimous, even towards his enemies."

"May you be immortal, lord", I said and inclined my head.

* * *

Later that evening we made our way back to our quarters under
escort of Shapur's guards.

"What will you do with the elephant?" the Primus Pilus asked
with a slight slur of the tongue.

"Maybe I will give it to Gordas", I replied. "He has always
desired to own one."

"Only the emperor is allowed to keep a live elephant", Vibius
enlightened us. "It is the law of Rome."

"Maybe we can eat it", Hostilius suggested. "I remember Cai
saying something about eating an elephant."

* * *

The palace complex was extensive. For long we were led along lamplit porticoes and down marble-clad corridors. Even at the late hour many people still moved about - cooks, cleaners, priests and guests arriving from far lands. I paid the strangers little heed.

From the corner of my eye, I noticed a figure that seemed familiar. On a portico, opposite a narrow courtyard, three men were similarly escorted by guards. Two men walked side by side, while the third trailed by three paces. The third man glanced our way, but we were in a particularly dark spot. As he turned to face the front, he passed by a lamp. I put two and two together, which caused a chill to run down my spine.

"You look as if you've seen a draugr, Domitius", Hostilius said when we entered the room.

"Do you remember the war leader of the Heruli, Roudolphos?" I asked.

"He is not a man one easily forgets", Vibius replied.

"And Naulobates?" I said.

"He is the one who saved us all when Cannabaudes killed Kniva", Hostilius said. "We owe him much."

"What do Roudolphos and Naulobates have in common with the Borani?" I asked. "And", I added, "what do all of them have in common with the Sasanians?"

"For the sake of the gods, Domitius", Hostilius growled, "spit it out."

I held up an open palm in an attempt to placate my friend.

"I believe I saw the two Heruli in the company of a Borani man", I said. "They were escorted to their room by Sasanian guards."

"Are you sure?" Vibius asked.

"No, the light was dim and I had had too much wine", I said. "But I saw the warrior markings on the neck of the third man. He is a Borani warrior for sure."

"The Heruli are mercenaries, and the treasury of the Sasanians is filled with Roman loot. They are here because Shapur wants them to fight at his side", I said.

"But they live north of the Dark Sea", Hostilius said. "How in Hades will they get here? If Shapur wanted to hire barbarians, surely there are tribes that are much closer."

"We need to find out", I said.

"How do you plan to do that?" Hostilius asked. "Do you plan on asking Shapur?" he added sarcastically.

"No", I said. "I will ask Hormizd."

* * *

The following morning we woke early, eager to start the journey back to Roman lands.

Hormizd arrived to see us off.

I took him aside. "Lord", I said. "I have fought side by side with the Heruli. The same men who now walk the halls of this palace."

It was a question, although not phrased as such.

For a long time Hormizd stared at me, then he said, "I am no traitor, but I owe you a life, Roman." He placed a hand on my shoulder, lowered his voice and said, "Take care of your family."

Then he clasped my arm in the way of the warrior and sent us on our way.

Chapter 20 – Moon (November 255 AD)

Hostilius glanced over his shoulder at the lumbering elephant. "I'm sure Shapur gave it to you to slow us down", he said. "Bastard."

"The Sasanians are hatching an evil plan involving the tribes north of the Dark Sea", the Primus Pilus continued. "Why else would Hormizd have warned you to take care of your family?"

"To attack Trapezus, the tribes would need access to boats", Vibius said.

"The Heruli have boats", I thought out loud. "But on such a long journey they will not be able to carry more than two thousand warriors – not enough to threaten the mighty fortress of Trapezus."

"Who else has boats that ply the waters of the Dark Sea?" Hostilius asked after a few heartbeats.

"Rome", I said.

"The Bosporans have hundreds of trading vessels", Vibius added. "It is supposed to be a client kingdom of Rome, but in these troubled times the Empire has neither the resources nor the inclination to meddle in their affairs. Come to think of it",

Vibius added, "I heard that a new king has recently come into power. There were rumours that he was aided by barbarian mercenaries."

I heard my friend's words, but thought little of it at the time.

Our journey up the Tigris was painstakingly slow. Days later, when we eventually reached the outskirts of Mesopotamia, we bade farewell to our escort of Sasanian horsemen. It is needless to say that our arrival at Singara caused quite a stir, as most of the legionaries had never before laid eyes on an elephant.

We were chomping at the bit to return to our families. The following morning I issued the necessary orders, and we thundered west, leaving the gift from Shapur, and its handler, in the care of a turma of nervous auxiliaries, tasked to escort the beast to Trapezus.

At every Roman fort we passed by we enquired about news, but there was precious little available.

Ten days later we arrived at the legionary fortress of Samosata. It was no longer the quiet place of weeks before. Thousands of Roman soldiers were camped north of the city beside the waters of the Euphrates. They were part of Valerian's army heading south and east to strengthen the various garrisons against the inevitable Sasanian onslaught.

That evening we dined with Legate Marius Perpetuus, who was the bearer of interesting news.

"I heard that the savages who live north of the Dark Sea have attacked the farthermost outpost of our coastal defences", he said, and drank deeply from his cup.

Immediately he had our undivided attention.

"Apparently the new king of the Bosporan Kingdom on the north coast of the Dark Sea cajoled a bunch of savages into helping him gain the throne. He promised to pay the barbarians from the captured treasury. But when he had achieved his goal, he found the treasury empty. The only way he could placate the barbarians was to give them a few ships."

He took another swallow of wine. "Imagine giving a savage a ship", he said, and issued a snicker. "What do they know of boats?"

"By some jest of the gods, a few boatloads of savages managed to crawl south along the coast", he said. "They attacked the Roman fort at Pityus. The single cohort that manned the walls gave the barbarians' arses a proper kicking and sent them packing."

"Can you even imagine that?" he added with a laugh and a shake of his head. "Those dumb savages using boats. Stupid bloody idiots. They ran back to their ships and rowed away. I'm sure most never made it to land again."

"So Trapezus has not been attacked?" Hostilius confirmed, fearing for the safety of our families.

"Don't be ridiculous, tribune", the legate said and waved away my friend's concerns.

* * *

Although our immediate fears for the safety of our families were laid to rest, we could not afford to keep the emperor waiting.

Legate Perpetuus informed us that Valerian was on his way south with the remainder of the Roman vexillations. For the time being, the emperor had taken up residence farther north along the limes.

We arrived before the walls of Melitene at around the middle hour of the third day after departing from Samosata. Soon I was seated in the presence of the emperor.

"You are the bearer of exceedingly good news", Valerian said after I had given him a watered-down version of the happenings. "I will stop over at Samosata for a few days, but then we will march south to Antioch - the Jewel of the East. If I take control of the city, it will reflect well on my campaign."

His words served to remind me that Valerian was above all a politician. Although the return of Antioch to the Roman fold was a hollow victory, he would use it to bring glory to his name.

"I wish for you to accompany me to Antioch", he said.

"I will do as you command, lord", I replied.

"But you fear for the safety of your family", Valerian sighed, divining my thoughts.

"I do, lord", I replied.

"Your fears are unfounded", he said. "I concede, the odd barbarian attack has come from the sea, but never have they invaded the coast in large numbers. You give them too much credit."

"A wise man once said that it is prudent to attack the enemy when he is unprepared, to appear where one is not expected", I replied.

Valerian was clearly angered by my stubbornness. He did not respond until he had composed himself. "I disagree, tribune. But I have not requested your presence only to ignore your advice." He gestured to a scribe to approach. "I wish for the garrison at Trapezus to be bolstered by ten thousand legionaries. There will be no siege of Antioch so we can afford to allow men to remain behind."

He waited until the scribe had finished the orders, then pressed his seal ring onto the molten red bitumen.

"Go visit your family", he said. "And hand my orders to the legate coordinating the movement of the troops. Join me in Antioch in thirty days."

"Thank you, lord", I said and turned to leave.

"Domitius", he said, stopping me in my tracks. "I appreciate that you gifted me the elephant. Ensure that it is well cared for. I will keep it for my procession through the streets of Rome, to celebrate our victory over the Sasanians", he said, smiled, and dismissed me with a wave of a hand.

* * *

Segelinde huddled close to me while we sipped heated wine. Similarly, Hostilius sat beside Adelgunde, little Maximian having fallen asleep on her lap.

"Sometimes it best to cook chicken in pot meant for ox", Cai, who sat beside Gordas on the couch, said in response to our tale.

The dining room of the spacious villa in Trapezus afforded us a panoramic view over the Dark Sea, or the *Pontus Euxinus* as the Romans called it. The rain pelted down in waves while the wind churned up the dark grey water.

Gordas rubbed his thumb against his forefinger, as if rubbing the air itself. "It is not nearly as cold as on the plains", he said, and took a swig of heated mead. "But here, there is a dampness in the air that moulds cheese and makes the spirit miserable."

Diocles looked up from where he was struggling to get the brazier lit. "Even the wood is damp", he said, blew into the firebox, and moments later started to cough due to the smoke.

"Try burning some of those scrolls", Gordas suggested. "They are old, dry and useless."

"Maybe it is best if you and Adelgunde join us in Antioch", I said to Segelinde before Diocles could reply to Gordas.

My wife and Adelgunde shared a glance. "We have spoken about it", she said and smiled sweetly.

"And?" I asked.

"We are comfortable in this house", she said. "Antioch was recently sacked by the Sasanians, so it will still be a mess. And what's to stop them from besieging the city again?"

Hostilius wetted his throat, a clear indication that he was about to offer his opinion.

"We just want what is best for Maximiam", Adelgunde said. "Don't you agree, husband?" she added, and placed her hand on his arm.

Hostilius stared at me in desperation, our plans of collaboration falling apart before my very eyes.

I raised my open palms in a gesture of reconciliation. "We are concerned about your safety", I said. "Gordas has seen Borani warriors in the city, and more than that, we already know that the tribes have access to boats."

"Has the emperor not bolstered the garrison with ten thousand men?" Segelinde asked. "More than two legions now guard the walls."

"It is true", I said. "But you must have noticed how many of the rich people from the surrounding countryside have been flocking into the city. In my experience it is a sure sign that there is trouble brewing."

"It is because they desire the safety of the great walls and the thousands of men manning them", she said.

* * *

Ten days later we departed the city without Segelinde, Adelgunde and Maximiam.

We decided to leave at noon, which would allow us to overnight twenty miles south of Trapezus in the foothills of the Anatolian Mountains. The day after, we would attempt to make our way across the treacherous passes.

After exiting the gates, I looked over my shoulder at the thousands of legionaries lining the walls.

Gordas noticed my concern. "To lose this city to the Borani, the Romans would need to be the biggest fools ever born", he said in an attempt to ease my mind.

"That is what I fear", I said, and turned my horse towards the mountains.

* * *

"Where is the elephant?" Hostilius asked when we were well on our way.

"I don't know, Primus Pilus", I said. "It should have arrived at Trapezus days ago. The emperor asked me to make sure that it is taken care of because he wishes to parade it in his triumph."

"Triumph?" Hostilius asked. "What triumph?"

"His victory parade through the streets of Rome once we have put the Sasanians in their place", I said.

"Let's hope the poor animal hasn't died of old age by the time that happens", he said.

The rain abated soon after, and the clouds scattered before a cold wind blowing in from the snow-capped peaks.

When dusk arrived, we made camp on a northerly slope where ancient cedars, firs and pines protected us from the icy breeze. We soon settled down beside a roaring fire. Gordas spitted cuts of mutton above the flames and Diocles filled our cups before settling down beside us.

I was sipping on my third cup when Diocles left our fire to gather more wood. When he returned, he indicated with his thumb over his shoulder. "The moon is rising over the Dark Sea", he said. "It is beautiful."

Gordas froze when he heard the words. "Why do you say that?" he asked.

"Because it is tinted with crimson", Diocles answered.

As one we rushed from the cover of the trees. Ominously, the blood-red orb hung above the faraway city.

"Smoke turns the moon red, Greek", Gordas hissed. "Have you not read that in your scrolls?"

We all knew that the Borani had come to Trapezus.

Chapter 21 – Borani (December 255 AD)

Towards the end of the third watch of the night we came across the first group of legionaries stumbling south along the Roman road. Even with only the dim light of the moon, the centurion who led a bedraggled mob of soldiers immediately identified us as senior officers.

It was not the right time to pass judgement on the fleeing soldiers – all we wished for was to gain information.

"At ease", Hostilius said when the centurion saluted and came to attention.

"Tell us all, centurion", I said.

"When evening arrived, we rotated the guard as usual, tribune", he said. "The men who came off duty went to the taverns and brothels."

"How many manned the walls?" Hostilius growled.

"One contubernium to every tower", the centurion replied.

"Only one man every twelve paces?" Hostilius asked.

"It wasn't my decision, sir", the centurion said. "It's what the duty tribune ordered us to do. He said that the double walls would protect us, that we needn't worry about them barbarians even showing up."

"When I did my rounds to make sure that the boys were alert, the savages attacked", he said. "My boys were good men, tribune, but the arrows came out of the darkness like a wave of death."

He removed his helmet, revealing hair clotted with blood. In the ghostly light the deep dent in the riveted plate was clear to see. "It felt like someone hit me with a hammer", he explained.

"When I came to, they had swarmed the battlements - not only a handful, but thousands, sir. The couple of us who still breathed had to fight our way to the gate", he said, and gestured to the motley group of followers. "If the savages weren't so occupied with looting, we wouldn't have made it."

"How did they gain the wall walk?" Hostilius asked, not convinced by the story.

"Once they had riddled the boys with arrows, they balanced the masts of their boats against the walls like ladders. Them savages climb like monkeys, sir – never seen anything like it."

"How many boats do they have?" Diocles asked.

"Hundreds, sir. They filled the beach as far as the eye could see", he said, his words accompanied by an appropriate gesture. "And they took the Roman boats that were still anchored in the harbour - the ones they hadn't burned."

I nodded for the centurion to continue.

"Once the barbarians were loose in the city, it was a slaughter, sir. Most of our boys were deep into their cups. You know how it is, sir."

"How many escaped?" Vibius asked.

The centurion thought on my friend's words for a span of heartbeats. "If it is a thousand, it is a lot, sir", he said.

* * *

We all knew the grim realities associated with the sacking of a city. Although violence and rapine are to be expected, the people of the city is a valuable commodity that is usually gathered, rather than killed. Having said that, oldsters or men regarded as a threat are normally done away with.

What had transpired could not be undone, but all knew that Hostilius and I would attempt to regain our families.

211

Trapezus was rich beyond belief, and it had been made a richer prize by the wealthy who had streamed into the city during the weeks before. The Borani and their allies had enough to occupy themselves with inside the walls. They were no fools and would not stray far from their ships.

We made our way to Mount Minthrion - the hill which overlooked the city. When the grey pre-dawn light arrived, we took in the scale of the devastation.

In my own mind I had discarded the thought of hundreds of ships, but the centurion's estimate had been close. "Five hundred and seventy-two", Diocles announced, pointing at the rows of hulls drawn up on the sand.

On the beach, all around the ships, hundreds of captives huddled together in large groups while a continuous stream of wagons moved into and from the city as the gathering of loot continued. The blackened carcasses of a few Roman ships were still smouldering in the harbour while many tendrils of smoke rose from the city – an indication that some invaders had lost their struggle against the base barbarian urge of putting things to the torch.

To the east of the city, between us and the ships, lay a sprawling barbarian camp of many thousands of tents.

I had prayed to the gods that the Heruli, who I still regarded as friends, were part of the raid. It would provide me with the opportunity to negotiate for the release of Segelinde, Adelgunde and little Maximian, if they still lived.

"I do not see the longboats of the Heruli", Hostilius said after a hundred heartbeats had passed, confirming my fears.

"One of us needs to enter their camp", Gordas said.

"I will go", I replied.

Gordas shook his head. In my heart I knew that I had the appearance of a Roman – clean shaven and hair cropped short. The Hun, on the other hand, would not draw a second glance from a fellow barbarian – especially given the diversity of the host.

"I will be back before noon", he said. "Take care of my horse if I don't return", he added, and melted into the undergrowth.

Chapter 22 – Raftaar

"The Hun should have been back already", Hostilius said while squinting up at the sky.

I noticed that I cast almost no shadow, and knew that it was close to noon.

My mind conjured up the most terrible of fates for Segelinde, and I could see that Hostilius was plagued by the same concerns over his wife and child. We said little, as we knew that our time was better spent praying to the gods.

Just then I noticed Kasirga's ears prick up, and a heartbeat later Gordas appeared from the cover of the surrounding vegetation.

There was no need to ask questions, as my Hun friend knew what was foremost on our minds.

"They live", he said, and a great weight lifted from my shoulders.

He held up a hand to stall our celebrations. "They are not bound in iron", he said, "but well-guarded along with the other slaves and loot of Lord Ulkos, the great overlord of the Borani."

"I am the only one who will not stand out among the people of the tribes", the Hun said. "You all look like Romans. You cannot simply ride into their camp – they will kill you on sight, long before you even reach the slave pens of Ulkos."

I could offer no argument in response.

At that moment, the gods intervened.

From the direction of the Roman road emanated a foreign sound – one that I had not heard in weeks. I knew then that Arash had answered my prayers.

* * *

"I think he says that you look like a slave who has stolen his master's elephant", Vibius said, translating the words of the handler as best he could. The strange man, half-turned to the rear, was assessing me critically from where he sat on the beast's neck.

I offered a scowl in reply.

The handler issued a string of words in Persian - or his bastardised version of the Sasanian tongue, to be more specific. Vibius listened with a frown, then responded at

215

length. It was clear that they struggled to understand each other. Finally the man broke into a smile, nodded, and tapped the elephant's great head with his stick. The beast seemed to understand the man better than Vibius did. It extended its trunk to assist its master to scamper to the ground. He trotted off and returned moments later, leading six packhorses.

Weeks before, I had taken no heed of the baggage that accompanied the elephant. Meticulously the handler of the beast laid out an array of cloth and leather-wrapped items. It dawned on me that the beast had been provisioned with extensive accoutrements.

He stepped back when he was done, bowed low, and indicated for me to choose the items I desired.

I pointed to sections of silver-plated iron and mail – the head and body armour of the beast. The handler closed his eyes and slowly inclined his head while pressing his palms together. I interpreted it as a sign of approval.

It took a third of a watch to clad the monster in mail and plate. We fitted purpose-made, razor-sharp blades to its blunted tusks and strapped spiked metal cuffs to its exposed lower legs. Thick-woven red cloth, adorned with golden thread, covered its massive body, all rounded off with golden tassels at the bottom edges.

I donned my Roman mail and armour, which Diocles and Cai had polished to a shine. With the help of Gordas I mounted the beast.

"He says that you look like a god", Vibius said, translating the words of the handler.

Once the driver, the mahout, had been briefed, we started down the hill towards the vast camp of the barbarians.

I would free my wife and Hostilius's family, or die trying.

* * *

The sentry rubbed his eyes and squinted at the approaching apparition. He stood his ground for another ten heartbeats, then cast his spear aside and ran in the direction of the camp, glancing over his shoulder to make sure that the beast was not gaining on him.

A multitude of warriors gathered at the perimeter of the tented camp, pointing in our direction. I noticed men stringing their bows, but I was not concerned - I knew the way of the tribes. The barbarians risked the wrath of their lord if they were to skewer me without a reason – this man, or maybe god, who had entered their camp.

The beast trundled down the path used by the carts. Wisely, none made a move to try to stop us. Many clutched their amulets while mouthing a prayer to whichever god they worshipped. Others retreated a step, or even kneeled in supplication.

The mob followed me, steadily increasing in number. They weaved their way through the tents lining the path until I came to a halt in front of a pavilion. A squat warrior, flanked by guards, stood outside the entrance beside a blazing fire. It was the same man I had seen in the torchlight in the White Palace of Shapur.

Ulkos, lord of the Borani, was nearly a head shorter than me. His neck was thick and his exposed forearms rippled with muscle. His lips were set in a permanent sneer, reminding me of the vicious dogs the Germani bred for combat. He wore the loose robes of the Scythians and the scale armour favoured by the peoples of the horse. His whole demeanour hinted at violence. Fittingly, his hand rested on the pommel of his sword.

I slid down the back of the massive bull elephant and thanked the gods when I landed on my feet in the slippery mud, eight paces from the barbarian lord.

"I wish to trade for three of your slaves", I said in the tongue of the Romans.

"What do you offer as payment, Romani?" he said in broken Latin.

"I wish to trade this beast", I replied in the language of the Steppes, and placed a hand on the elephant's tusk.

His eyes showed that he found my offer agreeable, but Ulkos was not the kind of man who relished the joy of a fair trade – even one that favoured him greatly.

"Why would I not kill you and take the beast for myself?" he asked.

I realised then that he had already made the decision not to barter. The only option left was violence – so I changed my tactics.

"If you believe that you can escape with your life before this beast rips you apart, you are a fool, Ulkos of the Borani", I said, and spat in the mud. "Like a dog, you eat from the hand of the great king of the Sasanians. While the brave warriors of

Rome are fighting against the Easterners, you attack their city whose walls are defended by the old and the weak. You are a coward - afraid to draw your blade and face a man with a sword in his hand."

"The Romani were once great warriors – a people of legend", Ulkos growled in Scythian. "But your race has grown soft. Now you build stone walls and hide behind them. Your emperor is a weakling who has forgotten that you have gained all by the blade. You teach your children how to speak rather than training them in the way of the sword and the spear."

Although the Borani chief's words rang true, I was there to save my family, not to have a discussion with a barbarian.

"You know nothing of the Romans, savage", I said. "You are like the swollen tick that curses the cow while it is sucking its blood. You are but a louse that we will crush under our heel."

Ulkos had not become the overlord of the Borani through his skills as an orator.

He drew his longsword.

I reciprocated. The flickering light of the flames accentuated the wavy forging line of the polished steel blade, which drew gasps of appreciation from the gathered warriors.

By the way Ulkos held his sword it was clear that he was no stranger to bladework. He moved forward, aiming a sweeping middle cut at my torso. I stepped in and met his blade near the hilt of my weapon to neutralise the incredible power behind the strike.

Our swords remained locked for three heartbeats.

Even with the slight disadvantage of leverage, Ulkos demonstrated his brute strength by forcing my blade to the ground. I retreated a step, unable to match his ox-like power.

He sneered with hubris and struck again from over his shoulder, an immensely powerful cut across my body. With the flat of my jian I guided the edge of his sword along its path.

And then I saw the sign that I had been waiting for. Far in the distance, close to the yellow moon, Gordas's fire arrow arced high in the sky above the Dark Sea. It also meant that Ulkos's reprieve came to an abrupt end.

Thinking me distracted, his weapon descended in a blur of motion. But the muscles in my legs, back and shoulders were tight as a drawn bow, waiting until he had fully committed to the blow.

Ulkos's blade sang as it cleft the air.

221

At the last moment I unleashed the pent-up power and lunged to the rear with my right leg. The rotation of my hips set my sword on its path.

I felt the draft as Ulkos's weapon passed inches from my face.

My sword came around in a full circle, striking like a bolt of lightning from the hand of a god.

Before Ulkos's severed head stopped rolling, I had regained my place on the elephant's back.

The mahout, who was called Raftaar, needed no further encouragement. The massive bull summarily charged into the crowd of horrified onlookers. Its great armoured head moved from side to side as it crushed and trampled all within its path. Men too slow to find refuge were flung through the air like rag dolls. Some were cut in twain by the razor-sharp blades moulded to its tusks.

I lay flat on the beast's back, holding on for dear life as it carved a swathe of death and destruction through the barbarian camp. In the wake of the charge, mangled tents fell onto glowing embers. Soon the warriors were dousing fires in an attempt to save their loot.

Once clear of the camp, Raftaar guided the elephant through thorny thickets impenetrable by men on foot.

But there was no need for concern – none of the warriors were fool enough to follow the crazed beast. Who knew what other evils lay waiting in the darkness?

Chapter 23 – Antioch

Although Gordas had freed the women before they could suffer any physical abuse, the emotional scars of being taken as slaves would remain for long. By the time we reached Antioch, Segelinde and Adelgunde, from an outward perspective, had returned to their old selves. Little Maximian, to the contrary, had taken only a day or two to forget the whole unfortunate incident.

Like the women, Antioch was slowly healing. Shortly after the Sasanians had departed, the process of rebuilding began.

The emperor had taken up residence on the famed Island of Antioch within the walls of the city. My retinue and I were allocated rooms within the imperial residence.

"We have accomplished that which we had set out to do", Valerian said. "Syria has been restored to Roman rule. I have also received word that the savages fled to sea when the legions arrived at Trapezus."

He gestured to an opened scroll carrying the seal of Gallienus. "There are good tidings from the West", he said. "My son and Aureolus's Illyrians have finally subdued the Franks. In terms of the peace agreement, the barbarians will provide us with two thousand five hundred warriors to serve as auxiliaries."

His mention of Aureolus's Illyrians rankled, but I kept my counsel. Although his name was not mentioned, I did not doubt that Marcus had a hand in the successes of Gallienus.

"It will be a waste of your talents to keep you in Antioch if there is no war to fight in the East", Valerian said. "My spies inform me that Shapur is occupied with internal problems. It will be some time before he turns his attention to the lands of Rome."

He handed me a scroll bearing his seal. "The legions in Pannonia and Moesia are still in disarray. The defences of the Danubian frontier need to be restored."

I must have frowned.

"There have been reports of a slackness, a rot, within the Danubian legions", he said. "I know of none better to root it out. I have decided to appoint you as the Inspector of Military Camps with full imperial authority."

"What about Legate Ingenuus who commands the Danubian frontier?" I asked.

"He is a good soldier, but I fear that he has been given too large an area to oversee. Do not be concerned, I am not throwing you to the wolves. An old friend of mine will join you in Sirmium – Senator Ulpius Crinitus, who you will report to."

I had seen the incompetence and hubris of the upper classes and the mention of the involvement of a senator did nothing to allay my fears.

Valerian noticed my lack of enthusiasm. "Trust me", he said. "He is not what you think."

* * *

Hostilius smacked a palm on the tabletop, spilling wine from his brimming cup. "Now that", he said, "is the best news I've heard in a long time. I've been itching to get my hands dirty again."

He hurried from the room and returned heartbeats later, reverently placing a wrapped item on the table. He flipped open the leather, revealing his trusty vine cane. "I've been saving it for a special occasion", he said, his voice filled with emotion.

"I am sure that the situation is not as bad as the emperor makes it out to be", I said, and I imagined I noticed a flicker of disappointment in Hostilius's eyes.

"Don't you worry, Domitius", Hostilius said. He picked up his vine cane and thumped the business end in his palm. "Things are always worse than what one expects them to be."

* * *

During the first week of March we departed from the harbour at Seleucia by the Sea near Antioch, on board the liburnian of Master Herminius.

Apart from a few expected transgressions by Scaevola, the voyage was swift and without incident. Three weeks later we arrived at Salona on the coast of Dalmatia.

Diocles was strangely quiet as we entered the port. Then I remembered that he was born near the city. I walked to where he was gripping the wooden rail, staring across the wide water.

"One day I will return to this city, legate", he said. "But not as a beggar", he whispered through his teeth. I had known Diocles for a while and recognized the look of determination in his eyes.

I nodded and placed a hand on his shoulder.

* * *

My aide was not the only one in a reflective mood. On our way north through the passes along the Via Argentaria, the Silver Way, Vibius was not his talkative self.

"I worry about Marcus", he said. "I cannot help to feel that I have abandoned him. I knew that my local knowledge of the East would be invaluable, but now…"

"None will blame you if you join him, Vibius", I said. "Marcus should consider himself fortunate to have a man like you as part of his retinue."

Vibius nodded. "I will depart soon after we get to Sirmium."

"Do not be troubled", I added. "I believe there is a reason why the gods have brought us together. Soon, you, Marcus and I will fight side by side again."

"That means that there will be war", he said.

"There always is", I replied, and kicked Kasirga to a canter.

* * *

Segelinde gasped when we exited the trees into the clearing around the villa of our farm near Sirmium.

Hostilius eyed me sternly. "Keeping things from your friends is a bad character trait", he said.

I had not told my friends or family that I had ordered the rebuilding of the villa months before. The sale of our property near Mogantiacum, added to the remainder of our gold, was enough to resurrect the villa which was destroyed when Phillip the Arab ordered it so.

We came to a halt ten paces in front of the sturdy gates.

"Ho there", Hostilius boomed in his primus pilus voice.

A hundred heartbeats later Egnatius appeared on the wall walk above the gates. He squinted in our direction, then disappeared again for another hundred heartbeats. Eventually the gates creaked open.

229

Egnatius came to attention and saluted. "Welcome tribunes", he said. "I trust that you have won a great victory."

"At ease, legionary. We have vanquished the barbarians and freed the East from their depredations", I said, playing along with the old man.

"Congratulations tribune", Egnatius said.

We dismounted, and on the command of the old man, servants appeared to unpack our belongings and care for the horses.

We took turns to rid ourselves of the dust and grime of the journey in the heated bath of the *lavatrina* adjoining the kitchen. Once we had dressed in clean tunics, Felix and Pezhman arrived after a day of toil on the farm.

Segelinde took charge, and soon the aroma of fresh-baked bread, grilled mutton and eastern spices emanated from the kitchen.

Although I could not retain the elephant, I did not return empty-handed from the court of the great king. Hostilius filled our cups with Basarangian wine, the finest vintage Sasania possessed.

It turned out to be a fine evening, filled with good food, great wine and even better company. But more than that – for the first time in years I felt as if I had come home.

Three days later, Hostilius, Vibius, Gordas, Diocles and I departed for the imperial offices in Sirmium.

Chapter 24 – Senator (June 256 AD)

Alexander, the secretary to the governor of Pannonia, embraced me like one would a brother.

"It is good to see you again, Lucius Domitius", he said, then turned to face Diocles, who greeted him in Greek.

Alexander raised his eyebrows and gave me a sidelong glance. "I see that you have finally woken up to the benefits of surrounding yourself with men of intelligence", he said, and bade us to be seated.

Before sitting down behind his desk, he walked to the door, opened it a crack, and peered into the hallway to make sure none were loitering outside.

"Emperor Gallienus has called Governor Ingenuus to Carnuntum in Upper Pannonia", he said. "He is dealing with the settlement of the Marcomanni south of the Danube."

The little Greek leaned in and lowered his voice. "The general is doing Gallienus's dirty work while the legions are falling apart."

"Has Senator Ulpius Crinitus arrived yet?" I asked.

"He has annexed the office of the governor", Alexander said, appearing decidedly uncomfortable at the mention of the senator's name.

"What do you know of him?" I said.

"Ulpius Crinitus is a long-time friend and confidant of Emperor Valerian", Alexander said. "He has recently spent time in Britannia and Hispania doing the emperor's work."

"Does he outrank Governor Ingenuus?" Diocles asked.

"He carries no rank", the secretary said. "That makes him even more intimidating. He acts on behalf of the emperor – Valerian has entrusted Crinitus with the imperial seal."

The words of the Greek roused my curiosity. What kind of man would Valerian trust so implicitly?

I did not have to wait long to find out.

* * *

Ulpius Crinitus was standing behind his desk when the guards ushered me into the office that would normally be occupied by the governor of Pannonia. The senator's arms were folded

233

behind his back, his fingers intertwined in a way that reminded me of a legionary standing at ease. He faced away from the door, staring out the window at the bustling city of Sirmium.

The skin at the back of his neck was brown and creased, like worn leather, and his thick silver hair cropped short in the style of the legions.

He wore the garb of a legate, yet his clothes appeared plain and workmanlike.

"Lucius Domitius?" he growled, without turning around.

"Yes, senator", I said.

He turned to face me.

His eyes were dark and piercing, his nose prominent and his lips thin. He must have seen more than fifty summers, but he was still lean and muscular.

My eyes were drawn to his gladius, adorned with a simple wooden pommel, worn smooth from many hours of use.

He noticed my interest. "Beech", he said. "Oak looks better, but it is not ideal."

"Oak corrodes the blade", I said, and noticed that my knowledge pleased him.

He picked up a scroll lying on the desk bearing the broken seal of Valerian. "The emperor informed me that he has decided to entrust his grandson to Ingenuus. Why, do you think, did he not ask you to mould the boy? You were after all the one he wished to have at his side when he faced the Sasanians."

Crinitus's revelation came as a shock.

"I do not know", I answered.

"Because", he growled, "Valerian believes that you are much too strict, that your harshness does not belong in our time. He sees you as one who would be better suited to days of old – to the times when men of iron ruled the Empire."

His words stunned me. Involuntarily my hand sought the comfort of the pommel of my sword.

"And that is the reason why I asked for you by name", he said, and pointed in the direction of the river. "The savages have smelled our weakness. They no longer fear us. Soon, innumerable hordes will spill across the Danube to join the feast – to pick clean the bones of the carcass of the Empire."

"The discipline and pride of Rome's legions have to be restored. If that cannot be achieved, the Empire will soon be nothing more than a memory."

Crinitus's knuckles turned white as his fist tightened around the scroll he still held in his hand. "By the gods, Domitius, the time for meekness has passed", he hissed, and slammed the desk with his other hand. "Valerian Augustus knows that only men of iron can rip the half-dead carcass of the Empire from the jaws of the savages."

His breathing slowly returned to normal, and he gently placed the scroll on the desk.

Then he grinned. "Finally", he sighed, "our time has come to pass."

* * *

"He sounds too good to be true", Hostilius said after I had shared my encounter with Crinitus. "But it is long overdue."

Gordas pulled his horse alongside ours. "It is better to spill the blood of a few to save thousands. In the lands of the Hun, a man who gainsays his commander does not live long enough to make more mischief."

Hostilius nodded. "The tail is wagging the bloody dog", he said. "The legionaries think that they rule the Empire. Order needs to be restored."

I was aware, and have personally experienced, the wanton cruelty commanders inflicted on the rank and file of the legions, but the words of the Primus Pilus and the Hun rang true. I knew that once rot had set in, it needed to be removed like I have seen medici do with a festering limb.

Soon the towering walls of the legionary fortress of Singidunum came into view.

"Well", I said, "let us then determine how bad the decay is before we decide whether we have to amputate."

We approached the gate, which contrary to regulations, had been left wide open.

Hostilius reined in beside the watch officer. "Give me your blade, centurion", he growled.

I noticed the hesitation in the centurion's eyes, but he wisely did as the Primus Pilus asked, and held out his gladius, hilt first.

"Sheath it", Hostilius barked after eyeing the steel.

The Primus Pilus kept his counsel as we made our way to the praetorium at the centre of the fort, but I knew him well enough to know why he pursed his lips.

Our orders, displaying the imperial seal, ensured that Hostilius and I gained immediate access to the quarters of the legate, who was clearly displeased by the interruption of his substantial lunch.

He read the orders, his expression changing from irritated to grim. "We do not live in the time of Divius Julius, inspector", he said. "If we were to employ the same, outdated, punishments for offences, we will have a revolt on our hands soon enough."

The legate leaned in as if to share a secret. "I still enforce the rules", he said, "but with the necessary discretion. I keep the troublemakers on my side." Then he winked, and added, "If you know what I mean."

I fixed Hostilius with a stare to keep him from voicing the obvious retort.

We soon left the chamber of the legate, allowing him to continue his lunch in peace.

Gordas and Diocles were waiting for us in the rooms reserved for imperial visitors and their retinues.

"The rot goes deep", Hostilius declared when he had pulled the door shut behind him. "The blade of the centurion at the gate was pitted with rust. I've seen enough."

I held up an open palm. "Let us spend a few days in the camp before we come to a conclusion", I said.

Hostilius scowled in reply.

We ended up spending eight days within the fort at Singidunum.

On the evening before the morning of our departure, I ordered the cook to bring food and wine to our chambers. Diocles sat at a desk while Gordas, Hostilius and I reclined on couches.

It was my Greek aide who spoke first. He had played the part of a disgruntled scribe and soon gained the confidence of his peers, who were equally disgruntled for the most part. Even without his deception they would probably have been more than happy to spread ill word of their superiors.

I was not interested in the normal complaints of long hours and too little pay, which Diocles only referred to in a cursory way. But then he said something that did interest me.

"According to the scribe of the head centurion of the second cohort", Diocles explained, "it is not the legate who has the most say in the legion, but rather a group of centurions."

"I've seen it before", Hostilius said. "A few criminally inclined bastards mix with the men who're most feared. Soon enough they have a racket going inside the legion."

He stood from the couch and paced around with his hand on the hilt of his sword.

"What else is there?" I asked.

"The mules and horses are underfed", Gordas said.

Diocles nodded. "The gang buys the fodder at half-price in exchange for gambling credit and on-sells it to farmers and bandits."

But my aide was not through. "The legion's physicians charge a fee to attend to the men", he said. "And some men have become like slaves to others due to unpaid debts."

"The barracks and the latrines are not cleaned properly", Hostilius added. "And I came across a brawl between two legionaries that was left unchecked and unpunished by the officers."

Hostilius gave me his 'I told you so' look.

"I will think on it", I said, and prayed to Arash to give me the wisdom to address the situation.

The following morning the god answered my prayers, but not in the way I had hoped.

* * *

"Did you manage to get a name?" Hostilius asked while wrapping his baggage.

The Greek smiled smugly. "Valerius Macednus", he replied. "He is the centurion of the third century of the first cohort."

The Primus Pilus raised his eyebrows.

"His clerk spilled the beans", Diocles explained. "Macednus had him flogged a few weeks ago for some minor transgression. He hates the man."

"I cannot condemn Macednus based on the word of a disgruntled clerk", I said. "We need more."

"I suggest you order his execution", Gordas said. "If he is innocent, there's no real harm done."

Huns.

I waved away his comment and mounted Kasirga.

Outside the gates, to the south of the fort, was a large vicus populated by retired legionaries and their families. While the townsfolk were going about their business, we walked the horses down the road, stopping for carts and toddlers crossing our path.

We had almost reached the edge of the settlement when we noticed a disturbance at the side of the road. A greybeard was trying to comfort a girl who was sobbing hysterically. I reined in and dismounted.

The grey-haired man noticed my approach. "I am sorry, legate", he stammered, "it's just that ..."

I held up my hand to stall his jabbering. "Tell me what happened", I said.

"I've been taking care of Julia since her mother died", he said. "The centurion was courting her, he was, and I thought he had honest intentions. Yesterday, while I was helping a friend mend his roof, the centurion beat her and dishonoured her."

I looked at the girl who had clearly been roughed up. She was comely, reminding me of my daughter.

I felt the anger stir deep inside.

"Who did this to you, girl?" I asked.

She looked at her father, who nodded his consent.

"Valerius Macednus", she said, and burst into tears.

* * *

Macednus returned my stare with defiance.

"She's half Roxolani", he said. "Half a bloody savage, sir. That makes her fair game, doesn't it?" he added with a chuckle and licked the spittle from his lips.

He leaned in. "I help the legate to keep the peace, sir", he whispered. "He would never risk a revolt, you know", he added as a veiled threat.

Unknowingly his words sealed his fate, removing the last vestiges of doubt from my mind.

I did not reply, but left Macednus in the cell.

* * *

"I cannot allow it", the legate of the IV Flavia Felix said. "There will be a revolt if we execute him."

"There will be no revolt", I replied, and went to speak with Gordas.

Chapter 25 – Justice

The Hun listened to my words.

"Do you believe that Macednus deserves a quick death?" he asked.

"No", I said. "But it will serve a purpose."

Gordas nodded.

"The Hun can show me which trees to cut while you update the legion's rolls", Hostilius said. "I will arrange for a sapper team to do the work."

Hostilius and Gordas returned to the fort early in the afternoon. Diocles and I made our way to where my friends were overseeing the arrangements.

At the front of the fort's parade ground, two holes had been dug in the hard-packed earth, sixty feet apart. Gordas had chosen two pine trees from the forest. The sapper team had cleared the branches, leaving two bare trunks, twenty-five feet in length. Two long, thick ropes were firmly attached to grooves cut close to the top of each trunk.

It took the best part of a watch to place the trimmed pines in the holes and compact the loose earth around the bases.

With the help of a team of eight carthorses, the top of one tree was pulled down and firmly tied to the base of the other trunk. We repeated the process until both trees were bent and secured, the ropes creaking under the enormous strain.

One rope still hung from the bent top of each tree. While we watched, the legion's smith arrived and affixed two iron shackles to the ends, which dangled in the gentle breeze.

Hostilius took a step back to admire our handiwork. He gestured to the ropes snaking in the wind. "All we have to do tomorrow is tie up a few loose ends", he said.

* * *

The following day, I said little on the way to Viminacium.

The execution was quick, but gruesome. Some of the legionaries, even men who were no strangers to war, vomited where they stood when the ropes had snapped taut.

"You sacrificed one man to save the lives of countless others", Gordas said. "There is no need to let it weigh upon your mind. If he had done the evil deeds in the lands of the Huns, it would not have been so easy for him. What do you think Octar would have done?"

The Hun was right, of course. No self-respecting chieftain of the Steppes would endure dissent within the ranks.

"The legionaries have too much power", Diocles said.

"The army needs to be large", Hostilius replied. "That's the downside of needing so many soldiers to protect the borders against the barbarians. There's nothing that can be done."

"The legions should be smaller", Diocles continued, "but more numerous. A group of a thousand soldiers will think twice before they revolt."

"It'll never work", Hostilius said and waved away Diocles's words.

"We will see", Diocles mumbled, fortunately not loud enough to carry to Hostilius's ears.

* * *

When we approached the legionary fort of Viminacium we found the gates locked and manned. The armour of the men

247

guarding the gate had been polished to a brilliant shine, the whetted tips of their spears gleaming in the sunlight. The legionaries did not open the gate before Hostilius boomed our credentials.

He leaned in while the gates swung open. "Either word travels fast, or the VII Claudia is a beacon of light in the midst of a sea of darkness", he whispered. "But I would put my coin on it not being the latter."

Everywhere, soldiers were engaged in some toil or other. None were loitering about.

"The legate of the IV Flavia Felix sent a messenger yesterday evening", Hostilius said, "and I'm sure that another messenger has travelled farther east."

The Primus Pilus was right. Word of the happenings at Singidunum had spread like wildfire.

We ended up spending seven days in Viminacium. The changes I ordered were adopted without any objections. No one had to be executed, none were flogged.

On our return to Sirmium sixty days later, I reported to Ulpius Crinitus.

The senator clasped my arm and placed a hand on my shoulder. "Valerian was right about you after all", he said. "You have put the fear of the gods into the men of the legions. I returned from Singidunum only yesterday. I am pleased to say that there is much improvement."

"Eradicating the culture of slackness will require more", I said.

Crinitus was no fool. He nodded, knowing what I was referring to. "We need a war", he said. "The men need to spill blood and win booty."

"I agree", I said, "but first I wish to make sure that they are able to win."

"Do what you need to", Crinitus said, "but know that the Goths have recovered from the defeat inflicted upon them by Aemilianus. There have been many minor incursions along the border, which is normally a prelude to a full-scale invasion."

"All I need is the winter", I said. "The men will be ready next season, by the time the month of the war god arrives."

* * *

During the months that followed we spent our time preparing the soldiers of Pannonia and Moesia for war. There were very few major lapses in discipline, mainly due to the increased emphasis on training – busy men have little time for the work of the Evil One.

Crinitus's presence in the province ensured that funding arrived regularly from Rome. My involvement ensured that the gold made its way into the stores and armouries at the frontier.

But the problems we experienced did not arise from our interactions with the legions. I would be lying if I said that it came from an unexpected source.

* * *

Three days before the Ides of September, Emperor Gallienus arrived in Sirmium with his son, Valerianus, who had shortly before been appointed as Caesar.

Valerianus had come to Pannonia to ensure that the family's authority was respected. Under the guardianship of Ingenuus he would learn to become an emperor – or that was what his grandfather and father hoped for.

Gallienus also made time to visit with Ulpius Crinitus, whose office was adjacent to mine.

When they raised their voices, I could not help to overhear.

"You are spending too much gold, Senator Crinitus", Gallienus said. "Do not think that wielding the seal of my father makes you the emperor."

Ulpius Crinitus was not a man who minced his words.

"The reason why your father has given me his seal, Egnatius, is because you are incapable of restoring order to the Danubian frontier."

I imagined Gallienus turn red in the face. "You will address me as 'Emperor'", he hissed and I heard the couch creak as he rose in anger.

"I have been bleeding for Rome since long before you played in the halls of my villa with a wooden sword, Egnatius", Crinitus growled. "I suggest you spend less coin on brothels and sculptors. I am no usurper, but not too old you give you a good thrashing."

A door slammed and I heard Gallienus storm from the room.

Moments later Crinitus entered my quarters.

"Did you hear that?" he asked.

I nodded.

"Pay him no heed", the senator said. "He is still the same petulant child as twenty seasons ago."

"I will invite him and his son to dinner tonight and make sure that there is more than enough wine, dancing girls and sycophantic poets. Tomorrow, he will approve the spend of gold and the whole incident will be forgotten."

Senator Crinitus knew Gallienus better than most. But he did not know the nature of Valerianus.

* * *

Hostilius stood outside the entrance, his dour disposition discouraging any unwanted visitors.

I heard a commotion as the emperor arrived to bid Crinitus farewell.

"Step aside, tribune", Gallienus said.

"The senator has taken ill, Lord Caesar", I heard Hostilius say. "We believe that it is the terrible pestilence."

It was well known that entering a bed chamber of a victim exposed one to the evilness that had taken hold of the unfortunate.

"I see", Gallienus said in a muffled voice, no doubt covering his face. "Very well then, I will arrange a sacrifice to assist his recovery."

The hurried footfalls of his entourage disappeared down the colonnaded porch.

Inside the chamber, Senator Ulpius Crinitus moaned in pain as the cramps wracked his prone frame. Diocles used a damp piece of linen to wipe away the saliva that kept running from his mouth. On the far side of the room Cai was frantically grinding up a mixture of herbs and salts in a small mortar.

"Panther cap mushroom", Cai said. "Poison take long before kill, but it strong."

When the Easterner was satisfied, he dissolved the powder into a cup of wine. I held up Crinitus's head while Cai poured a little of the liquid down his throat.

Eight days we spent in vigilance beside the bed of the senator. Every watch we administered the potion, until on the ninth day, Crinitus returned to the world of men and opened his eyes.

"What in Hades is happening to me?" he said while we helped him to an upright position.

"You were poisoned, senator", I said.

"When?" he asked.

"At the banquet you arranged in honour of Gallienus and his son Valerianus", I said.

Crinitus shook his head in disbelief. "Gallienus had five tasters, professionals who sampled everything. It is impossible for the food or the wine to have been poisoned."

He leaned in conspiratorially as if to share a secret. "I also take a dose of theriac every morning", he said. "It is the same recipe that Marcus Aurelius perfected."

"Did you eat or drink anything that was given to you by a guest, Lord Senator?" Diocles asked.

A frown creased Senator Crinitus's brow as he tried to recall the events of the evening. "No", he said. "Apart from sampling a priceless rare vintage of falernian from the emperor's own collection, there was nothing else."

"Who poured for you?" I asked.

"Valerianus", he said and the frown returned. "You are not suggesting that it may be the handiwork of the young Caesar?"

I shrugged. "'We will never know", I said. "But if the young Caesar is going to cause problems, Ingenuus, his mentor, will never put up with it."

"Do not be concerned, I will be back on my feet soon", he said, and promptly collapsed onto the floor while attempting to rise from the bed.

Chapter 26 – Letter (August 256 AD)

Senator Ulpius Crinitus read from the letter he had received from Valerian Augustus.

"In order that your unfortunate illness does not cause harm to the Empire, I wish for Lucius Domitius Aurelianus to take the defence of the lower Danube upon himself. Since my son, Gallienus, has restored peace along the Rhine, I will relocate the III Italica to the Danubian frontier when spring arrives."

He rolled up the scroll with trembling hands and sat down heavily on the couch, fatigued by the minor exertion.

"It is a wise decision", he said. "I am in no state to command troops. Even leaving my chambers is too much of an ask."

He picked up a cup of watered wine and took a small sip. "Are the legions ready to repel an attack from across the river?" he asked.

"They train every day", I said. "But we need more men and more coin to procure weapons and armour."

"My spies tell me that the Goths are preparing for war", Crinitus said. "They get bolder every passing year." He weakly slapped his knee in frustration. "Is there nothing we can do but hide behind our walls like sheep who know that the wolves will come?"

* * *

Not long after the Danube had frozen solid, the wolves came.

Hostilius, Gordas and I watched from the shadows, underneath ancient pines. In the distance, the Gothic horde streamed across the white river into the lands of Rome.

"They know that the harvest has been gathered", Gordas said. "Now they will gather their own harvest with spear and sword."

"There are too many", Hostilius said. "They outnumber us three to one."

I estimated their number at forty thousand, but did not say it out loud. "This is but a portion of the men Cannabaudes can field", I said.

"What do you suggest, Domitius?" Hostilius asked.

"We face them on ground of our choosing", I replied. "And then we fight them in the old way."

My words clearly pleased Hostilius. "I like it", he confirmed with a smirk.

"But why will we be victorious while men like Decius have failed with larger armies?" Hostilius asked.

"Because, Primus Pilus", I said, "we won't do anything stupid."

"And", Gordas interjected, "this time the favourite of Arash will not fight on the side of the tribes."

* * *

One Roman legion was stationed at each of the major forts of Singidunum, Viminacium and Novae. But it would have been madness to empty the fortresses of soldiers. Between the IV Flavia Felix, the VII Claudia and the XIII Gemina, we managed to gather twelve thousand legionaries while two thousand men remained at each fort – barely enough to man the walls and towers.

"When will the III Italica arrive?" Hostilius asked. "We need them - six thousand battle-hardened veterans."

"It could be weeks", I said. "Are we going to wait, and watch from the walls while the Goths destroy the land? Cannabaudes is not content with only gathering loot – he revels in the destruction." I pointed to the tendrils of smoke rising from the eastern horizon. "While we hide behind the walls, the people of Moesia are dying. Olive groves and vineyards, generations old, are burning."

Gordas and I had reconnoitred the train of the barbarians. "Tell them what we saw yesterday", I said.

"Thousands of horses, cattle, sheep and goats", the Hun said. "The line of Roman women and children captured as slaves is two miles long."

"I am tired of waiting", Hostilius growled.

"So am I", I said.

* * *

Gordas thundered towards the gate of the marching camp. He swung from his saddle even before the horse came to a halt inside the gates. Moments later the Hun joined Hostilius, Diocles and me on the rampart.

259

"The Goths are camped to the east of Nicopolis ad Istrum, where the Lyginus flows into the Yatrus", Gordas said. "They know we are coming."

"How do you know that?" Diocles asked.

"Goth raiding parties are returning to camp, but none are leaving", Gordas replied. "Cannabaudes is gathering his warriors."

"Did you find a suitable place?" I asked.

"Ten miles west of the Goth camp there is a narrow strip of flat, open land. To the north it is hemmed in by steep wooded hills, and to the south bordered by the forested banks of the Lyginus."

"How wide?" I asked.

"Less than a mile where it is narrowest, maybe a thousand paces across", he said. "It is at least eight miles long."

"Are they watching our camp?" I asked.

"Even now, the eyes of the Goths are upon us", Gordas said.

"Will you be able to leave the camp without being followed?" I asked the Hun.

"What do you think?" he said, and grinned like a wolf.

When darkness arrived, Gordas slipped from the Roman camp and rode north.

* * *

I was waiting on the rampart when he returned during the third watch of the night. The fresh scalp of a Goth scout hung from the Hun's saddle.

"I have spoken to them", Gordas said. "They will do as you suggest."

"Good", I said. "We march at first light."

* * *

When the first rays of the sun crested the eastern horizon, we turned off the Roman road that led to Nicopolis and headed west.

Gordas pointed to the Goth scouts atop the distant hills. "You have confused them by turning west", he said. "They think that we fear them."

261

The army struggled along rough tracks and across open fields. Just after the midday rest, we came across a greenway where we turned south. We passed a Roman village which had been looted and destroyed. The charred remains of the men and women too infirm to be taken as slaves lay among the smoking embers.

Although the march was long and taxing, there were none of the usual grumblings. The men of the legions were predominantly farm boys from peasant stock. Most would have grown up in or near villages similar to the one we passed.

Hostilius gestured with his head to the rows of legionaries marching behind us. "It is good that they see the handiwork of the savages", he said. "It will put iron in their sword arms."

We marched south for another six miles, arriving on the banks of the Lyginus at dusk. When it was too dark to continue working, one man in each contubernium was ordered to light a torch. At the start of the second watch of the night the camp was completed.

Hostilius sat down heavily on a chair, and with a nod, accepted a cup of wine from Diocles. "Many generals give in to the temptation and forego building a marching camp if they arrive late. Bloody fools", he sneered. "Digging a trench in the evening is better than digging a grave in the morning."

We retired early with the knowledge that on the morrow we would meet the barbarians on the field of battle – a battle that would see us outnumbered three to one. In the camp of the Goths, Cannabaudes would be feasting with his lords, giving thanks to the gods that they had delivered another Roman army into his lap.

But the gods can be fickle. While the high king of the Goths was getting drunk on Roman wine, Roman hands were toiling throughout the night to bring about his ruin.

Chapter 27 - Play

Eight thousand legionaries arrayed for battle - their right flank anchored by the northern bank of the Lyginus and their left by steep forested hills. The formation was tight, but necessary, as I knew what was to come.

Behind the main army was an unusually large reserve of four thousand men deployed in a similar fashion. A gap of ten paces separated them from the front ranks.

A dust cloud appeared to the east, announcing the arrival of the Goth cavalry. The horde of riders filled the width of the valley, their column more than a hundred paces deep.

Hostilius pointed at the sea of barbarian horsemen approaching at a canter. "Ten thousand at the least", he growled, and nudged Diocles with his elbow. "If you feel the urge to wet your braccae, you are not alone, Greek."

My aide did not offer his usual retort. His eyes were wide, fixed on the host of spear-wielding riders bearing down on us.

"Our boys will hold", Hostilius comforted him. "I just hope that you are right about Cannabaudes, Domitius."

I had gambled all, based on the assumption that the Goth king was no fool.

On my signal the signifier issued a note on the buccina. Simultaneously, thousands of Goth spears arced towards the Roman ranks. As one the legionary ranks formed a testudo, their large rectangular shields overlapping like the scales on a vest of armour.

The spears of the barbarians rained down on the protected Roman ranks. Again and again their javelins dimmed the sun, but the legionaries weathered the storm.

No horse will run into a shield wall. The barbarians reined in, and soon a mass of cavalry milled about in front of the Roman line. The Goths launched spears at the closed formation of overlapped shields, but to little effect.

I nodded, and the signifier who had been watching me, issued a command. The four thousand men of the reserve skipped forward, each launching one precious pilum over the heads of the men in the front ranks. Hundreds of Goths were bowled from their saddles. Horses, impaled by the thin iron shafts, groaned in pain and threw their riders.

The low moan of a ram's horn reverberated across the plain. Abruptly the horsemen turned their mounts and cantered back the way they had come from.

"Now The Crow knows that victory will not be easy", I said.

As the last of the Goth horsemen disappeared in the distance, the eastern horizon started to shimmer. "The whetted spears of the Goth foot", Hostilius explained, drawing a frown from Diocles. "Thirty thousand of them. If we try to hold, the line will break. The best we can do will be to give ground slowly."

I whispered a command to my standard bearer, who relayed my orders. In response, the reserve of four thousand legionaries abruptly turned around to face west, away from the front ranks. The centurions boomed the orders and they marched down the valley, coming to a halt five hundred paces farther.

"The die is cast", I said.

I had barely uttered the words when a cloud of dust appeared at our rear. Cannabaudes, being familiar with the terrain, had done what a skilled commander would do – he had sent his cavalry to strike us from the rear.

Hostilius glanced over his shoulder at the Goth riders bearing down on the reserve. "Our boys are only four ranks deep", he said. "They will not hold for long."

Moments later, the horde of thirty thousand Goth infantry closed with the Roman formation, the clash of blades echoing eerily off the distant hills.

The legionaries were well-trained, but eight thousand men cannot prevail against thirty thousand for long. Slowly the legionaries in the centre were pushed back, the line curving like a drawn bow. Step by step the flanks moved backwards in an attempt to maintain the integrity of the line, forcing the whole army into a steady retreat.

At our rear, the reserves were giving way against the pressure of overwhelming odds.

Hostilius pointed at the centre of the formation, only fifty paces from us, where the elite warriors of the Goths were cutting gaps into the Roman line. "I know the telltale signs, Domitius", he said with concern etched on his face. "Our line is about to break. If that happens, we are done for."

I swung from Kasirga's back and threw the reins to Diocles. With my gladius in my hand, I started pushing my way to the thick of the fight where a bull of a man was wreaking carnage.

The Goth champion fought without a shield, adroitly wielding a short sword with his right hand and a battle-axe with his left.

The big Goth slammed his axe into the shield of the legionary two paces ahead of me. The Roman soldier stepped in and thrust around the rim of his shield with his gladius. It was a well-executed manoeuvre. But the big Goth used the embedded axe as a lever and blocked the blow by forcing the shield across the body of the legionary – a move which requires massive strength. The big man stepped in as well, jerked the shield down, and buried his sword in the unfortunate legionary's chest.

I stepped into the gap.

The champion pointed his sword at me, bright blood still dripping from the blade.

"Are the Romans so desperate that they force old men to do the work of warriors?" he sneered in the tongue of the Goths.

The comment was meant for the ears of his fellows, rather than mine. In response, I flipped my gladius to my left hand and drew my jian.

"Are the Goths so desperate that they give blades to fools", I said, also using the barbarian tongue.

My words drew the attention of the Goth, whose sneer morphed into a feral growl.

"I am Eochar of the Roxolani", I hissed. "I am the god-messenger, the one who walks with Teiwaz. I have come to send your shade to the corpse hall of Donar."

I knew that the tales of my deeds were told around the cooking fires of the tribe. The Goth had no doubt heard them all. His complexion turned ashen and he retreated a step as his confidence evaporated. He stood undecided for a heartbeat, until his greed for fame got the better of his fear. He composed himself, roared a challenge, and charged with his axe moving in an overhead arc aimed at my head.

Only a fool would have tried to block such a powerful blow. I did what he least expected, and ran at him. The Goth realised that he would be late with the axe and tried to thrust with his sword. It was a mistake.

I moved to the right, narrowly avoided the blade, and cut the back of his leg as he passed me, severing the muscle and sinews.

A great cheer went up from the Roman ranks as the barbarian champion crumpled to the ground. A legionary pushed past me to close the line.

269

My attention returned to the injured Goth, just in time to see Hostilius twist his gladius as he withdrew his blade from the giant's throat.

"Thought you would need me to finish the job", he said, took me by the arm, and pulled me back to where Diocles waited with the horses.

But my intervention had not changed the inevitable outcome of the battle – it had only provided a temporary reprieve. But more importantly, also the chance for the legionaries to plug the holes in the line, which was still moving back under the relentless pressure of the Goths.

Hostilius watched with concern as both Roman lines were forced into retreat. "It is time", he said. "The savages are tired, but they sense victory. They will overrun us soon."

The signifier issued a series of commands which seemed to be ignored by the legionaries fighting for their lives.

Then, from behind the Goth footmen, a Roman buccina answered our call. The standards of the III Italica bobbed up and down as the legion advanced at a jog, eager to fall on the rear of the barbarian horde.

A ram's horn's low note followed soon after, and in response, half of the Goth warriors turned to repel the new threat.

Six thousand lead-weighted darts rose from the ranks of the III Italica and rained death on the confused horde. Wave after wave of darts wreaked havoc on the tightly-packed ranks of the Goths. When the tribesmen had lost all cohesion, the veterans of the legion smashed into their line.

But the Goth cavalry was about to overrun our rear.

A low rumble came from the west, followed by a wail of a dragon standard. The intensity increased, and a black line appeared, filling the valley from side to side. Three thousand black-clad riders bore down on the barbarian cavalry.

At the centre of the near perfect line, beside Gordas, rode a man with a white-plumed gilded helmet - Marcus Claudius and the Illyrians had arrived.

"By the gods", Hostilius mumbled. "I know they are on our side, but they still scare me."

The sky darkened as darts and arrows rained down on the Goths. The sun flashed off whetted spearpoints as the iron-clad riders lowered their lances. The large armoured horses slammed into the enemy riders, bowling over the smaller horses and impaling warriors with their long, thick spears.

Although we had shocked the Goths with the attacks on their rear, the fight still hung in the balance.

A roar akin to thunder erupted from the shadows on the slopes of the forested hills. A heartbeat later, more than two thousand throwing axes slammed into the flanks of the unsuspecting Goths. Haldagates and his Franks had hammered the final nail into their coffin.

* * *

When the last of the surviving Goths had fled the field, I sought out my friends. I embraced Marcus, Vibius and Haldagates in turn.

"Where is Aureolus?" I asked.

"He wished to join us", Marcus said, "but Emperor Gallienus summoned him to Colonia Agrippina to tend to an emergency."

"An invasion by Haldagates's kin?" I asked in jest, drawing a grin from the hulking Frank.

"Worse", Vibius said. "A new play opened at the theatre."

Chapter 28 – Loot (February 257 AD)

We scoured the battlefield in search of the body of The Crow, but found naught. There was no doubt that he had managed to escape.

"It will be a long time before the Goths will trouble us again", Marcus said, and held out his cup for a refill.

"It is true", I said. "The loss that the Goths suffered today will be a setback for Cannabaudes, but he will rise again. A day will come when the tribes will cross the river in strength. It may be a year from now, or even ten, but it will happen. On that day, Rome will face not forty thousand, but more than a hundred thousand. Mayhap more."

Gordas stared up into the night sky, no doubt seeing the terrible battle play out in his mind's eye. "I will sacrifice to the god of war to preserve my life so I may be part of such a battle", the Hun said, his voiced laced with emotion.

"As will I", Haldagates added.

"I will pray to Arash to allow us enough time to prepare for what is to come", I said.

It took many days of scouring the countryside to rid the land of the Goths who failed to reach the sanctuary of the northern bank of the Danube.

Freeing the slaves and distributing the loot was no easy matter. It soon became evident that my personal involvement was required. Naturally, I called on Hostilius for assistance as he was a man of the world.

The Primus Pilus gripped his vine cane tightly with his right hand, the business end tucked under his arm. "You're learning, Domitius", he said. "Distribution of the loot is as important as winning the battle – if not more important."

He lowered his voice, as if imparting a secret. "The trick is to give the men enough, but not too much. If one overfeeds a dog, he becomes fat and lazy", he said. "On the other hand, if one starves one's hounds, they soon turn on you, and rip you apart limb from limb. The same applies to the boys under the standard."

"What about being fair to the peasants who lost their livelihoods?" Diocles asked.

"Fairness is a Greek concept that only exists in the addled minds of philosophers", Hostilius said. "Just like that absurd system called democracy they like to bandy about."

The Primus Pilus held up an open palm to stop my Greek aide's inevitable retort. "What one wants to achieve is to return enough to the peasant farmers so they are able to survive the rest of the winter. They also need enough to enable them to plough the land and purchase seed for the coming season."

"So, you do care about the peasants?" Diocles asked.

"Don't be ridiculous", Hostilius said, and waved away the Greek's words. "It's to ensure the army has food for next year's campaigning."

Eventually, when all the booty had been tallied and the Roman slaves released, I decided to return half of the loot to the peasant farmers whose future hung in the balance. One quarter was sent to the treasury in Rome, and the rest distributed among the soldiers.

* * *

Once the III Italica, auxiliaries and vexillations had set out to their places of origin, we rode west to Sirmium in the company of Marcus, Vibius and their Illyrians.

Senator Crinitus, who had not yet fully recovered from his ordeal, embraced me when I entered his quarters. He clasped arms with Hostilius, Marcus and Vibius.

"I have written to Emperor Valerian", he said. "And I thanked him for sending you and your friends to me. How I wish I could have been there when you destroyed the horde."

"You honour us with your praise", I said.

"It is I who have been honoured by your presence and by that of your comrades", Crinitus replied, and it was clear that his words came from the heart.

At that moment the doors to the senator's chambers burst open and the young Caesar, the son of Gallienus, stormed into the room. He was flanked by two praetorians.

"I have been informed that the loot gained in the victory against the Goths had been divided", he sneered. "You have distributed the gains which belongs to the Empire to peasants and slaves. And you have done this without my approval."

Valerianus pointed his finger at me. "My father warned me about you, Domitius. You don't know your place. Don't let this happen again."

Involuntarily my hand moved to the pommel of my sword.

Caesar turned, stormed from the room, and slammed the door shut.

We were all left speechless.

The young Caesar had barely departed when there was a knock at the door.

"I have tried everything in my power", General Ingenuus said and sat down heavily on the couch. "Initially, I thought it a great honour to be allowed to mould the young Caesar. Now I believe it is a curse. I do not know for how long I will be able to endure it."

Not long after, we rode from the gates of the city, heading for my farm.

"I've seen the look on Ingenuus's face", Hostilius said. "He's going to slit that little bastard's throat soon. Mark my words."

For once, I agreed with Hostilius. "And then?" I asked.

"Then we will have a choice", Marcus said. "Either do the right thing, or make sure the Empire survives."

* * *

Marcus and Vibius agreed to take advantage of our hospitality and remained as guests on the farm for ten days. On the morning of their departure to Germania, we all shared a cup of heated wine.

"Why are you not returning to Mediolanum?" Diocles asked. "Is that not where the Illyrians are based?"

Vibius nodded. "It is good to show the Germani that the black riders have not left for good", he said. "And we will take new recruits with us when we ride south, across the passes. This season we aim to bring the Illyrians up to full strength."

Hostilius whistled through his teeth. "Ten thousand?" he asked.

"Yes", Marcus said. "The horses and the armour have already been procured. All that remains is to train the recruits that have been selected."

"After all these years Rome will have a cavalry force of note to call upon", Vibius said. "It is ironic", he added, "that we have the Illyrians at our disposal when there are no wars left to fight."

Chapter 29 – Fimbulwinter (August 257 AD)

Egnatius shuffled closer, followed by an impatient imperial messenger.

"Legate", he said, inclined his head, and handed me a scroll.

I broke the seal of Valerian Augustus and read the missive.

I nodded to the man, who frowned in response. "My orders are to wait for a written reply, legate", he said.

I passed the scroll to Diocles. "Read it", I said, "and accept the invitation in the appropriate manner."

Segelinde and Cai were busy in the kitchen, preparing a dish using exotic spices that I had procured in Ctesiphon.

"We have been summoned to travel to Rome in the spring", I said.

"Who are the 'we' you are referring to?" Segelinde asked. Too late I realised my error.

"All of us, of course", I replied.

She smiled sweetly. "That is truly good news, husband", she said. "There are many things that cannot be found in the shops in Sirmium. I cannot wait to spend our portion of the spoils that you have gained from Cannabaudes's defeat."

I had not had the heart to tell Segelinde that I had foregone my share of the loot in favour of the peasant farmers.

A knock at the door saved me. "There is a barbarian at the gate, legate", Egnatius announced. "Should I scare him off?"

Hostilius and I went to investigate, knowing full well that the old man's eyes were not always trustworthy, especially after dark. We hurriedly climbed the steps that provided access to the walkway while strapping on our swords.

Outside the main gate, a mounted Roxolani warrior was waiting patiently. He was dressed in the way of the Scythian nobility, wearing loose-fitting embroidered garments.

"Open the gate", I shouted, and servants rushed to give effect to my command.

I embraced the visitor in a bear hug. "It is good to see you, Lord Elmanos", I said.

"And I you, Lord Eochar", he said, and clasped arms with the Primus Pilus. "It was not an easy journey."

"I am surprised that you were allowed to enter Roman lands, my friend", Hostilius said. "The Goths' actions have ensured that no Scythian is welcome south of the Danube."

"I tried to enter as a trader", he confirmed. "But I was turned away."

The Roxolani are a proud people. His demeanour indicated that he did not take kindly to having to skulk around like a thief in the night.

"It cost one gold aureus to get me across the river in a fishing boat", he confessed, "and another gold coin for my horse."

I knew that for a Roxolani noble to endure this humiliation, the reason for his visit must have been important. "Come", I said. "Join us for dinner, my friend. You are welcome at my hearth."

It was unusually cold for the time of year, which prompted Diocles to light both braziers in the dining room. Once we were all seated on the couches, sipping wine from our cups, Elmanos told his tale.

"Since you have returned Prince Belimar to his kin, the Roxolani and Quadi have maintained good relations. Although the Scythians and the Germani have never been the greatest of allies, Bradakos and Belimar's mutual respect for you was the cornerstone of their friendship."

"A few moons ago, we received word of Quadi raids on Roxolani camps", Elmanos said. "Bradakos and I called for a meeting with Belimar in order to put a stop to the Germani's depredations."

Elmanos shook his head in disbelief. "The Belimar we met with was not the same man as the one we had dealt with before. He had turned bitter, as if some unknown evil was consuming him. He was rude and insulting. Belimar told us that the Quadi and their kin, the Marcomanni, was bound to Rome by marriage. He informed us that if we retaliated against the Germani, it would be as good as an attack on Rome itself."

"So what did you do?" Hostilius asked.

"We ambushed the Quadi raiding parties and killed them all, of course", he said.

"I believe that I am the one to blame", I said, and shared the tale of Gallienus's marriage to Pipara, who was betrothed to Belimar before the emperor took a fancy to her.

Elmanos listened intently. "Belimar is an evil man", he concluded. "Why did the Roxolani herdsmen have to die because of the Roman emperor's lust? Neither can you be blamed, Lord Eochar."

"I knew no good would come of Gallienus's dealings", Hostilius growled.

"There is more", Elmanos said and Diocles filled his empty cup. "As a consequence of killing the Quadi raiders, Rome has suspended all trade with the Roxolani. It was ordered by General Ingenuus."

Elmanos shook his head. "Our people suffer as a result."

"And you wish for me to speak with Belimar?" I asked.

"Yes", he replied.

* * *

Late the following morning Hostilius, Gordas, Cai, Elmanos and I headed north. Diocles had left for Sirmium at first light to inform Ulpius Crinitus of what had transpired. The senator and I shared the same view of the world - I knew that he would not object to my actions.

When we arrived on the southern bank of the Danube, a military barge was waiting.

We crossed the river, with an icy easterly whipping up white spray from the surface of the grey water. The centurion in charge of the barge pulled a fur from a wooden trunk. "Never seen it this cold in August", he said, and wrapped the cloak around his shoulders.

My companions sensed my mood so we spoke little. I knew not what words I would offer to Belimar, or even if he would be inclined to meet with me.

Cai offered counsel drawn from his wealth of wisdom. "Best not to remove fly from friend's forehead with axe."

Hostilius, who was riding on my left, heard the words of the Easterner. "That", he said, "would be good advice to give Belimar."

Cai took no notice of the Primus Pilus's words. "Go talk with friend", he said. "See what happen."

As always, my friend's words were simple yet wise.

When we had cleared the forested banks of the Danube, I kicked Kasirga to a canter. The wind that rushed through my hair blew away the last vestiges of my dark mood. I caught myself grinning, relishing in the strength of my horse as he powered across the endless sea of grass.

In the distance, a small cloud of dust gave warning of approaching riders. As a precaution I pulled my bow from its case to string it, but Elmanos smiled and shook his head.

It turned out to be none other than my daughter, Aritê, who led a group of fifty warriors. She vaulted from her horse in a show of athleticism that brought a smile to Gordas's face.

Wisely, I did not try to outdo her, but swung from the saddle and caught her in an embrace. "It is good to see you, Father", she said.

"Are you happy?" I whispered, too softly for the others to hear.

"I am", she said.

While Aritê greeted Gordas, Cai and Hostilius, I studied her. She had changed much in the two years since last I laid eyes on her. The Roman girl was gone forever, replaced with a confident Scythian warrior.

I did not fail to notice that Aritê made sure to ride at my right when we entered the camp of the king. My reputation was well-known among my mother's people. Seeing her riding next to me in the place of honour would do much to increase her prestige with the tribe.

Soon we found ourselves beside the hearth of the king. There was no need for decorum, as we were all family.

"Word has reached us of a great battle", Bradakos said while slaves filled our cups with Roman wine. "They tell of a Goth army slaughtered in the lands of Rome. A great general of the Romans defeated a Goth champion in single combat before summoning dark riders straight from the land of Hades."

He slapped my back. "We miss you, Eochar", he said. "We all do."

"Then let us remedy that", I said, and emptied my cup with one long swallow.

It turned out to be a fine evening. I had been too occupied with the affairs of Rome to realise how much I missed being among my mother's people.

* * *

Hostilius took my arm in a grip of iron and shook me awake. "Don't stick a blade in me, Domitius", he said, "but if we don't get up now, we might as well not go hunting."

I remembered the promise I had made the evening before, groaned, and slipped from the furs.

"By the gods", I said, "it is as cold as in the lands of the Huns."

"It's the wine talking", he said, and waved away my complaints.

I passed him the bucket of water.

Hostilius took it with a frown, then noticed the frozen mass inside. "Maybe it's a little colder than usual", he said. "But it's not too cold to hunt."

Not long after, we rode west. Hostilius, Gordas, Elmanos and Aritê led the way, followed by Cai, Bradakos and me.

"When she returned to us, many whispered behind her back", Bradakos said. "Some called her a Roman, others called her a Goth."

Bradakos's words were troubling.

"But your daughter has your blood, Eochar", he said, and grinned. "Those tongues are silent now. Or rather, those tongues have been silenced."

"She is respected, and feared", he said. "Not only for her skills with the sword and bow, but for her mind."

I decided to broach a subject I had long been curious about. "Do you have plans for her?" I asked.

Bradakos immediately knew what I was referring to. "She has a double claim to the throne", he confirmed with a nod. "Her great-grandfather was Apsikal, and she is also my granddaughter, although it is through adoption."

"But?" I asked, sensing that there was more.

"Elmanos has proven his loyalty to me", he said. "He is my kin and has a claim through blood."

I knew where this was going. "You are wishing for Elmanos to marry my daughter?" I asked.

Bradakos smiled. "It may be so", he said. "But I know that it will be easier to tell the sun to set in the morning than to convince your daughter to do something against her will."

Just then Elmanos raised an open hand and reined in. He gestured to the tree-lined banks of a river. Bradakos took his

289

heavy spear in his hand and nudged his horse forward, falling in beside Hostilius.

"What you think of Bradakos's wishes?" Cai asked.

"I think that feeble men wish", I said. "Men like Bradakos will."

Cai grinned in response. "You are closer to Dao than it appears", he said and nudged his horse to follow in our friends' wake.

* * *

Bradakos speared a thick cut of boar with the tip of his dagger and raised his cup to Hostilius. "It was a fine kill", he said. "Your prowess as a hunter has become legendary among my people."

Hostilius beamed at the compliment and raised his cup. "I have learned from the best", he said, which drew a grin from Bradakos.

Just then a messenger entered, flanked by a guard. He approached and whispered words into the ear of the king. The man bowed low and disappeared the way he had come.

"Tomorrow we ride", Bradakos said. "Belimar of the Quadi has agreed to meet with us."

We were all tired from the hunt. Knowing that we would depart before sunrise, we retired to our furs. I struggled to fall asleep, and when I did, I was plagued by nightmares.

Hostilius kicked my leg. "You were screaming like a stuck pig, Domitius", he said.

"I make tea", Cai said.

The Primus Pilus walked over to the hearth to get a fire going. "It's still early", he said, "but we might as well get up", he added, and fixed me with a scowl.

"I have a bad feeling about today's meeting", I said. "The Germani are a strange people. Once one has fallen from their graces, they do not easily forgive."

"Huns don't forgive", Gordas confirmed. "We do not have a word for it in our tongue."

"Neither do the Germani", I said. "They seek compensation, wergild, to right a wrong."

"No need speculate", Cai said. "We know before sunset."

It was dark and bitterly cold when we rode from the camp. In addition to the king's entourage, which included my companions and me, a group of fifty oathsworn accompanied us. To my surprise, their leader was none other than Aritê. My daughter, kitted out for war, acknowledged my presence with a curt nod.

We rode across the plains as swiftly as only Scythians can, arriving at the place of parley by early afternoon. The Germani had been there for a while. They had set up camp at the edge of the treeline bordering a stream.

"Water the horses five hundred paces upstream", Bradakos commanded his oathsworn. "I wish to speak with the Germani today. Do not set up camp until we return."

Bradakos, Elmanos, Gordas, Hostilius, Aritê and I rode towards the Quadi camp. The Germani had noticed our arrival, and soon six mounted men made their way towards us.

The two groups reined in when five paces separated us.

"Welcome to the lands of the Roxolani, Lord Belimar", Bradakos said.

"It is interesting to know that you regard this land as your own", Belimar replied.

It was not the words of a man seeking peace and friendship.

"Why have you asked to meet with me?" he said, looking me in the eye.

"I had hoped that we could put the past behind us", I said. "There is no reason for you to punish the Roxolani."

"I had given your actions much thought", he said. "And there is a way for you to make amends. You will have to make good my loss – it is the way of the Quadi."

I nodded, as the payment of wergild was not unusual in the lands of the Germani.

"How much do you want?" I asked.

"I do not wish for gold", he said, and issued a snicker. "I wish to have the hand of your daughter, Aritê. I wish to wed her."

For a moment I was stunned, as I had not expected his words. The culture of the Scythians was different to that of the Germani. Aritê was her own person and would marry whom she wished.

Before I could answer, Bradakos growled. "We cannot give you something that does not belong to us."

"What is the worth of a king if he is unable to command his subjects?" Belimar sneered.

I was irritated by Belimar's words and felt the anger stir deep inside. Nonetheless, I kept it under control.

"Do you wish to marry me, Scythian whore?" he sneered at my daughter.

Needless to say, I lost the fragile hold over my anger. Twenty heartbeats later Belimar lay at my feet, my blade pressed against his jugular. Around me lay the bloodied corpses of five of his oathsworn.

"End it", I heard Gordas call from behind me. Strangely his words had the opposite effect and I regained control of my senses.

"Do not think that you can insult me just because I used to call you friend", I growled.

"I wish to ask you a question", I said. "Is there peace between the Quadi and the Roxolani?"

Belimar nodded, his eyes filled with fear. The movement caused the razor-sharp blade to draw blood.

"Good", I said. "I will report to Governor Ingenuus that the Quadi and the Roxolani are at peace."

"My work here is done", I said and vaulted onto Kasirga's back.

"And", I added, "I give you your life as wergild for the loss of your betrothed, King Belimar."

* * *

"You should have killed him", Aritê said.

"You spend too much time in the company of the Hun", I replied.

"Now Belimar fears you", Elmanos said. "He will think twice before he raids our lands."

"Let us ride for home", Bradakos commanded. "We have to celebrate the conclusion of the peace."

* * *

The following morning, the tribe's medicine woman shuffled into my tent unannounced. When I was a boy, she had been an old woman. Now, she could best be described as ancient.

She leaned on a linden walking stick, staring at me through a curtain of lank, wispy hair. "I have a message for you, god-

295

messenger", she said, and laughed at her own jest. Her cackling continued for much too long, hinting at a deep-seated malady of the mind.

Her laughter morphed into a wheezy cough. Then a shiver wracked her fragile frame and I noticed that she wore only a thin dress.

I pitied her and draped a fur around her skeletal shoulders, receiving a nod of appreciation in return. "The eastern tribes believe that a great winter will usher it in", she said, and there was no mistaking the fear she tried to disguise.

I knew she was not through and allowed her to compose her thoughts.

"Snow will blow in from all the directions of the wind", she croaked, and gestured with a bony finger. "And then, afterward, the wars of men will come. Wars innumerable", she added and I thought I noticed sadness in her eyes.

She stopped talking, as if she had forgotten why she had come in the first place.

"You spoke of a message?" I asked.

"Ask your Roman father for help", she said. "He has the ear of your king, you know."

"My father is dead", I replied.

"Not for long", she said, and smiled a toothless smile.

She turned to leave, but then Hostilius spoke from where he sat silently at the far side of the tent.

"You said that the great winter is a prelude", he said. "To what?"

She ignored the Primus Pilus's words, but paused as she pushed aside the felt flap, allowing a gust of freezing air to enter the tent.

"Beware the Fimbulwinter, Roman", she said, and it sounded as if she was reciting another's words. "It ushers in the doom of all."

Chapter 30 – Honour (October 257 AD)

Aritê agreed to accompany us on our trip back to the farm in Sirmium, but refused to even consider joining us on our journey to Rome, which would come to pass in the spring.

"I wish to spend time with my mother", she said, "but I will have no part of the decadence and debauchery of Rome."

"Don't use those words when you speak with your mother", I said. "She is looking forward to visiting the city."

"You have betrayed your roots", she said, and there was iron in her voice.

"Do not forget who your grandfather was", I said. "You know that he sacrificed all for Rome. He died defending you and your mother."

Aritê still remembered her grandfather, Nik, who loved her with all his heart.

"I spoke in haste", she said.

"A part of him lives on in you", I said. "I see him in your eyes. You are Roxolani, but never forget that you are Roman as well."

We spent another week enjoying the hospitality of the king. On a cold, wet morning, six days before the Ides of October, we said our goodbyes to Bradakos and headed south towards the lands of Rome.

We had barely left the Roxolani camp when it started to snow.

Gordas pointed to the west. "I have never seen the snow come from there."

"I'm starting to think the old crone was right", Hostilius said.

"Valerian has regained much of the lands in the East", I said. "The Germani fear our cavalry and therefore they remain north of the Rhine. The Goths will need time to regain strength."

"For the first time in years I do not see conflict looming on the horizon. I know the wars will come eventually", I added, "but I cannot see it happening soon."

None offered a reply. Even Cai remained silent.

* * *

Segelinde was overjoyed by the arrival of Aritê.

During the months she spent at the farm there was little tiffing between mother and daughter. Aritê was content in the knowledge that, come spring, she would return to her life with the Roxolani – the life she had chosen.

All agreed that the winter was the coldest in living memory – so cold that even the hardy tribes did not cross the Danube when it froze over. They preferred to huddle around their hearths drinking mead and ale and telling stories of their deeds.

And, of course, they planned.

But the star of Rome was rising again for the first time in fifty years. The defences of the Rhine and the Danubian frontier were being bolstered. Raiding the riches of the Empire was becoming increasingly difficult.

The wild men north of the rivers knew that, bar a disaster, Rome would once again become invincible. So they did the logical thing and beseeched their gods to intervene on their behalf.

* * *

In early spring of the following year I escorted Aritê to the northern bank of the Danube where, as agreed months before, Elmanos and fifty of the king's oathsworn were waiting.

"I have spoken with Governor Ingenuus and informed him that the Quadi and the Roxolani are at peace", I informed Elmanos. "I told him that I had heard it from the lips of King Belimar."

"Come spring, you will be allowed to trade your goods and cattle once again", I added.

In truth, I had not spoken to Ingenuus directly, but informed Ulpius Crinitus, who had volunteered to meet with Ingenuus. The governor knew that Crinitus had the ear of Valerian and he readily agreed to lift the trade ban against the Roxolani.

Seven days later Hostilius, Gordas, Cai, Diocles, Segelinde, Adelgunde, Maximian and I departed for Rome. Senator Ulpius Crinitus requested to join our entourage. He had regained some of his former strength, but spent most of the days in the company of Segelinde, Adelgunde and Maximian inside the four-horse coach.

On the afternoon of the eighth day on the road we entered Siscia. It was not our first visit to the city, and I led the way to the inn of Hortensius, the rumourmonger.

"Congratulations on your promotion, Legate Domitius", the innkeeper said while servants scurried about to tend to our horses and baggage. "Word of your great victory against the savages has spread to the far corners of the Empire."

"You must be Senator Crinitus", Hortensius exclaimed when the senator stepped from the coach. "It is an honour to meet you."

"Legate Domitius has told me about your special talents", Crinitus said. "Thank you, Lord Senator", he said, beaming. "It is true, my hospitality is legendary around these parts."

"Then I would love to sample it", the senator replied.

Come evening we all congregated in the dining room of the inn, reclining on the soft couches. After slaking our thirst on a fine vintage, large platters arrived from the kitchen. As an entrée, we enjoyed tunny in a pepper, lovage and date wine sauce, complemented by fish liver pudding drizzled with olive oil, and fresh-baked bread as a side. The highlight of the dinner was wild mountain sheep roasted in a raisin wine and thyme sauce, accompanied by stewed Damascus plums.

Once we had gorged ourself on the food, Hortensius arrived with a small amphora of wine to go with the dessert of cheese, figs and dates.

We exchanged news and gossip with the innkeeper who greedily gobbled up any tidbits that were thrown his way.

It was late in the evening when a servant entered after a knock at the door. Hortensius frowned and dismissed him with curt words.

"Please, lord, a messenger has arrived", he said.

Hortensius shook his head and approached the servant who still stood in the doorway. The man whispered words into the innkeeper's ear.

When Hortensius retook his seat on the couch, he had turned as white as a bleached tunic. "A terrible tragedy has befallen us", he said. "The young Caesar Valerianus is dead." He leaned in and whispered conspiratorially. "And the word is that Governor Ingenuus is responsible."

It took a handspan of heartbeats to recover from the shock.

Hostilius stood then, his face emotionless. "Ingenuus will take the purple", he said. "He is a dead man either way. We must leave without delay, before Ingenuus closes the borders and we find ourselves on the wrong side of a doomed rebellion."

* * *

Nik had taught me that there are few things that cannot be procured with sufficient gold.

In spite of our efforts to reach the safety of Emona, we were stopped at the border two days later.

"I cannot allow you to cross, legate", the officer on duty said. "Governor Ingenuus has commanded it so."

I placed a purse, bulging with gold, on the table and pushed it across to the centurion. It was the last of our coin that Segelinde had wished to spend in Rome.

The centurion scooped the bag from the table. "Tonight, at the end of the second watch", he said. "The password is 'honour'".

* * *

"Where do we go now?" Hostilius asked once we were safely in the province of Noricum.

"We go to Rome", Crinitus said. "The emperors will decide what will happen next."

The seal of Valerian gave us access to imperial accommodation in Emona. We debated the future late into the night, warmed by the heat of blazing braziers. Once Hostilius had helped Gordas to his quarters, Ulpius Crinitus and I were the only ones who remained.

"Lucius", he sighed, "I believe that the poison is killing me."

He held up an open palm to stall my response. "I wake up with terrible pains in the night", he said. "Sometimes there is blood."

"My wife and daughter died many years ago – they were taken by the plague. I have no heirs and I have not come across anyone that I deem worthy to carry my name. Until now."

He took a long swallow from his cup. "I know that you are of humble birth", he said. "It is the only thing holding you back. If you carry my name, the line of the great Traianus, there is no limit to the heights you may reach."

"I would like your oath, senator", I said.

He frowned in response.

"That you will never repeat my words to anyone", I said.

Ulpius Crinitus drew his sword and placed his hand upon the steel. "I swear it, as Mars is my witness."

I told the him the story of my life. How my father had sacrificed everything to save the Empire.

"Out of respect for my father, I cannot take the name of another, senator", I said when I had told him all.

He placed his hand on my shoulder. "And that is the reason why I wish to adopt you as my son", he said.

It was my turn to frown. "Surely", I said, "Roman law does not allow adoption without acceptance of the name?"

He grinned. "The one man who is above the law is my friend", he said. "Valerian will allow it if I ask."

Chapter 31 – Sponsor (April 258 AD)

On the morrow, we departed from Emona. The Via Gemina took us south and west, into the foothills of the mountains. By late afternoon we descended to the way station at the far side of the Pear Tree Pass.

Hostilius dismounted and looked back the way we had come. "It is the *bura*", he said, indicating the light breeze. "I've heard it starts like this, but in a third of a watch it will rip the trees from the hillside."

I doubted the Primus Pilus's words, but no sooner had we settled into the comfortable accommodations when the full might of the wind arrived.

"I have heard stories of men blown from their horses and others impaled by branches", Hostilius said as we huddled around the brazier. "I'm starting to think that the medicine woman spoke the truth. Since winter, all we've had is bad news."

"There is no official word of Ingenuus declaring himself emperor", I said. "And I haven't heard about any wars."

"It will come", Hostilius said. "This thing with Ingenuus will not blow over."

By the time we retired to the furs, the storm had not abated.

I woke up tired, as the howling wind had kept me awake for most of the night. We were forced to spend another night at the way station to allow the garrison to clear the road of fallen trees.

Two days later, after following the valley of the Vipava, we arrived at the Roman bridge spanning the Isonzo River. We spent a comfortable evening in the town on the eastern bank, departed early, and arrived at the outskirts of Aquileia the following afternoon.

We rode through lush countryside. Apple, pear and prune orchards lined the sides of the road. The budding trees were covered in blossoms of white and pink, saturating the air with a pleasant scent.

"Gods", Hostilius said, "but it feels good to be back in Italia. Can you imagine barbarians running amok through these lands?"

As always, Gordas glared at the riches with longing in his eyes. "Every tribesman north of the Great River dreams of plundering Italia", the Hun said.

He gestured to the surrounding villas and farms. "When the ox is being fattened for the feast it believes that it is blessed by the gods", he said. "Even when the blade is about to pierce its flesh, it still remains in denial."

He took a swig from his wineskin, then wiped the droplets of red liquid from his scarred chin with the back of his hand. "In the land of the Hun we expect the wolves to attack. When it does not happen, we thank the gods, but still we prepare for the inevitable. These people would do well to do the same."

After departing from Aquileia, we travelled south along the coastal road until we reached Ariminum, from where we followed the Flaminian Way to the greatest city on earth.

* * *

Valerian patiently listened to the request of Ulpius Crinitus.

For a span of heartbeats, he did not reply.

"I will sanction your request", he said. "But I wish to announce it at a more appropriate time. At the moment we are all preoccupied with the events in Pannonia."

He held up a scroll. "Ingenuus's troops have raised him to the purple", Valerian sighed. "My people have confirmed it."

"Gallienus fears for the life of his second son, Saloninus", Valerian added. "When we were informed of the death of Valerianus, Gallienus immediately departed for Colonia Agrippina on the Rhine frontier. He took Saloninus with him."

"Is that wise?" Crinitus asked. He was a close friend of Valerian, one of few men who would dare question the emperor's actions.

Valerian pursed his lips, and he must have reminded himself why he valued Crinitus, who was no sycophant.

"Soon, I will leave for the East", he said. "Saloninus will be tutored by General Postumus, whom I trust implicitly."

"Did you not trust Ingenuus implicitly?" Crinitus asked.

Again, I noticed that Valerian was not accustomed to this treatment. "Ingenuus did not murder my grandson", he said.

"But neither did Ingenuus manage to prevent someone else from opening your grandson's throat in the night", Crinitus countered.

"That is why we are taking additional precautions", Valerian said. "The praetorian prefect, Albanus, has accompanied Saloninus to the Rhine frontier. He will remain to protect my grandson while Gallienus rides east."

"Where is Gallienus riding to?" Crinitus asked.

"He is gathering forces from the Rhine frontier", he said, "to crush Ingenuus before the mutiny spreads any further."

The emperor noticed my questioning stare.

"You disagree, Domitius?" he asked.

"The Germani will spill into our lands as soon as they know of our weakness", I said. "The Franks have been dealt a blow, but Chrocus of the Alemanni has been biding his time. His scheming mother, Braduhenna, will not have forgotten the insult."

"The Germani fear our black riders. The savages will believe that a contingent of Illyrians are still in the area, although Gallienus is taking the entire corps", Valerian said. "The seasoned men stationed in Germania as well as the recruits still in Mediolanum – all ten thousand of them."

"Gallienus is blinded by his grief for his son", Crinitus said. "Allow Marcus Claudius to remain near Mogantiacum with three thousand Illyrians."

Valerian shook his head. "The die is cast, my friend", he said. "The Illyrians have long departed for Pannonia."

"I will ride north tomorrow", I volunteered. "To assist with the fight against the usurper."

The emperor shook his head. "You will do no such thing", he said. "Marcus Claudius is a competent legate. I have full confidence that he will advise Gallienus well."

"I called you to Rome to honour your loyalty to the Empire, Legate Domitius. You have defeated the Goths, enriched the farmers and bolstered the treasury of Rome without lining your own pockets with gold."

"I wish for you to serve a term as consul in the near future", he said. "But the senate will never approve if you have not sponsored the required events. I have arranged for races to be held at the Circus Maximus, to be followed by a banquet to which senators and equestrians will be invited. I have arranged for prizes, lavish gifts, and two white bulls for the sacrifices."

"You and your retinue will remain as guests in the imperial palace, where all your needs will be catered for. I have issued instructions to the city prefect to provide you and your family with a purse heavy with gold."

I did not expect the honours that Valerian had bestowed upon me, and was at a loss for words.

"There is no need for gratitude", he said. "The Empire can never repay you for what you have done."

* * *

"Not even Hades himself will keep me from attending", Hostilius said. "By the gods, Domitius, I never dreamed that you would sponsor a race day."

"Neither did I", I said.

There was a knock at the door and Hostilius, who was the closest, answered.

"There is a man who wishes to speak with Legate Domitius", the praetorian said.

"What is his name?" Hostilius asked.

The praetorian appeared decidedly uncomfortable, a clear sign that he had been bribed to deliver the message. "I believe he is called 'Father'", the guard said.

Pumilio had aged since I had last seen him. His silver hair and fine clothing marked him as a man of status.

"You look like a bloody senator", Hostilius said and embraced our friend.

"That's because I am one", Pumilio said, and grinned. "Adopted into the illustrious line of the Corvinii", he added.

He waved away our questions. "In Rome, it's all about coin", he said and held aloft a scroll.

"I've been invited to a day at the races sponsored by you, Umbra", he said.

"The treasury is paying", I said. "I do not have enough coin to sponsor it."

"When we had nothing, you shared your gold with us", Pumilio said. "You gave Felix a new life and your gold paid for a stone for Bellus. Were it not for you, Umbra, I would never have reunited with my mother. It is my turn to give. Allow me the honour to contribute – I will ensure that it is the finest races Rome has ever seen. I will arrange for teams from the farthest ends of the Empire. My gold will pay for singing rope-dancers, gazelles, hounds, mimes and acrobats. Men will talk about it for years to come."

"You might even make a few coins from gambling on the day", Hostilius said.

Pumilio issued a shrewd smile in reply.

Chapter 32 – Senate (July 258 AD)

Another spasm shot through my prone body. Involuntarily my knees pulled up to my chest. I felt the bile rise, but the plague had robbed me of the strength to move.

With surprising adroitness, my friend from Serica turned me onto my side and held my head over a bucket. When the last of the fluids had dripped from my mouth, he dabbed away the blood with a moist linen cloth.

"Drink, Lucius of the Da Qin", Cai said, and I swallowed the vile mixture from the cup he pressed to my lips.

There was a faraway knock at the door, followed by the sound of Cai's footsteps.

"Is there any change?" I heard Hostilius say.

"Lucius very strong", Cai replied.

"May I sit with him?" Hostilius asked.

"No", Cai answered. "You sick tomorrow if you do."

I imagined the Primus Pilus scowled, which prompted an explanation from the Easterner.

"When boy, bleeding sickness swept through village", Cai said in his broken Latin. "I close to death, but gods decide that it not my time. Plague not make sick twice."

"Will he live?" Segelinde asked and I heard her sob.

"Not Cai who decide", he said. "Best sacrifice to gods."

I heard the door close and my friend sigh softly as he retook his seat beside my bed.

* * *

The poppy juice took effect and I felt my shade distance itself from my pain-ridden body.

An eery silence descended upon the room.

The door creaked open and a hulking form ducked into the chamber. I heard the familiar hissing sound of iron scale as the warrior's massive chest expanded and contracted with breath.

"Why should I allow you to live, Scythian?" he growled in the guttural tongue of the Sea of Grass, and I noticed his hand go to the hilt of his sword.

317

"So I may honour you on the field of battle, lord", I replied.

Arash slowly nodded, a smile breaking his scarred visage. "Then let it be so", he said. "Repay me in blood."

"But there are no enemies to fight, lord", I said.

"Then I will remedy that", the god replied.

* * *

Cai propped another cushion behind my back.

"Did you see him?" I asked.

"Not see with eyes, but felt", the Easterner answered and placed a hand upon his chest. "When I feel god leave room, bleeding stop suddenly."

"Everything has a price", I said.

"What god want?" Cai asked.

"Blood", I replied.

"Best pay then", he said.

* * *

Three days later I was able to hold down food for the first time in ten days.

Cai had proclaimed it safe, so Hostilius, Gordas, Diocles and Segelinde sat beside my bed.

"Any news from Pannonia and the war against Ingenuus?" I asked.

"Very little", Hostilius said. "Gallienus and his army have crossed the border into Pannonia, but he is yet to get to grips with the usurper. Ingenuus is no fool. He knows the area around Sirmium like the back of his hand – it could be months before there is a pitched battle."

"Anything else?" I asked.

"I've heard that the Franks are up to their old tricks", Hostilius said. "Apparently they've crossed the border near Colonia Agrippina. Postumus should be able to deal with the incursion. I just hope that Gallienus has left him with enough soldiers."

"News of Roman weakness spreads", Gordas said.

"I fear that you are right, friend", I said.

319

"You all leave now", Cai said and waved them from my chamber. "He need rest."

Cai made sure I consumed two bowls of thin chicken broth, then closed the shutters. "Rest", he said, and shut the door behind him.

I woke with a start when Hostilius opened the shutters and light flooded into the room.

"By the gods, Domitius", he said. "You've been sleeping for more than a day. Enough is enough!"

Gordas walked through the door a heartbeat later. "Have you told him?" he asked the Primus Pilus.

Hostilius shook his head.

"The Alemanni are pouring across the Rhine fortifications", he said.

"How many?" I asked.

Hostilius's expression turned bleak. "Some reports mention fifty thousand", he said, "others swear that their numbers are more than a hundred thousand."

"Tell him the bad news", Gordas said.

Hostilius pursed his lips and struggled to meet my gaze. "And in the wake of the Alemanni, another tribe has crossed the border."

I realised that I was holding my breath.

"The Juthungi follow the Alemanni", he said. "No one knows their numbers, but all talk about a horde innumerable. Like a plague of locust, they cover the land to the horizon, as far as the eye can see."

I tried to rise, but there was no strength in my legs and I collapsed back onto the bed.

"The great winter will usher in the doom of all", Hostilius whispered, his hand reaching for his amulet.

"No", I said. "It is the doing of Arash. The god of war and fire is seeking recompense."

* * *

I had fallen ill three days after the successful conclusion of the circus day. Valerian had wished for me to accompany him to the East, but my malady made it impossible. In my stead,

321

Ulpius Crinitus volunteered to join Valerian's entourage as his military adviser.

A week after the turning point, I was still confined to my bed, but improving by the day.

"Any word of Valerian?" I asked.

Diocles held a scroll aloft. "Do you wish to read it yourself, legate?" he asked.

"No", I said, "give me the gist of it."

The Greek broke Valerian's seal and spoke while he ran his finger along the writing. "Valerian Augustus has arrived in Antioch", he said. "He is overjoyed at the news of your recovery and congratulates you again on the success of the races that you have sponsored. The Sasanians are readying their armies to campaign against Rome."

"Is that all?" I asked.

Diocles looked me in the eye and placed the scroll on his desk. "The emperor has heard about the invasion of the Alemanni and the Juthungi. He believes that the gods have intervened to place you in Rome at this time, legate. You are charged with the defence of the city."

"It may not come to that", I said. "The barbarians are still ravaging the lands north of the passes."

"Rome is the biggest prize of all", Diocles said. "For half a thousand years the sheep has been fattened", he said, reminding me of the words of the Hun. "No, legate", he added, shaking his head. "The Germani will not turn back of their own accord – someone will have to do it for them."

I offered no reply because I knew that my aide was right.

* * *

The following morning I managed to get out of bed by myself.

On unsteady feet, I went to speak with Hostilius, whom I found in the company of Diocles.

"We need to start preparing", I said. "The praetorians and the II Parthica will have to march north, to the passes. The only way we will be able to stop the invaders is by blocking their passage through the Alps."

"We require the approval of the senate to remove the praetorian guard from the city", Diocles said, displaying his knowledge of the workings of the Empire.

I did not doubt the accuracy of his statement. "Then let us submit a written request to the Fathers of the City", I said. "Surely they will see reason."

Due to the urgency of the matter, the senate debated my request and responded in writing later the same day.

"Legate Lucius Domitius Aurelianus

The Conscript Fathers have debated the threat to the safety of the commonwealth. It is our divine duty to ensure the survival of the Sacred City. Therefore we cannot allow the legions to desert us in our time of greatest despair.

If our exalted prince, Valerian, has appointed you as the saviour of Rome, who are we to gainsay him? We place our trust in you, Lucius Domitius Aurelianus, general of Rome, who is famed for his valour and bravery on the field of battle.

For our part, we will make enough gold available from the treasury to enable you to be successful. We will ascend to the temple and beseech the immortal gods to aid you in the defence of the Sacred City of Rome."

Diocles rolled up the scroll and placed it on his desk.

"I'm not surprised", Hostilius said. "Most of those fools don't even know what a barbarian looks like. All they are worried about are their trading businesses, their expensive villas and their estates close to the city. They care naught for the peasant farmers."

"Just take the legions", Gordas suggested. "Surely the Roman warriors will follow you."

I shook my head. "We have laboured for years for the survival of Rome", I said. "I will not behave like a usurper."

"There has to be another way", Diocles said.

"How can twelve thousand men halt a hundred thousand warriors on open ground?" Hostilius asked.

"Best general win battle without fight", Cai said, no doubt quoting the wisdom of the ancients. "Remember, all war based on deception. When weak, make enemy think you strong."

And then the god planted and idea inside my mind.

"How many people call this city their home?" I asked.

"More than a million", Diocles answered.

"How many men between the ages of sixteen and sixty?" I said.

"I estimate three hundred thousand", Diocles said. "Including slaves, servants and freedmen."

"You cannot expect an untrained slave, baker or miller to face a Juthungi warrior, Domitius", Hostilius said. "You of all people should know that."

"That is why you are going to train them", I revealed.

"It can't be done", he said, his expression resolute.

"What can't be done?" I asked.

"There is not enough time to teach them how to wield a spear or sword", Hostilius said, accentuating his words with a scowl.

"I agree with you wholeheartedly", I said. "That is why I have other things in mind."

Chapter 33 – Alemanni (September 258 AD)

"Where were you this morning?" Hostilius asked.

"Diocles and I paid a visit to the head of the tailors' guild", I said.

"And the Illyrian armour?" Hostilius asked.

"The blacksmiths will have it ready for fitment in three weeks", I said. "One complete set."

"How many horses do we have?" I asked Diocles, who during the past weeks had proven himself an administrator par excellence.

"Twelve thousand horses with riders", he said. "Most are peasant farmers and their plough horses. More are arriving every day."

"Excellent", I said.

"And the wood?" I asked.

"The prefect of the grain supply has authorised a third of the fleet to be diverted to Gaul, in order to import additional timber. We should have nearly thirty thousand available when the time comes."

"Lead?" I asked.

"It is proving difficult", Diocles replied. "But since the rumours of the barbarians' crossing of the Alps have started to trickle into the city, people have been lining up to sell us their cookware. Even the winemakers have given up their lead pots. We are buying everything we can lay our hands on."

"The praetorians and the II Parthica are training north of the city", Hostilius said. "I've combined the urban cohort and the *vigiles* – together they number about five thousand. With Pumilio's help, I've been able to scrape together another legion's worth of retired drunks and amputees. They'll get into the swing of things soon enough."

"And the others?" I asked.

"Our initial seventy thousand have been whittled down to fifty thousand", Hostilius said, his vine cane tucked under his right arm. "But the ones who remain are getting there, although it is a painstakingly slow process."

"Pumilio has arranged for all charioteers who reside in the city to aid Gordas with the training of the riders", I said. "It's progressing as planned, although most of the horses are old and not capable of moving faster than a trot."

* * *

While the bravest warriors in the lands of Rome killed one
another in Pannonia, the Alemanni and Juthungi laid waste to
the provinces of Germania Superior, Noricum and Raetia.
Towns and farms that had taken centuries to establish were
destroyed without a thought – all razed to the ground.

When there was no more loot to be had north of the Alps, the
savages streamed through the passes along the Roman roads.
Soon, tens of thousands of Germani spilled into the ancient
lands of Italia.

The barbarians had timed it well – it was the time of the
harvest. Most of the inhabitants fled before the approaching
horde. Farmers abandoned fields golden with barley, emmer,
millet and spelt. Vineyards and orchards, heavy with ripe
grapes, olives and fruit were left untended. They loaded
whatever they could onto wagons and buried their tools and
implements where the Germani were unlikely to search.
Livestock were culled in haste, the meat cured and packed for
the journey. Prize bulls and rams were tied to wagons. The
remaining animals were taken to the mountains in the hope
that they would remain hidden from the savages.

"The horde has arrived in strength in the fertile Valley of the Po", Diocles announced one morning. "It will take them weeks, maybe months, to gather the loot."

"They will move with speed", I contradicted the Greek. "The war leaders of the tribes are no fools. They know that the passes will soon be blocked by snow. They have two, maybe three months to fill their wagons with plunder and their purses with gold. Half of the horde will remain in the Po Valley and strip the land bare. The others, their best warriors, will come south to plunder Rome."

"The Germani will not spend the winter in Italia", Gordas confirmed. "They will wish to return to their longhouses to drink mead and Roman wine beside their hearths. They will long to winter amongst their own people, to share the tales of how they had ravaged the lands of the once mighty Empire, while blood-stained coins carrying the image of the emperor dangle from leather thongs around their necks."

"Which means we have little time before they arrive", Hostilius said.

* * *

Five days after the Ides of August we received word.

"The horde is moving south along the Flaminian Way",
Hostilius said. "Fifty thousand footmen and twenty thousand
riders. We have fourteen days, maybe less."

"Are we ready?" I asked.

"As ready as we will ever be", he replied.

"Any news of Gallienus?" I asked.

"It seems that Ingenuus's forces are trapped in and around
Sirmium", Diocles said. "A battle is imminent, but they will
never be in time to aid us, even if they were to sprout wings."

* * *

Segelinde helped me fit the armour Diocles had polished to a
brilliant shine the evening before. When she was done, she
took a step back to admire her handiwork.

"You look like a general of Rome", she said in near perfect
Latin.

There was a knock at the door. Servants from the imperial
kitchen entered, carrying trays of fried smoked pork, boiled

eggs, cheese and freshly baked bread. Hostilius, Gordas, Cai and Diocles appeared moments later.

"One can smell this from a mile away", Hostilius said, and took a rasher of pork from a dish.

I poured each of us a cup of wine and watered it down by half.

"This may be our last meal", I said, and raised my cup to my friends.

Gordas bit down on a soft-boiled egg and the yolk exploded in his mouth with a pop. "The gods determine the days of our lives long before we are born", he said, grinning with egg-stained teeth. "Today is as good a day to die as any."

"Did you deliver the message to Master Herminius?" I asked Diocles.

"Yes, legate", he said. "He set sail as soon as I handed him the scroll."

"Is all arranged?" I asked Hostilius.

"The men are assembling beyond the city limits, on the flat ground that borders the Flaminian Way. We will form up north of the Milvian Bridge that spans the Tiber", the Primus Pilus confirmed.

We said our goodbyes and made our way down the Palatine Hill, from where we turned north onto the Via Flaminia.

When at last the sun appeared from behind the eastern horizon, seventy thousand men were neatly arrayed, ready to give battle. Or so it appeared.

Less than a watch after sunrise the lands to the north darkened, announcing the arrival of the horde of the Juthungi and Alemanni.

"Here they come", Hostilius said. "It is now or never."

The Primus Pilus, Diocles and I nudged our horses and slowly rode towards the enemy. We reined in five hundred paces from the Roman line. Just when I thought that the barbarians would ignore our attempt at parley, a ram's horn issued a note, and the great barbarian army halted. From among the ranks of the Germani, three mounted men appeared and slowly made their way towards us.

"Do they know when?" I whispered to Hostilius.

"They know", he said. "We have trained to do this a hundred times."

When the barbarian war leaders were fifty paces from us, the buccina issued a command. The Roman soldiers, who were arrayed in three large blocks, many ranks deep, widened their front to match that of the barbarians'.

The commands of centurions echoed across the plain. Twelve silver eagles bobbed up and down as the great Roman army reorganized itself. With practised efficiency the soldiers executed the commands, hinting that the men facing the barbarians were veterans all.

I noticed the effect the faultless manoeuvre had on the approaching barbarians. The confident grins fled from their bearded faces while their eyes scanned the battlefield, no doubt counting the legionary standards highlighted by the polished silver *phalerae* affixed to the thick shafts.

Just like the silver eagles, the *phalerae* and the eagle standards were fake. Hostilius and his underlings had painstakingly trained for months. But they had not practised with the sword or spear, they had only trained to carry out the one manoeuvre they had just executed flawlessly. Behind the thin line of shield-bearing legionaries, drawn from the praetorians and II Parthica, stood oldsters, young boys and men who had never wielded a blade.

"I am Gundon of the Juthungi", the big, bearded leader riding in the centre growled in the tongue of the Germani.

His long blonde hair was fashioned in a topknot, in the style of the northern tribes. His clothes were of good quality, his armour workmanlike. There was no doubt in my mind that he was a formidable man – a man who led a horde numbering more than a hundred thousand.

"I am Domitius of the Romans", I replied in my best Germani. "And you are not welcome in our lands, Gundon of the Juthungi. Let us draw our blades and settle this the old way", I said.

The bearded man snarled, "You are the one who wears the clothes of the Romans", he said, "but you have the eyes of a Scythian. You are the one who walks with the god of war, the one who commands the black riders."

He swept his hand across the plain, indicating the legions arrayed in battle formation. "I am not fool enough to fight you, Roman", he said. "The Franks say that you have made a pact with the Dark One – none can best you with a blade."

"But I see that your dark riders are absent", Gundon continued with a smirk. "I have heard that Roman princes are slaughtering each other in the eastern lands bordered by the Mother River. My people tell me that the dark riders have gone east to join your emperor."

A low, unearthly wail echoed across the plain north of the Tiber. The western skyline darkened with a long line of horsemen, the whetted blades of their lances glinting in the sun - their armour black as pitch and their faces hidden behind dark helmets.

It was a trick, of course. Gold from the treasury had paid for thousands of farmers and their plough horses to be clad in black robes and skullcaps. From afar it was indistinguishable from the armour worn by the Illyrians. Their lances were pieces of rough-hewn timber, the ends clad in thin sheets of beaten lead.

Gundon turned his head. Not even his thick beard could hide the twitch that settled in the sinews of his jaw. "It is not possible", he whispered, as if speaking to himself. "You have summoned an army not of this world."

"They are men of flesh and blood", I said and turned to Hostilius. "Summon one of my men so we can show the Germani that his childish superstitions are unfounded."

Hostilius blew a note on the buccina and a single rider detached from the line of horsemen who had halted more than five hundred paces from us.

Gordas, clad in full Illyrian armour, thundered towards us. He rode like a man possessed, like only a Hun can, coming to a halt ten paces from us. Tied to his saddle was a strung horn bow and three full quivers. He vaulted from his horse and went down on one knee. "Great lord", he said in the guttural tongue of the Huns. "How may I serve you?"

"Remove your helmet so our enemies can see that you are a man of flesh and blood", I said.

Gordas gripped his blackened iron helmet with both hands and pried it from his elongated skull, revealing his features to the Germani warlord and his two underlings.

Gundon and his oathsworn issued a collective gasp – a normal reaction for men laying eyes on a Hun for the first time.

"It is no man", Gundon mumbled as Gordas galloped away, howling like a wolf.

"Why do you think no army has sacked Rome in half a thousand years?" I asked. "Rome is favoured by the gods. You have won loot, honour, and reputation, Gundon of the Juthungi. Now you will lose it all because of your greed."

I turned my horse. "Give the order to attack", I said to Hostilius. "Let us show the Germani what thirty thousand black riders are capable of."

"Wait", Gundon said, and in response I turned my horse to face him.

* * *

A third of a watch later the last of the Germani warriors disappeared in the distance.

"It is a great victory, even if we did not swing a blade", Hostilius said. "But it feels hollow. We have saved the Sacred City but the Germani have visited destruction upon our lands. They need to be taught a lesson."

"Even if I wished it, I cannot allow them to leave Italia", I said.

Hostilius's brow morphed into a frown.

"The god of war healed me from the plague", I said. "I need to repay him."

"With gold?" he asked.

"No, Primus Pilus", I said. "With blood."

Chapter 34 – Blood

The senate, relieved that the city had been spared, declared a great victory in the aftermath of the confrontation with the tribes. Public sacrifices were performed daily, and celebrations held throughout the city. Meat, bread and wine were distributed to the populace, all paid for by the treasury.

Our role in the conflict was soon forgotten, and the senate claimed the victory for themselves.

Fourteen days after the tribes had been turned back from the gates of the city, my aide arrived with a missive carrying the seal of Gallienus.

Diocles unrolled the scroll. "The usurper is no more", he said, sharing only the gist.

His words saddened me, as Ingenuus was a competent general – his skills would be sorely missed in the days to come.

"A large, pitched battle was fought near Sirmium", Diocles said. "The Illyrians carried the day, but General Marcus Claudius was wounded."

The Greek noticed the anguish on our faces and continued immediately. "His wound is light", he said. "Like Achilles of old, Legate Claudius was wounded in the heel."

Hostilius, Cai, Gordas and I issued a collective sigh of relief.

"Emperor Gallienus has received your message and he is marching back to Italia at speed", Diocles said. "He wishes for you to meet him at Aquileia."

Small bands of barbarian stragglers were still raiding the area north of the Eternal City. It would have been foolish for a handful of men to venture into the countryside. Fortunately, there was another option.

Master Herminius realised the urgency of our mission. Aided by his fast liburnian, and the skills he had accrued during his many years at sea, we completed a two-week journey in fewer than ten days.

On a rainy, dark afternoon we moored at the massive river port of Aquileia. The ship's master bade us farewell while he watched Scaevola secure the prow to a mooring ring.

The city's fortifications had been well-maintained because of its involvement in the conflict between Emperor Thrax and the senate years before. This served the city well, as the barbarians had not even attempted to attack its mighty walls.

Before we entered through the massive port gates, I noticed activity on the western bank of the Natiso, north of the city, where ten thousand horsemen were executing manoeuvres.

Hostilius gestured with his chin towards the black riders. "Looks like the emperor beat us to it", he said.

* * *

Gallienus gripped a thick scroll in his hand – in a way one would wield a weapon. For a moment I thought that he was about to attack me with it.

"Do you know what you have done, Legate Domitius!" he shouted.

I had not the faintest idea what he was referring to. "No, Lord Emperor", I said.

From the corner of the chamber, I heard Aureolus issue a snicker.

"For years, my father and I have been labouring to restrict the power of the senate", he said. "Work that you have undone in weeks."

"Lord?" I asked.

He dismissed my confusion with a flick of his hand. "I forget that you are but a half-barbarian soldier", he said. "Maybe I am partly to blame for expecting too much of you."

"Tell him, general", the emperor said.

Aureolus pouted his lips, and I had to suppress the urge to draw my blade. "General Domitius", he said. "Although you managed to keep the proverbial barbarians from the gate, you allowed the senate to bask in the glory of a great victory."

"What else could I have done?" I asked. "Should I have fled the city and left it at the mercy of the Juthungi?"

Gallienus and Aureolus exchanged a knowing glance, hinting that they preferred the latter.

"Do not interrogate me, Domitius", he said and waved away my words. "What is done, is done. Now, all that we can do is to salvage what little glory is left."

"Your friend, Marcus Claudius has remained in Sirmium", Gallienus said. "It will allow him the time to recover from a minor wound. In the meantime, I am in need of a cavalry commander who can temporarily stand in for him. You fit that bill."

I glanced at Aureolus.

"General Aureolus is a strategist", Gallienus said, noticing the question in my stare. "He is far too valuable to be placed in harm's way. I need someone to be the tip of the spear."

Before I could offer a reply, he added, "Serve me well, and I will overlook the mistake you made. General Aureolus will furnish you with your written orders tomorrow. You will have to excuse us - we have to attend a performance at the amphitheatre tonight."

* * *

"So, he is prepared to forgive us", Hostilius growled, his face as red as a beet.

"Yes", I said.

"We can be with the Roxolani in fewer than ten days", Segelinde suggested.

The Hun said naught, but continued to slide the blade of his dagger across the surface of a whetstone.

"Stay your hand, Gordas", I said.

343

He shrugged and grinned like a predator, revealing his unspoken intentions.

"Gallienus means well", I said. "He has defeated the usurper and now he is willing to punish the Germani."

"He seeks glory", Diocles said.

"He requires glory to keep a high standing with the army", I countered.

Cai mostly refrained from offering his opinion, but when he did, we listened.

"Do not forget that peasant farmers are ones who suffer most", the Easterner said. "Rome needs to defeat tribes, or predations will carry on for months. It not about Gallienus or glory. It about ending suffering of farmers. Nik fought all his life to help common people, he never concerned about who win glory."

I was shamed by my friend's words. "Cai is right", I said.

None gainsaid me.

* * *

"The horde is heading towards Mediolanum", I said. "They will not cross the mountains along the Via Claudia Augusta, but rather the western passes."

"Impossible", Aureolus sneered. "I do not believe those dirt tracks can even accommodate a cart, never mind a wagon."

"The Germani are used to travelling on paths that are less than ideal", I said.

"You have fallen for their ruse, Domitius", Gallienus said. "The savages wish to lure us away from the safety of Verona."

"Have you inspected the defences of the city recently?" I asked.

Both Aureolus and Gallienus appeared concerned.

"Why do you ask?" the emperor said.

"Because the wall is crumbling in many places, lord", I replied. "If the barbarians were to launch an assault, it will not hold them for long."

"Maybe you are correct in your assessment after all, Legate Domitius", Gallienus conceded. "I suggest that the legions advance to Verona at double pace. That will ensure that we are able to destroy the barbarians before they make their escape through the western passes."

"Augustus is wise indeed", Aureolus said, and inclined his head to Gallienus.

Four days later, three Roman legions arrived outside the walls of the city. Although we were in Italia, I insisted that they construct a marching camp beside the one used by the ten thousand Illyrians.

In Marcus's absence, I was in nominal command of the Illyrians, although I still had to defer to Aureolus. On the same day that the legions arrived, Hostilius and Gordas returned from scouting out the movement of the Germani.

"The Juthungi have started their ascent into the foothills of the Alps", Gordas said. "Their wagons are heaped with loot. Many slaves accompany them. The route is treacherous - it will take long for the last of the tribe to enter the passes."

"How long?" I asked.

The Hun thought on my words for a span of heartbeats. "Maybe five days", he said. "Seven if it rains."

"And the Alemanni?" I asked.

"They are camped on the banks of the Adda, north and east of Mediolanum", Hostilius said. "United, the tribes are too numerous to defeat."

"We will wait until the last of the Juthungi have committed to the passes", I said. "Then we will fall on Chrocus and his Alemanni."

* * *

Roman armies seldom attacked during the hours of darkness. There were good reasons for it. The most important being that Roman legions on the offensive often found themselves deep within barbarian territory where every peasant hiding in a hole would alert their fellows to the imminent threat. It was not the case within Italia.

We slowly made our way west along the well-maintained Roman road between Bergomum and Mediolanum. The last of the Juthungi, who had camped on the western bank of the Adda, had ventured into the mountains the day before. Our scouts reported that the Alemanni had spent the previous day packing their loot and making arrangements to follow their brethren.

Gordas, Hostilius and I had used the Illyrians as a screen during the last days. Enemy scouts who ventured farther east than Bergomum had been killed, captured or driven off in an attempt to hide our intentions.

The Alemanni knew that the legions were still at least fourteen miles away. They found comfort in their superior numbers and knew that the Romans would be unlikely to attack a force that outnumbered them two to one.

At the end of the second watch of the night, the three legions were in position – one mile from the enemy camp. It took another watch to line up for battle, deploying in such a way that the ranks faced west. For the following two thirds of a watch, the legions moved closer as silently as they could, knowing that to achieve total surprise was the only way to counter the superior numbers of the Germani. When it was light enough to distinguish shapes, the Romans were five hundred paces from the edge of the Alemanni camp.

To travel silently with ten thousand horses is not possible. Therefore, the Illyrians followed a mile behind the legions. As soon as the light allowed it, the ranks of legionaries parted.

"Lord", the runner said, gasping for breath. "We are ready."

I nodded to the signifier, who raised the dragon standard. Immediately, ten thousand Illyrians kicked their horses to a gallop. It took only moments for the ram's horn to sound the alarm, but it was too late. A galloping horse covers twelve paces every heartbeat. Within a hundred heartbeats the Illyrians had seamlessly passed through the gaps between the centuries and the first volley of ten thousand lead-weighted darts rained down on the confused enemy camp.

I took four arrows from my quiver. A dark-haired man stumbled from a tent twenty paces in front of me. He wore only a tunic, a Roman gladius in his hand. Before he had gained three steps he pitched forward, a shaft skewering his neck. Another ran at us with his spear drawn back. An armour-piercing arrow slammed into his skull before he disappeared under the hooves.

When the shrill note of a buccina ordered the retreat, the dark riders loosed a final volley. They thundered north, parallel to the line of eighteen thousand charging legionaries. The heavily armoured Roman infantry poured into the barbarian camp. The legionaries were mostly of peasant farmer stock. They knew of the atrocities that the Germani had inflicted upon their kin. Gallienus had ordered no slaves to be taken, but even if he had, I doubt whether his commands would have doused the red-hot vengeance burning in the veins of the Romans.

By the time the sun crested the horizon, the Alemanni army was no more.

Gordas, Hostilius and I rode through the enemy camp, our horses picking their way through a sea of corpses.

"I believe that you have settled your debt, Domitius", Hostilius said, staring at the sea of dead. "I don't know if it is possible, but you might even have overpaid."

Chapter 35 – Baths (February 259 AD)

"I believe that you should have coins minted to celebrate your great victory, lord", Aureolus said.

Gallienus was clearly pleased by the words of his greatest supporter.

"Mayhap a winged horse, accompanied by the words 'Germanicus Maximus'", the emperor said.

"A splendid idea", Aureolus replied.

Gallienus turned to face me. "I nearly forgot why I summoned you, Domitius", he said. "You know that my father wanted you to join him in the East months ago", he added, and took a deep swallow from a jewelled chalice. "But your untimely malady made that impossible. Now that you have recovered, he wishes for you to do as he had intended."

"I will depart tomorrow, lord", I said.

"Good", he replied and dismissed me with a flick of his wrist.

I turned to leave, but paused to ask a final question. "What about the Juthungi north of the Alps, lord?"

"It is no concern of yours, Domitius." He sighed and added, "But if you must know, I have elevated Postumus to governor.

In the spring I will take the Illyrians across the mountains. Between us, we will crush what remains of the invaders. My son, Saloninus, will aid him."

As I walked from the chamber, Gallienus and Aureolus shared a whispered jest. Both burst out laughing. I found it hard to imagine that the humour was not at my expense.

* * *

The master of admissions looked up from his seat inside the foyer of the private baths of the imperial palace of Byzantium.

"Ah, Legate Domitius", he said, and inclined his head. "Valerian Augustus is expecting you."

I walked through the door to find Valerian and his retinue seated on couches beside the steaming baths.

"Legate Domitius", the master announced before closing the door behind him. An uncomfortable silence descended on the gathering.

The emperor rose from his seat and all followed. "Lucius Domitius Aurelianus, I have called you here to thank you on behalf of the commonwealth. You have saved Italia from the

352

power of the Germani and delivered us from the depredations of the Goths."

He gestured to a grand ivory chair on which were heaped sets of fine clothes and armour. "In return for your great achievements I present you with four complete general's outfits, two proconsul's cloaks, two togas – one embroidered with gold, the other with palms, and, of course, an ivory chair. This is but a gesture of our gratitude."

I approached Valerian and went down on one knee. "I have suffered wounds with patience and exhausted my sworn comrades and our horses", I said. "I have shed my blood for Rome, not only to gain the approval of the commonwealth, but also of my own conscience."

Valerian knew that my words came from the heart. He raised me to my feet and placed his hand on my shoulder. "It is good to see you Lucius", he said. "I will speak with you later, but there is one more announcement to make."

The emperor raised his golden goblet and his entourage reciprocated.

All assembled retook their seats. A man seated at the back stood then, and I noticed that it was Senator Ulpius Crinitus.

"Lord Valerian", he said. "It has long been the custom of Rome for men of high birth to choose the most courageous men as their sons. It allows men like me, who has no offspring, to gain honour from borrowed stock."

When the laughter had died down, the senator continued. "I wish to ask your approval to adopt the man you have given to me as a deputy. Valerian Augustus, do you give the order that Lucius Domitius Aurelianus may gain the sacred duties and the legal rights of Ulpius Crinitus?"

Valerian stood and embraced me and Ulpius Crinitus in turn.

He handed me a thrice-bound leather diploma which bore the imperial seal. "I have granted your request", he said in a low voice. "You will keep the name arranged for by your father, the name which was paid for in his blood."

* * *

Following months of war and turmoil, the time we spent in Byzantium was godsent. I walked the city in the company of my wife, trained with Cai and Hostilius, and explored the countryside riding alongside my Hun friend.

Three days after the Ides of February, I was summoned to attend a private dinner with the emperor and Senator Crinitus to discuss the upcoming campaign against the Sasanians.

"I wish to seek the senate's approval for you to be appointed as consul for next year", Valerian said.

"I accept, lord", I said. "As long as I will still be able to fight the enemies of Rome."

"That is exactly what you will do", Valerian replied. "Shapur is up to his old tricks. He has crossed the border and managed to take the fortress of Dura Europos. I believe his armies will move north come spring. There will be no shortage of enemies to kill."

We were sampling a course of seafood when an urgent missive arrived.

Valerian unrolled the scroll. Within the span of ten heartbeats his complexion took on the colour of his bleached tunic.

"Regalianus, the man who replaced Ingenuus as governor of Pannonia and Moesia, is staging a revolt", he said. "And what is more", he added, "he attacked the Roxolani when they collected their annual tribute and claimed it for himself."

"My forces are fully committed in the East", Valerian said. "Gallienus and Postumus will have their hands full dealing with the Juthungi and the Franks along the Rhine. There is no simple answer for this. Rome has no troops to send against Regalianus", he sighed.

"Not even the gods can help us now", he added, and buried his face in his hands.

"You mentioned that Regalianus has made enemies of the Roxolani", I said.

Valerian nodded.

"Then maybe I will be able to help if the gods are occupied", I said, and swallowed down an oyster with a mouthful of white.

* * *

A mounted patrol intercepted us soon after entering the lands of the Roxolani.

The first sign of trouble was when I attempted to speak with their leader – a warrior whom I knew only by sight. The man held up an open palm and shook his head. I immediately realised that he was acting on the command of the king.

356

"This isn't a good sign", Hostilius said.

Cai nodded his agreement.

By the time we arrived at the Scythian camp, my mind had conjured up a score of possibilities – one worse than the other. Relief flooded over me when I saw Bradakos waiting for us in front of his tent. The concern returned with a vengeance when I noticed that my daughter was absent.

Bradakos stood with arms folded across his chest, reminding me of the way he used to look at me when I was a boy.

The king of the Roxolani acknowledged Hostilius and Cai with nods. "Come, Eochar", he said. "We ride."

He must have noticed the horror in my eyes. "Aritê is well", he said, "but she does not wish to see you."

I vaulted onto Kasirga's back and followed Bradakos from the sprawling camp. As soon as we had cleared the last tents, he kicked his horse to a gallop. We rode in silence.

For the best part of a watch we thundered across the endless plains, until we reached a river which I suspected was the Tisza. Bradakos turned his horse towards the east and ascended a low hill overlooking the grey water. The king swung from the saddle and I dismounted as well.

Then I laid eyes on what we had come for – a large mound of earth already overgrown with winter grass. Bradakos carelessly let go of the reins of his horse and I followed suit. The king continued until we stood atop the barrow.

For long, Bradakos said naught, but stared at the sea of grass surrounding us.

"Elmanos died when the Romans stole our gold", he said. "He was like a son to me." The king did not try to hide the tears which dripped onto the grave of a man whom I had called friend.

The presence of Arash overcame me. As if in a dream, I slipped my jian from its scabbard and drew the razor edge across the palm of my left hand, then rammed the tip deep into the sacred ground near the feet of the king.

I fell to my knees, gripped the hilt of the sword with both hands, and bowed my head to the god of war and fire while the blood flowed down the blade, soaking into the dark earth.

"I will not rest until the scalp of the murderer adorns my saddle", I hissed in the tongue of the Sea of Grass.

Bradakos acknowledged my oath with a nod, lifted me to my feet, and embraced me. "Some said that you had become Roman", he said. "They were wrong."

It was dark when we arrived back at the Roxolani camp. I found Hostilius, Cai and Gordas sharing mead around a blazing fire while juicy cuts of mutton hissed above the open flames.

Cai took one look at the blood which was still dripping from my fist, hissed something incomprehensible in the tongue of the East, and left to retrieve his potions.

Gordas did not seem to notice my arrival, as his full attention was focused on running a whetstone along the blade of his dagger.

Hostilius regarded me with a sidelong glance while picking a piece of gristle from his teeth. "So, who needs killing, Domitius?" he asked, and passed me a brimming cup.

"Regalianus", I said.

I could have imagined it, but when Hostilius mentioned violence, a ghost of a smile played around the corners of the Hun's mouth.

To be continued.

Historical Note – Main characters

Eochar - Lucius Domitius Aurelianus, or Aurelian as he is better known, I believe, was the most accomplished Roman to ever walk this earth. Some would disagree, which is their right.

In time, all will be revealed, but for now I will leave you with a few quotes from the surviving records.

From the English Translation of the (much-disputed) *Historia Augusta Volume III*:

"Aurelian, born of humble parents and from his earliest years very quick of mind and famous for his strength, never let a day go by, even though a feast-day or a day of leisure, on which he did not practise with the spear, the bow and arrow, and other exercises in arms."

"... he was a comely man, good to look upon because of his manly grace, rather tall in stature, and very strong in his muscles; he was a little too fond of wine and food, but he indulged his passions rarely; he exercised the greatest severity and a discipline that had no equal, being extremely ready to draw his sword."

"..."Aurelian Sword-in-hand," and so he would be identified."

"... in the war against the Sarmatians Aurelian with his own hand slew forty-eight men in a single day and that in the course of several days he slew over nine hundred and fifty, so that the boys even composed in his honour the following jingles and dance-ditties, to which they would dance on holidays in soldier fashion:

"Thousand, thousand, thousand we've beheaded now.

One alone, a thousand we've beheaded now.

He shall drink a thousand who a thousand slew.

So much wine is owned by no one as the blood which he has shed."

Marcus - Marcus Aurelius Claudius was an actual person, famous in history, and I believe a close friend of Lucius Domitius.

Cai is a figment of my imagination. The Roman Empire had contact with China, or Serica, as it was called then. His origins, training methods and fighting style I have researched in detail. Cai, to me, represents the seldom written about influence of China on the Roman Empire.

Primus Pilus Hostilius Proculus is a fictional character. He represents the core of the legions. The hardened plebeian officer.

Gordas – The fictional Hun/Urugundi general. Otto J Maenschen-Helfen writes in his book, The World of the Huns, that he believes the Urugundi to be a Hunnic tribe. Zosimus, the ancient Byzantine writer, mentions the Urugundi in an alliance with the Goths and the Scythians during the mid-third century AD. (Maenchen-Helfen's book is fascinating. He could read Russian, Persian, Greek and Chinese, enabling him to interpret the original primary texts.)

Vibius Marcellinus was an actual person. He will feature more later.

Segelinde – the Gothic princess, is an invention. However, Ulpia Severina, the woman who was married to Aurelian, is not.

Lucius's Contubernia – Ursa, Silentus, Pumilio and Felix. They were not actual people, but represent the common soldiers within the Roman Legions.

Diocles – was an actual man. The son of a freedman who became one of the great men in history.

King Bradakos of the Roxolani never lived.

King Chrocus of the Alemanni – was the king of the Alemanni during the reign of Valerian. Gregory of Tours mentions that his mother was evil. **Braduhenna** was not her real name.

362

Haldagates was a Germanic chieftain (mentioned in the Historia Augusta) fighting under the command of Aurelian somewhere between 253 AD and 260 AD. He might have been a Frank.

Postumus was a Roman legate of Batavian descent who emerged as the dominant figure on the Rhine during Valerian's reign.

Ingenuus was a Roman legate in charge of the Danubian frontier during the rule of Valerian.

Aureolus was a Roman military commander placed in charge of the mobile cavalry corps under Gallienus.

Senator Ulpius Crinitus was a senior Roman general/politician in the time of Valerian. Some believe he is an invention of the authors of the Historia Augusta.

Historical Note – Roxolani storyline

Emperor Valerian travelled to Rome to cement his position with the senate soon after Aemilianus was killed by his own soldiers. He was welcomed by the senate because he was one of their own.

One of the first decisions Valerian made was to appoint his son, Gallienus, as co-emperor. Gallienus was also appointed to serve as consul for the year 254 AD.

Valerian and Gallienus then restructured the defences of the Empire. Gallienus was given the responsibility for the Rhine and Danubian borders. Postumus soon emerged as the dominant figure on the Rhine frontier and Ingenuus on the Danubian frontier. Aureolus is believed to have been placed in charge of the newly formed cavalry corps.

In 255 AD the Marcomanni breached the Pannonian Limes. The reason for the breach is not known, although the Marcomanni were allowed to settle in Pannonia Superior to act as a shield against future barbarian incursions. The agreement stipulated that Gallienus take Pipara, the daughter of Attalus, as wife (concubine). It is unknown whether she was given to Gallienus as a hostage, or whether the emperor was in love with her, and demanded her hand in marriage in return for allowing the Marcomanni to settle in Roman lands. I choose to believe the second option, as the *Historia Augusta* states that he loved Pipara.

Was there a war between the Juthungi and a Marcomanni/Quadi federation at the time? There is no evidence as such, apart from the fact that the Marcomanni seemed to have required a safe haven south of the Danube due to a threat to their ancestral lands. During this time the Semnones became known as the Juthungi, which hints at a newer generation (maybe more warlike) taking control of the tribe. Many great battles, equal or greater than those of Rome must have been fought between the barbarian tribes. Very few are recorded in written history. I placed the battle between the Juthungi and the Marcomanni alliance southwest of the Moravian Gates near a town called Hranice, in the eastern Czech Republic. My inspiration for this battle was the tactics employed by Hannibal at the Battle of the Trebia, fought between Rome and a victorious Carthage in 218 BC.

During this time Valerian left Gallienus in charge of the West and set off to reconquer the East. There is no written account of this process but I believe that Valerian would have used Trapezus as a base to kick off his campaign.

There are no surviving written records detailing any major Roman victories during Valerian's foray to reconquer the lost Eastern Provinces. But... there is an account in the *Historia Augusta* mentioning that Aurelian was sent as an envoy to the Persian king, from whom he received gifts, including an elephant of unusual size. This anecdote is undated, which left me with the freedom to assume that some of the conquered territory was willingly returned. I invented the lion hunt and the capture of Hormizd as a reason behind the gifts.

Hormizd, who later became shahanshah of the Sasanians, was the second son of Shapur. Bahram, his elder brother, succeeded him. Many still view Bahram as a usurper.

Shapur and Hormizd were tolerant of other religions. Bahram sided with Kartir, the priest of Ahura Mazda (Zoroastrian religion), when he came to power. After gaining the throne, Bahram had Mani, the father of Manichaeism, jailed and killed.

During 255 AD Valerian wrested Syria from Sasanian control. Whether by the sword or by negotiation is not known.

During 255 AD a novel threat to Roman territory emerged – seaborne barbarian invasions on a grand scale. *Zosimus* provides an account and mentions various groups including Goths, Scythians and Borani. No one knows who the Borani

366

were, but some historians believe that they were, to a large extent, made up of '*latrones*', or brigands/pirates of various origins, including ex-Roman legionaries. These barbarians were apparently employed by Pharsanzes to gain the throne of the Bosporan Kingdom, which provided most of the ships for the attacks.

Did the Sasanians have a hand in these attacks? There is no evidence to support it, but given the situation, it would have been a strategically sound move for Shapur to pay the Bosporans to provide ships to the barbarians for an attack on Roman forts.

The first seaborne barbarian attack in the Black Sea region began at the Roman fort at Pityus. The attack was repelled. From there the barbarians travelled south and sacked Trapezus, which was a formidable fortress with a double wall. The garrison had been bolstered with ten thousand additional soldiers to repel a possible attack, but *Zosimus* tells us that *"the soldiers were addicted to sloth and inebriety, and that instead of continuing on guard, they were always in search of pleasures and debauchery."*

The attack most probably included a siege. Please forgive me, but I had little patience for a protracted siege.

The barbarians took many inhabitants of Trapezus as slaves and looted an incredible amount of wealth from this affluent city. Some of the legionaries escaped through the main city gate.

Of course, Aurelian did not attack the Borani all on his own on the back of an elephant, but it would have been a pity to let the elephant go to waste without a bit of fun.

During this time, Aurelian was appointed as Inspector of Military Camps. He came under the patronage of Ulpius Crinitus who held a position of authority in Pannonia and Moesia.

There is a reason why Hostilius refers to Crinitus as "being too good to be true". Some historians believe that Ulpius Crinitus was an invention of the writer of the *Historia Augusta*. I choose to believe otherwise.

The *Historia Augusta* mentions Aurelian executing a soldier (who had abused a woman) by tying him to bent trees which ripped him apart. Although this seems barbaric, it was no harsher than crucifixion, which saw the victim suffer for much longer. It is said that Aurelian was so feared by the soldiers that once he had punished offences in camp, no one offended again.

During 256 AD Valerianus (aka Valerian II), the son of Gallienus, was appointed as Caesar and placed under the tutorship of Governor/General Ingenuus in Sirmium. History tells us very little of this young man, other that he died at around 257/8 AD while in Ingenuus's care.

Sometime during the latter half of the 250's Ulpius Crinitus fell ill with an undisclosed malady. The Goths invaded across the Danube and the responsibility of repelling the attacks fell onto the shoulders of Aurelian. The *Historia Augusta* mentions that Aurelian was placed in command of a Roman legion, eight hundred heavy cavalry soldiers, as well as a mix of auxiliaries. Amongst the Germanic auxiliaries was a chieftain named Haldagates.

The battle on the banks of the Lycinus (Rositsa) is my invention to put meat on the bones of the words of Valerian as quoted in the *Historia Augusta*: *"The commonwealth thanks you, Aurelian, for having set it free from the power of the Goths. Through your efforts we are rich in booty, we are rich in glory and in all that causes the felicity of Rome to increase."*

During this time, there is evidence of hostilities between Rome and the Sarmatians (Roxolani and Yazyges). I invented the disagreement between Eochar and the Quadi king as a reason.

Early in 258 AD, Valerianus (Valerian II, son of Gallienus) died. The circumstances surrounding his death remain unclear. It might have been that Ingenuus had a hand in the young Caesar's death, or that Ingenuus usurped due to fear that he would be blamed for what had happened. The date of Ingenuus's insurrection is not known, but estimated to be anywhere from 258 AD to 260 AD.

Later during 258 AD, Gallienus's second son, Saloninus, was sent to Colonia Agrippina under the guardianship of the praetorian prefect, Albanus (aka Silvanus).

Gallienus gathered vexillations from Gaul, Germania, Raetia and Noricum. In addition, he was accompanied by Aureolus and the newly formed cavalry. *Cassius Dio* mentions that Marcus Claudius was wounded in the heel during the battle with Ingenuus.

The Germanic tribes took advantage of the war between Gallienus and Ingenuus. In 258/259 AD the Franks crossed the limes and raided deep into Germania Inferior. Similarly, the horde of the Alemanni and the Juthungi invaded Germania, Raetia and Noricum. *Zonaras* estimates their numbers at 300 000. I have downplayed this slightly.

The Alemanni and Juthungi then flooded across the Alps into the Po Valley, marching on Rome. Somehow the tribes were repelled by an army assembled by the senate. The details of Aurelian's involvement are fictional, but not impossible. Some historians believe that the successful repulsion of the Germani made Gallienus jealous of the glory won by the Roman Senate, giving rise to his exclusion of patricians from senior military posts.

On their way home to Germania, the Alemanni were intercepted at Mediolanum (Milan) by Gallienus's army which had successfully put down the rebellion of Ingenuus. In the famous battle of Mediolanum, the Romans triumphed over the Germani, slaughtering thousands.

The remnants of the Germani invaders, mostly Juthungi, were intercepted north of the Alps and defeated by a Roman army.

The scene at the baths in Byzantium is based on an undated story in the *Historia Augusta*. I thought it appropriate to include it, although there are doubts regarding the accuracy. The *Historia Augusta* claims that Aurelian was adopted by Ulpius Crinitus. Adoption of deserving men into influential families was common practise in the Roman world.

Historical Note – Random items

- Gallienus is credited with the formation of a large mobile cavalry corps, referred to as the Dalmatian cavalry.

- The Batavi were legendary for their horsemanship and swimming skills. They were said to be able to swim with full armour. Some regard the Batavi as the ancestors of the Dutch.

- The Germani believed that storks possessed human souls and that their presence was a good omen, as they provided protection.

- What did the top of a third-century Roman fort wall look like? No consensus exists among historians on the appearance of Roman battlements. My conclusion is that the soldiers on the wall walk would have been protected by a waist-high breastwork topped with intermittent merlons, designed to protect a single legionary. I support the theory that the crenellations (gaps) were wide, and the merlons (upright portions) narrow. Niederbieber's wall measured in the region of 930 metres, and the fort is said to have housed a thousand soldiers. Many of the soldiers would have manned towers and gatehouses, or operated artillery.

That did not leave enough men to stand shoulder to shoulder on the wall, hence the requirement for broader crenellations. Some reconstructions include traverses, which protected the defenders from attacks from the side.

- When dark clouds and lightning appeared above one of the opposing forces in a battle, the Germani believed it to be a sign of favour from Donar (Thor), who would assist them to gain victory.

- Hostilius's new spear is inspired by the kovel spearhead, adorned with runic inscriptions. It was found in the Ukraine and dated to the middle of the third century AD. The inscription has been translated to mean "target rider", or "thither rider", either a magical invocation or maybe the name of the spear or its owner. The original spearhead was lost during WWII.

- Authentic Quadi names are scarce. The name I used for the Quadi lord, Gabinius, belongs to a fourth century Quadi king.

- Who were the ancestors of the Germanic people of Western Europe? Many theories exist which are predominantly based on linguistic evidence. In recent years the advancement of genetic analyses, coupled with the availability of samples, added an additional dimension. There were many waves of migrations of peoples, but it appears that four thousand five hundred years ago the people of the Yamnaya culture of the Eurasian Steppes overran large tracts of Western Europe, insomuch that the DNA of modern Europeans still display a significant Yamnaya content. Wodanaz (Odin or Wodan) translates to the 'Lord of the Raging Horde'. Some believe that Odin, who possesses many shamanistic elements, originated on the Eurasian steppes.

- The Semnones is believed to mean 'the chained ones'. *Tacitus* mentions sacred groves where none may enter unless chained. He talks about 'the supreme and all-ruling deity'. Wodan is not mentioned by name. It is believed that the Semnones ruled over a hundred cantons (districts) which could each call on a thousand warriors. The Semnones became known as the Juthungi (the descendants). They later integrated into the Alemanni.

- The last wild Zubr, or European bison, was killed by poachers in Russia in 1927. Fifty animals remained in captivity. Following a successful breeding programme, they have since been re-introduced into the wild. In

2019 seven thousand five hundred animals roamed the forests and plains of Europe.

- The description of the saddle that Lucius receives from Bradakos is based on the reconstruction of an ancient Scythian saddle unearthed in the Pazyryk barrow.
- For fun, I have included a few nautical terms of yesteryear which most probably originated long after Roman times, but could be linked to the ancient past.
  - The phrase 'square meal' originates from the square wooden platters ancient sailors used when eating a large warm meal on a ship.
  - A kedge is a light anchor.
  - Brining of meat as required on ships, hardens the fat. Although it is still edible, it has to be chewed for long. 'Chewing the fat' means talking interminably.
  - 'Combing the cat' refers to running one's fingers through a scourge between strokes to untangle the tails.
- The proverb of 'how to eat an elephant' is attributed to Kung Fu-tzu, also known as Confucius.
- The *Legio XV Apollinaris* was stationed at the fort of Satala during the 250's. Quintus Atilius served in this legion, although not during this time.

- I based my lion hunt on the ancient text found in the Near East, as well as a silver Sasanian dish displaying the king hunting lions from horseback. The Assyrian 'Lion Hunt of Ashurbanipal' palace reliefs indicate that lion hunting was a ritualistic affair reserved for royalty.

- The Severan Bridge, spanning the Cendere River in Turkey, is 390 feet long and 23 feet wide. This single-arched bridge was built around the year 200 AD and is still in good condition.

- Ahura Mazda, the Lord of Wisdom, was the chief deity of the Sasanians. His antithesis was called Ahriman. Traditionally, Ahriman's name was written upside down.

- The ruins of the legionary fort and city of Samosata have been inundated by 385 feet of water from the lake behind the Atatürk Dam which was constructed during the 1990's. Satellite photos taken before the flood reveal the extent of the city. The wall was three miles long and enclosed an area of five hundred acres. According to *Theodoretus's Historia, Ecclesiatica (Book 4, Chapter 13),* the Euphrates bordered the walls of the city.

- The wall of ancient Nineveh is worth a mention. It was 7.5 miles long. The base was constructed of stone, 20 feet high. On top of the stone foundation was a mudbrick wall, 33 feet high. The thickness of the wall was 49 feet. Although the area was first settled in 6000 BC, the Neo-Assyrian king, Sennacherib (700 BC), made it the greatest city in the world.

- The Arch of Ctesiphon (Taq Kasra) is the only remaining part of the ancient city. The arch, which used to be the audience hall of the Sasanian kings, is the largest vaulted brick arch of the ancient world. Historians are divided about the date of its construction – some believe that it was built by Shapur I during the middle of the third century AD.

- Based on a recorded discussion between a Sasanian high king and his page, Babylonian and Basarangian wine were deemed the best.

- "May you be immortal", was a favoured way of responding to the Sasanian shahanshah.

- How did ancient Europeans fight with the sword? Did they just swing wildly, like one would imagine a barbarian would? I came across interesting research done on bronze age swords. Scientists asked trained modern swordsmen to spar using fighting techniques recorded in medieval times. The wear on the replica bronze swords were remarkably similar to the wear on the original blades, indicating that swordsmen of ancient times were well trained in similar techniques, rather than barbarians just swinging a blade.

- The Via Argentaria (Silver Way) was the name of the Roman road through the Dinaric Alps connecting Salona to Sirmium. Silver was transported from the mines east of Aquae Sulphurae (modern day Ilidža in Bosnia and Herzegovina) to the Roman mints at Salona and Sirmium.

- Apparently, the phrase 'spill the beans' originated in ancient Greece where a secret voting system existed. Either white or black beans would be added to a jar. Sometimes the jar was dropped, prematurely revealing the outcome of the vote. Seeing that Diocles was Greek, it was an appropriate comment.

- The Legio IV Flavia Felix was based at Singidunum during this time. Valerius Macednus, an attested member, died while fighting in the East. Although I used his name, he was not implicated in any unsavoury dealings.

- It is written that Marcus Aurelius took a daily dose of special theriac (anti-poison agent) containing cinnamon. It was a special concoction prepared especially for him by his famous physician, Galen.

- The Balkan Mountains south of the old Nicopolis ad Istrum were also known as the 'Old Mountain'.
- The ancient name of the Rositsa River (which flows a few miles south of Nicopolis) is the Lyginus.
- I placed the fictitious battle against the Goths between the modern villages of Nikyup and Pavlikeni in northern Bulgaria, just west of the old Nicopolis ad Istrum.
- When conditions are favourable, a wind called the *bura* blows through certain valleys in the Julian Alps. The wind is funnelled through gaps in the mountains and can reach velocities in excess of 100 mph.
- The Milvian Bridge across the Tiber was built in 206 BC. It is still in use.
- The Septimer Pass north of Milan was not the main Roman route across the Alps, but was in use during Roman times.

Historical Note – Place names

Saalburg in Germania – Twenty-five miles northeast of Mainz, Germany.

Nida in Germania – Frankfurt, Germany.

Colonia Agrippina (previously Ubiorum) – Cologne, Germany.

Mogantiacum (or Mogontiacum) on the Limes Germanicus – Mainz, Germany.

Niederbieber – Roman fort on Limes Germanicus, fifty miles northwest of Mainz.

Holzhausen – Roman fort on Limes Germanicus, twenty miles northwest of Mainz.

Vindobona – Vienna, Austria.

Carnuntum – Petronell-Carnuntum, Austria.

Gate of the River – Moravian Gate, Eastern Czech Republic, near Hranice.

Arelate – Arles on the Rhône, France.

Messana – Messina, Sicily.

Byzantium – Istanbul, Turkey (formerly Constantinople).

Trapezus – Trabzon, Turkey.

Satala – Roman fort close to Sadak, Turkey.

Erez – Erzincan, Turkey.

Zimara – Roman fort close to Bağıştaş Dam, Turkey.

Melitene – Roman fort close to Malatya, Turkey.

Samosata – Roman fort close to Samsat, Turkey.

Zeugma – Roman fort and crossing of Euphrates near Belkis, Gaziantep, Turkey.

Carrhae – Harran, Turkey.

Resaina – Ceylanpinar, Turkey.

Singara – Sinjar, Iraq.

Nineveh – Mosul on the Tigris, Iraq.

Ctesiphon – Salman Pak, Iraq.

Antioch – Antakya, Turkey.

Seleucia by the Sea – The seaport of ancient *Antioch*.

Sirmium in Pannonia - Sremska Mitrovica, Serbia.

Singidunum – Belgrade, Serbia.

Viminacium – Near Kostolac, Serbia.

Novae – Svishtov, Bulgaria.

Nicopolis ad Istrum – Near Nikyup in northern Bulgaria.

Siscia in Pannonia – Sisak, Croatia.

Ariminum – Rimini, Italy.

Mediolanum – Milan, Italy.

Bergomum – Bergamo, Italy.

Author's Note

I trust that you have enjoyed the eighth book in the series.

In many instances, written history relating to this period has either been lost in the fog of time, or it might never have been recorded. That is especially applicable to most of the tribes which Rome referred to as barbarians. These peoples did not record history by writing it down. They only appear in the written histories of the Greeks, Romans, Persians and Chinese, who often regarded them as enemies.

In any event, my aim is to be as historically accurate as possible, but I am sure that I inadvertently miss the target from time to time, in which case I apologise to the purists among my readers.

Kindly take the time to provide a rating and/or a review.

I will keep you updated via my blog with regards to the progress on the ninth book in the series.

Feel free to contact me any time via my website. I will respond.

www.HectorMillerBooks.com

Printed in Great Britain
by Amazon